WALKIN'
THE DOG

G·K
Hall
&Co.

Also by Walter Mosley
in Large Print:

Always Outnumbered, Always Outgunned
Gone Fishin'
A Little Yellow Dog
RL's Dream
Black Betty
White Butterfly
Red Death
Devil in a Blue Dress

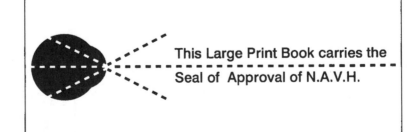

This Large Print Book carries the
Seal of Approval of N.A.V.H.

WALKIN' THE DOG

WALTER MOSLEY

G.K. Hall & Co. • Thorndike, Maine

Published in 2000 by arrangement with
Little Brown & Co., Inc.

G.K. Hall Large Print Core Series.

The text of this Large Print edition is unabridged.
Other aspects of the book may vary from the original edition.

Set in 16 pt. Plantin.   21446

Printed in the United States on permanent paper.

Library of Congress Cataloging-in-Publication Data

Mosley, Walter.
    Walkin' the dog / Walter Mosley.
        p.   cm.
    ISBN 0-7838-8961-5 (lg. print : hc : alk. paper)
    ISBN 0-7838-8962-3 (lg. print : sc : alk. paper)
    1. Afro-American men — California — Los Angeles —
Fiction.   2. Philosophers — California — Los Angeles —
Fiction.   3. Ex-convicts — California — Los Angeles —
Fiction.   4. Los Angeles (Calif.) — Fiction.   I. Title.
PS3563.O88456 W35 2000
    813'.54—dc21   99-089945

This book is dedicated to W. Paul Coates.

contents

blue lightning

At first he thought the trill and bleating note was part of a dream. A sweet note so high it had to be the angel that Aunt Bellandra said the blue god sent, "to save the black mens from fallin' out the world complete. He got a real high voice like a trumpet an' he always come at the last second, after a fool done lost his job, his money, his wife, his self-respect and just about everything else he got. Just about dead," Bellandra proclaimed, clapping her hands together loudly, "an' that's when the angel sing."

Back when he was a little boy, Socrates feared his tall and severe auntie. But he was also enthralled by her stories about the black race in a white world under a blue god who barely noticed man.

"When he almost gone that angel just might make his move," she'd say. "And when a black man hear that honied voice all the terrible loss an' pain fall right away an' the man look up an' see that he always knew the right road but he never made the move."

Again the high note. This time strained a bit. This time a little warble in Socrates' sleep.

"But not everybody could hear it. Some dope

7

fiends too high an' some mens hatin' too hard. Sometimes the angel is that much too late and his song becomes a funeral hymn."

Socrates jerked himself upright in the bed, opening his eyes as wide as he could. He was afraid that the music he heard in his dream was really the dirge of that tardy angel — that he'd died in the night and it was too late for him to make up for all the suffering he'd caused in his evil years.

He sat up on his fold-out sofa bed. There was a slight whistle in his throat at the tail end of each breath, a whistle that blended into the high notes of the trumpet playing somewhere outside.

The music was like crying. A long sigh breaking down into a cascade of tears and then gasping, pleading notes that seemed to be begging for death.

The luminescent hands on the alarm clock told the ex-convict that it was three thirty-four. In less than an hour and a half he had to get up and get ready to go to work.

He listened for the song in the notes but the horn went silent. Socrates let his eyes close for a moment, then opened them briefly only to let them close for a few seconds more. He was considering putting his head back down on the couch cushion when the horn sounded again. This time it was playing a slow blues; a train coming into the station or maybe just leaving.

Socrates' sleepy nod turned into appreciation for the music. He swung his feet over to the edge of the bed, stepped into the overalls that were on the floor and stood up, pulling the straps over his shoulders. He slid his feet into the large leather sandals he'd found in a trash can on one of his delivery runs for Bounty.

Leather slapping against his heels, Socrates walked out of his apartment door and into the small vegetable garden that led to the alley. The black dog raised up on his two legs and dragged himself to his master's feet.

The horn song was coming from the left, from the lot where a warehouse once stood. The warehouse had once supplied the two furniture stores, now abandoned, that flanked Socrates' sliver of a home — a corridor between the two stores that had been walled off.

Outside, the trumpet notes were loud and clear. The music took on an angry tone in the open air.

The night stars seemed to accompany the song. Socrates wondered why he didn't get up before dawn more often. The night sky was beautiful. There wasn't anyone out and it was peaceful and he was free to go anywhere with no metal bars or prison guards to stop him.

The burned-out lot was vacant but it wasn't empty. Two rusted-out cars, several large appliance boxes, various metal barrels and cans, piles of trash and even a rough and ready structure stood here and there designed by the temporary traveler, the homeless or the mad.

Socrates couldn't see the musician but that

blues train continued rolling. His aunt Bellandra's words were still cold in his mind. Leaving the black dog behind the gate, Socrates walked toward the lot, leather heels slapping and gravel crackling in his wake. Everything seemed to have reason and deep purpose — the yellow light in Mrs. Melendez's window, the cold from the night breeze on his shoulders that he felt without shivering.

He stopped at the edge of the lot and watched the half moon just above the horizon.

Baby bought a new hat, Socrates imagined the notes were saying. *She bought a yellow dress.* They were the words to a song the barber used to play on the phonograph on Saturdays when his half brother Garwood would take him for his biweekly buzz cut.

She's gonna ride that Greyhound bus and take away my best.

"Hey!" Socrates shouted and the music stopped. "Hey!"

The answering silence was like a pressure on Socrates' eardrums.

He didn't know why he'd come out into the dark night unarmed, out in the dangerous streets of his neighborhood. Three weeks earlier a woman had been shot to death, execution style, and dropped in the alley. The neighbors said that all she wore was a silver miniskirt and one red shoe. He'd forgotten the name but she wasn't even twenty, brown and slender except that she had large breasts. When he heard of her death,

Socrates' first thought was that when she was born he had already been fifteen years in an Indiana prison cell.

Something hard and metal fell. Socrates moved quickly in his awkward shoes.

"Stay 'way!" A small man leapt over a toppled water heater and ran the length of the lot through to another alley. By the time Socrates reached the end of the lot, the little man was gone.

◼ ◼ ◼ ◼

"Looks like your watch must be a little slow today, Mr. Fortlow," Jason Fulbright said in way of greeting. It was seven fifty-seven A.M.

"Say what?" Socrates answered, none too friendly. Fulbright was a tan-colored black man with thick lips that he compressed into the thinnest disapproving frown that he could muster. He showed Socrates his own wristwatch, tapping the crystal.

"It's almost eight," he said, his high voice like an accusing catbird. "You're on the seven forty-five shift aren't you?"

"My bus driver must'a got it mixed up today," Socrates said in a bit milder tone. He liked his job. He felt good coming in to work every day. He needed that paycheck too.

"Your bus gets you in too late. You should take an earlier one," the young man said. "Even if you get in a little early at least you'll be on time. Yes sir, if you want to make it in this business you got to take the early bus."

11

Fulbright clapped Socrates on the shoulder. Maybe when he felt the rock-hard muscle of that upper arm he began to realize that he was in over his head.

"Don't put your hands on me, man," Socrates uttered on a slight breath.

"What did you say?"

"I said, keep your hands to yourself if you wanna keep 'em at all." All the reserve he had built up, all the times he told himself that men like Jason Fulbright were just fools and not to be listened to — all of that was gone. Just a few hours of missing sleep and a strong dream — a fool playing his trumpet in the middle of the night — that's all it took, one bad morning, and Socrates was ready to throw everything away.

Unconsciously Fulbright took half a step back, but Socrates could see in the man's face that he still intended to say something else. And no matter what he said it was going to cause a fight. Not a fight but a slaughter. Fulbright was tall and strong from playing sport, but he didn't know the meaning of the kind of violence he called up in the ex-con. Socrates couldn't shake the fists out of his hands.

"Good morning, Jason, Socrates," Marty Gonzalez, the senior store manager said.

Fulbright and Fortlow had to turn away from each other in order to return the greeting.

"Mr. Gonzales," Jason said.

Socrates merely nodded. He liked the fire plug manager. Marty had once shown Socrates a pocket watch he carried that held a picture of his great-grandsire, Ernesto Gonzalez, pasted opposite the timepiece. He remarked on how much he looked like his ancestor from Sonora but how little like him he was.

"I don't speak Spanish," Marty had said. "Been to Vietnam but never to Mexico. My wife was born in Denmark. My kid has blue hair and thinks that Taco Bell is all he needs to know about Chicano culture."

Now he stood between them.

"What's happening?" the dark-eyed manager asked.

"I don't know what the heck's going on to tell you the truth, Mr. Gonzalez," Jason began.

He was going to say more but Marty cut him off. "Uh-huh. Hey, Jason, why don't you go and make sure that the twins did a shelf count and order form last night?"

"Okay, Mr. Gonzalez. If that's what you want." Jason fixed his brown and red striped tie and gave the two men a questioning stare.

"Yeah," Marty said, clapping Jason on the shoulder. "You just go on and check out the twins' work."

The twins were Sarah Shulberg, a Jewish girl who lived on Spalding Drive, and Robyn Craig, a light-skinned Negro child whose father was a plastic surgeon with an office on Roxbury. Sarah and Robyn did everything together. They dressed alike, talked about cute boys. Their mothers took turns driving them to work and home again.

"I swear I'ma break that mothahfuckah's head right open he don't get up offa me," Socrates said loudly as Jason walked away.

Marty gestured with both hands for his employee to lower the volume.

"I know," the manager said. He was broad but short and had to look up to address the big man. "He's a prissy prick."

"You better talk to him, Marty," Socrates said. "He come up here sayin' that my watch must be busted, that I better get on a earlier bus. Man, I take the first bus leave in the mornin' an' I ain't ever even owned no watch."

"It's okay, Socco. Jason's just a kiss ass. He don't know."

"He gonna find out soon enough he keep on fuckin' wit' me like that."

"What's bothering you, Socco?"

"Nuthin'," the big man said. "He just made me mad, that's all."

Marty nodded and looked down at his feet.

"Yeah, he's a bitch all right," the manager said. "Why don't you'n me and Hector unload the big truck this mornin'? Give us somethin' to do."

Socrates liked unloading the big truck that delivered on Monday mornings. Tons of groceries had to be pulled off onto the loading dock at the side of the store. It was hard work but Socrates was a strong man. More often than not he was the strongest man in the room.

14

He lifted and toted, stacked and wheeled thousands of pounds off the truck that day. Hector La Forna and Marty Gonzalez had to take turns just to keep up with the big, bald, black man. He worked until the sweat was glistening on his head. He knew he'd be sore for a week because even though his muscles were strong they were still old and reluctant.

"Lets break for lunch," Marty suggested at eleven fifteen.

"Lunch ain't till twelve twenty for the seven forty-five shift," Socrates reminded him.

"Fuck that. Let's get some corned beef sandwiches from the deli and go over to the park. I'll tell Jason that he can be in charge while we're gone. That'll give him such a hard-on that his wife'll send me a thank-you card."

The little patch of green across the street from the Bounty supermarket had a park bench and table, a bronze statue of a nameless prospector and a boulder more than nine feet high and almost as broad, all shaded by a very old and green pine. Marty bought the sandwiches, with beer for after the meal. Socrates accepted the apology for Jason Fulbright's behavior and relaxed for the first time since three thirty-four that morning.

After some solid eating and drinking Socrates nodded and blinked. Maybe he napped for a minute or three. In the stupor he leaned a little too far forward and had to jerk up quickly to

15

keep from falling.

Marty was grinning at him.

"What time is it?" Socrates made to stand but relaxed when Marty put up his hand.

"It's about a quarter to one."

"I'm a half hour late. What's Fulbright gonna do wit' that?"

"What's wrong, Socco? Why're you so nervous today?" Marty's eyes were so black that they seemed like bullet holes to the ex-con.

"Wrong? Lotsa stuff is wrong. All kinds a shit. I seen in the paper last night where the cops beat up a whole truckload of illegal Mexicans again. Right in broad daylight. Right on TV. But nobody cares. They didn't learn nothin' from them riots."

"But that's every day, Mr. Fortlow," Marty said. "What's wrong today? I mean, they didn't kick your butt."

"You mean they didn't try. 'Cause you know, man, the next mothahfuckah try an' kick my ass gonna be dead. Cop or whatever. I don't play that shit. How about that for wrong?"

Marty Gonzalez was lying on his side, propped up on an elbow.

"What?" Socrates asked after a few moments' silence.

"I didn't say anything."

"You wanna go back?"

"Whatever you say, Socco." Marty shrugged one shoulder but otherwise stayed still.

"You ever worry that you might be goin' crazy,

Marty?" Socrates didn't even know what he'd been thinking until the question found words.

Marty nodded. "Every time my wife's mother comes to dinner until about an hour after she leaves."

Socrates' laugh sounded like far-off explosions, a battery of cannon laying siege to a defenseless town.

"You always been a fool, Marty?"

"I guess so. What about you?"

"Yeah, I guess," Socrates rubbed his rock-breaking left hand over his pate. "Fool to begin wit' now it looks like I'm comin' back for another shot at it. You know I was gonna break Jason's face for 'im if you didn't show up."

"And I almost let you do it too." Marty smiled. "You'd be doing that brother a favor but I'd surely hate to lose you, Socco. You're the only full-grown man in the whole store. Outside of you, it's just women, kids and kiss asses."

Socrates laughed again. "Yeah," he said. "I know what you mean. Uh-huh. Sometimes I wonder how some'a these men get dressed in the mornin'. An' here I got to listen to this shit just to make four ninety-five a hour."

"That's all we're payin' you?" Marty actually seemed shocked.

"Yeah. Don't you know what you pay people?"

"Uh-uh. They cut the checks by grade downtown. But I thought you'd at least be a grade four by now. You been here over a year. That boy you look after, Darryl's making four sixty."

"Shit. I'm lucky to have a job." Socrates looked left and right then pulled himself up and on to his feet. "We better be gettin' back."

Marty stood up too. He put himself face to neck with the big black man. "Gibbs is leaving the produce department to go downtown. He's going to supervise the southwestern purchasing area."

"Yeah. He deserves it, I guess."

"I need a new produce manager." Marty's eyes did not blink.

"Uh, yeah, I guess you do. Benny lookin' to move up. He got a wife and kid."

"How old are you, Mr. Fortlow?"

"Me an' sixty's kissin' cousins."

"And you work harder than two Jason Fulbrights."

"Not if I sit out here suckin' beer all day." Socrates bit his lower lip with a row of powerful yellow teeth.

"You could be my produce manager, Socco."

"Naw, Marty. Not me. I just come in and do what I'm told. Pick that up, put that down — that's me."

"You're the best man I got, Socco. And I need somebody I can trust in produce. Produce and meat — they're perishable and need a responsible eye on 'em."

Socrates turned away from his supervisor and looked across the street at the huge supermarket with its vast parking lot. It seemed very far away.

"We better get goin', man," Socrates said to his boss.

▰ ▰ ▰ ▰

Socrates and Darryl worked next to each other on checkout counters five and six, bagging groceries for the four o'clock rush.

"How you doin' in school, little D?" Socrates asked his young friend.

"S'okay I guess." The boy concentrated on the number ten cans of tomatoes he was placing at the bottom of the bag.

"Okay good or okay bad?" Socrates pressed. He could bag twice as fast as any child in the store. His hands did his thinking for him — a trait that brought him more trouble than help over the years.

"I already brought my report card home to Mr. and Mrs. MacDaniels. They got it."

Socrates finished putting his six bags into the wire cart for a small white woman. He recognized her face but couldn't recall her name.

"Can you help me, young man?" The white lady smiled at Socrates while skinny Darryl struggled with the heavy bag he'd loaded. Socrates could have told the boy that he was putting too many big cans in one bag but Darryl needed to learn for himself.

"Sure," Socrates said to the little white woman in the synthetic brown pants suit. "Happy to."

When Socrates returned Darryl was still working counter six but the only other opening was on number fourteen. They worked through the rush until it was time for the late afternoon break. Darryl was the first to get the nod from the assistant supervisor of the late shift, Evelyn Lau.

Darryl left through the deli department. Evelyn always kept Socrates on until the end because he was the best worker at Bounty; the only one who could bag for two checkout counters at the same time.

After Evelyn gave him the nod, Socrates found Darryl smoking cigarettes with some of the other children around the Dumpster at back of the store.

"Come on, we gotta talk," Socrates told the boy.

Darryl dropped his cigarette and crushed it with his Nike shoe.

They walked around to the ice-making machine at the other side of the store and stood there for a while watching the blue skies darken.

"How much that shoe cost you, boy?" Socrates asked.

"Regular one sixty for a pair, but I got these for ninety on sale." There was pride in the boy's voice but he squinted and flinched a little because he could hear a lesson behind Socrates' question.

"And you gonna stamp out a cigarette with a rubber-soled shoe that cost you a whole week's salary."

"It's mines. I bought it." Darryl said. But the

defiance was only in the words, none of it in his tone.

Socrates was the only man that had a right to hit him, that's what Darryl thought. Even though Hallie and Costas MacDaniels were his foster parents, Socrates was the one who had taken him out of a life of gangs and forgave his mortal crime. The social welfare department wouldn't let a convicted felon adopt the boy, but Socrates looked after Darryl anyway and made sure that he had a chance.

"You work two weeks for shoes you shouldn't be burnin' 'em like that. Bad enough yo' feet outgrow 'em in six months. I mean where you think money come from anyways?"

Socrates could see that Darryl was angry but he didn't mind.

"And what about that report card?" Socrates asked. "You gonna tell me about that?"

"I got dees and stuff."

"An' what stuff?"

"You know."

"What's wrong?" Socrates wanted to know. "Don't you do your homework?"

"They'ont like me, that's all. They just don't care. I'ont know what they be talkin' 'bout. An' if I ask they'ont even say." The glower in Darryl's eyes reminded him of the boy who spent so much time with his Aunt Bellandra.

"Why ain't they gonna like you, Darryl? It's a school. You a student. It's their job to tell you what things mean."

21

"But they don't. I just don't get it. They think I'm stupid, that's all."

"You not stupid," Socrates said. "You not. But that ain't gonna help if you fail in school. I mean what you gonna do if you fail?"

"I could work right here wichyou. People work here. Mr. Gonzalez do."

"If that's what you want," Socrates said. "If that's what you want. But don't make it all you could have. Ain't no shame in bein' a grocer but it's bitch and a half if they think that that's all you're good for."

◪ ◪ ◪ ◪

Socrates made German potato salad for his dinner that night. He boiled six potatoes and fried bacon on his butane camping stove. He used two tablespoons of good vinegar with mustard and minced onion, garlic powder, and a pinch of cayenne for seasoning. He ate until he couldn't swallow any more.

Then he pulled on his fatigue pants and jacket, stepped into his high army surplus boots, and put two pints of Myrtle's brand brandy in the inside pockets of the lined army coat. In the vacant lot he climbed into a Westinghouse refrigerator box carrying a red plastic milk carton box for his seat.

The sun was down and there was a chill in the air but between Myrtle's brand and Uncle Sam Socrates was snug and warm.

He used the oversized bottle cap for his shot glass and poked a hole in the box to see the night sights. He had brought a half gallon plastic milk container to use as a urinal. Socrates was on a mission like a small boy camping in the backyard, or a sniper laying in wait.

He nodded out now and then, talking to his Aunt Bellandra in a brandy stupor on the plastic milk crate.

"Does the angel play for white men?" the boy Socrates asked.

"No, baby," Bellandra replied in a surprisingly gentle manner. Socrates thought that she must have been drunk to be so friendly like that. "White men don't need that angel, neither do white women nor black ones either. It's just black men so hardheaded that they cain't do right even by themselves."

"Oh Reggie! Oh yeah!" a woman's voice cried. "Oh do that! Do that! Yeah."

Socrates came awake to the sound of the lovers. The young woman's pleas got him half hard in his refrigerator box and he had a difficult time getting the right angle with the milk container to relieve himself. After a while he got it right but the stream was noisier than he would have liked.

"What's that?" a man, probably Reggie, said.

"Uh, what?" asked his girlfriend.

Socrates managed to stop urinating but the last few drops were as loud as tapping fingers on a tight drumhead.

"Who's that?" Reggie called out.

Socrates stifled a giggle thinking about how he

was hiding in a box way past midnight. There he was with some clown swinging his dick in the night air and calling him out.

"Who's there? Motherfucker, I find you an' I'm'onna cut you too!"

Socrates zipped up his pants because he didn't want to fight with his business hanging out.

"Sh! You hear that, Tanika?"

"Let's go, baby. Maybe it's Arnold."

"Motherfucker!" Reggie shouted. "Is that you?"

Socrates wondered what those children would think if he stood up and busted out of his box, if he broke out on them and yelled boo.

But no. That's not why he was there. He took a sip of brandy and listened to the footsteps of the sneak lovers recede.

"Beety beety dwa dwaaaa! Dwa dwaaaa!" the horn said. Just that fast sleeping Socrates was awake and sober and so excited he began to sweat.

He put his eye up next to the hole and looked. At first he couldn't see anything because his eye was still asleep. But the horn kept playing and he kept looking until finally he saw a foot, a toe-tapping foot that beat out a fast tempo for the slow sweet tune.

Socrates ripped the box apart and was on the small wide-eyed horn-player, a lion on a lamb.

"What who you want?" the little colored man cried. "What?"

24

He was more gray than brown, more boy than man. He was old and tiny and slender like a child.

Socrates raised the small man by the shoulder and cried, "What the fuck you doin' out here playin' that gotdamned horn in the middle'a the mothahfuckin' night like a fool?"

He didn't mean to say all that. He didn't care why the man was there.

"Lemme go, brother," the man said. "I ain't got nuthin' but this beat-up horn an' it ain't worth two dollars."

Socrates sucked down a deep breath and tried not to squeeze too hard. His grip was a bone breaker, a skull buster. His hands were weapons trained from childhood for war.

"I don't want your horn, man," Socrates said after a few breaths. "It's just your music woke me up. I'ont know why, I mean why I'm out here. What's your name?"

"Hoagland. Hoagland Mars."

"My name is Socrates, Socrates Fortlow."

Hoagland Mars nodded and eyed his attacker with concern.

"You wanna drink, Hoagland Mars?"

Socrates took the second pint of Myrtle's brand from his army jacket, cracked the seal and passed it over. The musician smacked his lips over his first sip and took another before passing it back.

"That's the right stuff right there," he said.

They went back to Socrates' small home after

a few sips. Hoagland sat at the kitchen table playing his two-dollar horn and tasting the cheap brandy. Socrates glowered and plodded toward drunk but Mr. Mars didn't seem worried at what his host might do.

"Yeah, man," Hoagland opined, "I played behind T-Bone Walker and right besides Lips McGee. I played the Dark Room in Chi and all through Motown records. You know I figure you could hear my horn a hunnert times every day on the oldies radio station. Shit."

Socrates was surprised that Hoagland had such thin lips. "A black man, a horn player," he told Stony Wile a few weeks later. "And he had lips like a white girl ain't never been kissed."

Near dawn Myrtle and Hoagland's horn both ran dry. The little man was flagging, head dipping halfway to his knees.

"What you do with all that money?" Socrates asked.

"Spent it," the musician said. "Spent every dime. Real brandy and real blondes. Stayed in hotels where the ashtrays cost more than my whole Mississippi cotton-pickin' family could pull down in a year. Huh. Shit. I'd drop a hundred dollars on a handkerchief or tie. You know I done lived."

"So why you out in a alley in Watts tonight?" Socrates asked. "What brought you down here?"

"Black man cain't keep nuthin', brother. All we could do is borrah an' you know the white man wan' it all back — wit' interest."

26

Socrates didn't wake up until ten thirty-five. His pocket change was missing from the kitchen counter. Twenty dollars he kept in a sock in a shoe under the sofa bed was gone. He didn't remember pulling down the bed or falling in it. He hadn't heard Hoagland Mars stealing and neither did he care.

Socrates got to work at twelve fifteen. The first thing he saw was Jason Fulbright headed straight for him down the center aisle. But before Jason reached Socrates Marty Gonzalez grabbed the assistant manager by the arm and talked to him, told a joke, it seemed, and then sent him on his way.

The stocky manager greeted Socrates and smiled. "You look a little better," Marty said.

"Say what?"

"I told Jason that you told me yesterday that you were sick and had to see the doctor. You know I'd forget my head if it wasn't for my neck."

"I'll make it up, Marty. I'll stay late and help the twins with their inventory."

Socrates skipped lunch and both his breaks. He worked straight until eight forty-five and then hurried out of the sliding doors.

"Socco!" Marty called at the big man's back. "Hey, Socrates."

"I gotta run, Marty. I got to catch the eight fifty bus. The next one is over a hour from now."

"Hold up," Marty said. "I'll give you a ride down to Venice and you can catch the two eighty-three."

He slapped Socrates hard on the back and walked him out to his Ford Explorer. In the high driver's seat Socrates rode with no seat belt looking out at the dark streets of Beverly Hills.

"Car's nicer than my place," Socrates said. "Bet you pay more on insurance than I pay rent."

"What's your rent?" Marty asked.

"Nuthin'. I used to pay this dude but he musta died or sumpin'. But you know the place ain't worth much, it's just a space between two empty stores."

"Yeah, well," Marty said as he swerved past a red Bonneville that had loud bass music playing out of its open trunk. "I guess you can't beat that."

"Yeah," Socrates said, not really agreeing.

"So, Socco," Marty said. "What about that produce job?"

"I got a job. I mean I know it's a low hourly wage but I get tips for deliveries and I know if I get sick that somebody can take my place."

"I looked up your record. Today's the first time you were ever even late as far as I can see. You've only been sick twice."

"Man, I was four hours late today, I'm almost sixty, and you don't know me. How you know that you could trust me with that kinda responsibility?"

"I want you to be one of my men, Socco,"

28

Marty said. "I need people who I can rely on to roll up their sleeves, people who work."

Marty took a left on Olympic heading east. The wide street was lined with low apartment buildings and nice single-family homes. Not many streetlights and not much traffic to speak of. They made good speed down toward Fairfax.

The car, Socrates thought, was as quiet as a tomb.

"No," he said as they turned south of Fairfax. "You let Benny have it, Marty. And just call on me for anything extra you need."

"You sure?"

"Sure as sin on Sunday."

There was silence past Pico and Saturn and Pickford. Silence across Airdome and Eighteenth and all the way down to Venice. But when they pulled up to the bus stop and Socrates opened the door Marty said, "Gibbs isn't leaving for six weeks. I won't make my decision until the day he's gone."

Socrates swung one leg out of the door and then turned back to his boss.

"Why you want me, man?"

"I like working with you, Mr. Fortlow. I trust you."

"You don't know nuthin' about me."

"I don't know anything about anybody down at the store. We work together, that's all. It's none of my business what you do some place else."

"I'll think about it," Socrates said. "But I don't

29

know. I mean if you give the job away before I get back to ya it'll be okay by me."

"Six weeks," the store manager repeated. "You got till then."

◤ ◤ ◤ ◤

The bus ride took over two hours. He had to transfer twice. The connections were slow but Socrates didn't care. He was used to wasting time. All convicts were.

When he got to his place he had the feeling of coming home. Home to his illegal gap. Home to a place that had no street address, a jury-rigged electrical system, plumbing that turned off every once in a while, sometimes for weeks. It was a hard place. Sometimes when he was hungry, before he had a job, he had thought that jail might be better than starving freedom; jail or death. It was a place he slept in, a place to read or drink or almost cry. But it had never been home. It had never been hearth or asylum but now it was both of these things. For the first time he was thankful for what little he had. He was safe at least for one night more.

promise

Nineteen years after Levering Jordan died, and nine years after his own release from prison, Socrates was bagging groceries when he remembered the promise he'd made.

Longarm Levering Jordan had been Socrates' back for five years in the Indiana slam. He was in for fifty-six years but prison had a way of killing some men early. It didn't matter that Levering was tall and powerful. Strength was an asset in the penitentiary but that didn't mean you'd survive.

"Brawn, brains, nor beggin' could keep you alive in here if you was born to be free," old man Cap Richmond had always said. Cap had gone down for assault on a white woman in an armed robbery in 'forty-nine. He got seventy-four years for his crime. By 1988, when Socrates was let free, Cap had seen a thousand murderers come, serve their terms and leave.

"Seventy-four years for a slap," Cap would say. "Din't even knock out no tooth."

Levering never got used to being locked down. Any night that Socrates awoke in his own tight cell he knew that he could look out of the metal grid and see Longarm across the way, his fingers laced with the steel cage, his eyes willing the walls to break open.

Maybe it was five years without sleep that finally took the toll on Levering. In the last months he was skinny and weak. One of the big rats that came out at night could have knocked him over. But the rats didn't bother and the predators among the convict population knew better than to mess with a friend of Socrates Fortlow.

"Socrates'll kill ya," was the phrase most often used to explain to new cons how they should deal with him. Even the guards came in threes when Socrates had to be disciplined or *managed*.

When Levering was dying, the chaplain, a woman named Patricia James, had three guards bring Socrates to that special room in the infirmary where they brought prisoners to die.

It was a nice room for a prison. Gray nylon carpet and a picture of flowers on the wall. The window had bars but they were widely spaced and the sun, they said, came in almost all afternoon on a clear day.

"Even if you dyin'," the bookmaker B. B. Moffat once said, "they got ya. Put you in a room to let you see what you ain't never gonna have again. Give you a carpet an' then bring you to the grave."

Socrates sat on a stool next to the dying man's cot. The gaunt-faced Levering smiled once and then gestured for Socrates to lean close.

"Hold it," one of the white guards said.

"Leave him alone," Chaplain James commanded with a whisper. "Have respect for a man when he's dying."

Socrates bent forward and looked into Death's eyes.

"I want you to plant me a tree," Levering wheezed.

"What kinda tree?" Socrates asked.

"A African tree if it grow where you live. But any tree that can get tall. Maybe one with flowers."

"You got it."

"An' another thing, man."

"Yeah?"

"Right after you plant it I want you to fuck me a girl."

Socrates smiled for the first time in a long time.

"No lie, man," Levering said. "She got to be pretty, she got to be black, an' she got to be young. All right? You gonna do that for me?"

"I will if I can, man. But you know by the time I get outta here my thing might not get out no mo'." Socrates laughed for real and Levering shared his joke.

"They kill ya every way they can," the dying man said. "But even if you can just slap up against it that's okay. I just wanna tree an' some love for me somewhere. You know I been sittin' here lookin' at the sun an' thinkin' on it."

It was the sunlight flowing through the windows at Bounty supermarket that jogged Socrates' memory. He had spent ten more years in prison after Levering died. They gave him parole even though they didn't have to. Unlike Cap, Socrates' victims were black and the Indiana Department of Corrections decided that twenty-seven years four months and sixteen days was the price for that crime.

He'd been free for nine years but that didn't mean a thing. Socrates had cut off everything from his old life. He had no old friends or debts. He was through with Indiana, prison, family and friends. His pledge to Levering got swept away with everything else.

Also, Socrates never thought that he'd be able to honor that pledge. It was just a friendly laugh at the end of a good man's life.

But standing there putting spicy Italian sausages and Lysol disinfectant in a white plastic bag, Socrates realized that he had a debt to pay.

◢ ◢ ◢ ◢

"Can I help you?" the small white man asked, emphasizing each word.

"That's why I'm here."

"The job we have has already been taken," the flabby-faced man said.

"Ain't this a nursery?" Socrates asked.

The man squinted behind his thick rectangular lenses as if he was being addressed in a foreign language that he could not even identify.

"You sell these here plants, right?" Socrates

34

asked, gesturing at the potted plants around the outside lot.

"Yes?"

"Well I come here to buy one, or order one."

"Ooooooh." The word made the white man's lips pucker. That combined with his eyes, magnified by the lenses, made him look like some sort of albino bottom fish. "Something for your yard?"

"Ebony tree," Socrates said. He decided to keep the talk to a minimum, do his business and get out of there before something made him mad.

"Very rare, tropical." The nursery man became excited. He took off his glasses and wiped them on the dirty green apron. "Not indigenous. From India and Africa and Ceylon. Can't grow here at all. It's the heartwood you know. The heartwood's what they want." He shook his head. "No we don't have that. Can't grow it."

"Ain't there some kinda American ebony trees?" Socrates splayed out his fingers to inhibit his fist-forming reflex.

Again the lumpy faced fish stare. "Why yes. Not true ebony but almost the same thing. Comes from somewhere in the Caribbean I believe. Trinidad . . ."

"Jamaica," Socrates said. "I called you yesterday evening an' you said that there's ebony in Jamaica that might could grow here in L.A."

The fish smiled at Socrates.

"I want a Jamaican ebony tree," the ex-con said.

The smile remained but no words or gestures accompanied it.

"I want to buy a Jamaican ebony tree."

"We don't have any."

"I thought that you could get any plant from anywhere in the world. Ain't that what your ad say?"

"It's very difficult to find a plant like that and it can be very expensive. Maybe a shrub palm or a rosebush . . ."

"I got a rosebush already. I want what I said."

The fish slowly became a man. Lips relaxed, eyes narrowing down to some kind of reasonable size. As the gardener became human so, it seemed, did Socrates in the gardener's eyes.

"My name is Antoine," he said.

"Socrates. Socrates Fortlow. I don't wanna cause no problem, Antoine. I just want what I want. You know I live on the other side of town but this was the only place seem to know how to get it."

"You probably talked to Joseph," Antoine said. "He knows about exotic plants. I can have him look up this Jamaican ebony of yours and call you."

"Um. Well you know my phone line is out. Phone company said that the lines is all busted up and they'd have to give me a new number. But I could come back in a couple'a days. When's this Joseph gonna be in?"

36

"On Friday." The nursery man's face had changed again. This time he was trying to read the story behind Socrates' eyes.

"I'll see ya then," Socrates said. "Tell'im I'll come on Friday.

◪ ◪ ◪ ◪

It was Tuesday, meat loaf day at Iula's diner on Slauson.

Socrates got there late, about nine. He climbed the rickety aluminum stairs to the restaurant, which was constructed from two old-time yellow school buses welded together side by side and hoisted above Tony's Mechanical Repair Yard.

Socrates liked to eat his meat loaf alone, but after seven Iula's was always full of people. She cooked soul food like in the old days. Collard greens and fried fish, corn bread and hog maws. She made black-eyed peas and blue crab gumbo every Friday. And there were always three kinds of homemade pie: lemon, apple and mince; sweet potato, pecan and pineapple. She had pumpkin pie and strawberry-rhubarb, even green tomato pie sometimes in the summer.

Iula could cook.

She had broad hips and smiling lips, freckles and orange-brown skin. Gold on her teeth and no rings on her fingers. She was Socrates' girlfriend — sometimes. And sometimes just his friend.

"Hey, Socco," Bernard Williams hailed.

Bernie, a liquor store salesman, sat next to

Stony Wile and Stony's woman-on-the side, Charlene. Bernie was older than Socrates, tall and dark. Stony was much lighter, brawny and closer to the ground. Charlene was all that beauty could be in a black woman, at least that's what Socrates thought. She was long like Bernie but not tall or awkward. She had dark skin and sculptured lips, a high forehead and eyes that looked right down into your heart.

Charlene was born to be a high-society woman but her parents were down-home Baptists who believed in hell and God with only human beings to separate them. So she paid dearly for every stick of lipstick and glimpse in the mirror. Beauty was wanton in her mother's eyes and the love of beauty was a sin. Charlene learned to hate her natural elegance and to find men who treated her like trash.

Now in her forties, when Charlene's wild oats should have been cultivated by some minister or well-to-do businessman, she was still in the streets trading a slapper for a shouter, turning in good men for tramps.

"Hey, Bernie, Stony," Socrates said. He looked at Charlene and she made the slightest kiss with her lips. The ex-con looked away, momentarily shy. When he looked back, she was smiling at the discomfort she had caused.

"Mr. Fortlow," she said sweetly.

"How you tonight, Charlene?"

"Stony wanna stop me from drinkin'. You think I need to change, Mr. Fortlow?"

Socrates didn't want to insult Stony by flirting with Charlene so he just shook his head to say that she was fine the way she was. But there was something too strong, even in that little head movement, and Stony stared down angrily at his meat loaf and greens.

"Come on an' sit down with us here," Bernie offered. They were at a booth by the window.

Socrates sat next to the liquor salesman and took in the bus.

Iula sat behind the long counter that ran the space where the buses were joined. All seven stools were occupied. He recognized Veronica Ashanti and Topper, one of the last black undertakers on Central Avenue. There were a few others whose names he knew, the rest were familiar but no more. Many people were standing around waiting for takeout or seats. But Iula was taking her time talking to Tony LaPort, her landlord and ex-husband, at the end of the counter. She could afford to take it easy because she had hired Charles Rinnet to work in the back bus, which served as the kitchen, during the heavy hours between seven and eleven.

She had once offered Socrates that job but he was still afraid of his hands back then. The hands of a killer had to be careful of what they did.

"What you doin', Socrates?" Bernie asked. "You still workin' at that supermarket?"

"Yeah, yeah. Still packin' them bags. How's Harold?"

"Cheap as a motherfucker," Bernie complained. "You know I asked him for a two-dollar raise after nuthin' for three years an' he told me I could leave."

"Yeah?" Socrates was interested.

"Uh-huh."

"So what you do?"

"I worked out my week and quit. You know they said that when black men owned businesses it was gonna be better but I went over to Zimmerman on Sixtieth and he hired me like that." Bernie snapped his long fingers.

"But I thought you was still with Harold?" Socrates asked.

"I am," Bernie replied. "Harold came to me, *to me*. Because you know nobody like him. The only reason they come to that store is 'cause I know how to respect peoples. An' here he is worse than a white man."

"You got your two dollars?"

Bernie nodded his head like a bass man on a groove. "Motherfucker gimme three."

Socrates laughed deeply. Charlene leaned toward him over the table, drawn to his powerful pleasure. She was wearing a blue sweater that was tight and V-necked.

Socrates turned to Stony and asked, "So, Stony, what's happenin' with you?"

"Nuthin'," the ex-ship welder said petulantly.

Socrates shook his head and stood up.

"I got to go talk to I," he said.

"You gonna come back, Socrates?" Charlene wanted to know.

40

"Maybe in a little while. But first I got to see what I can see."

Iula noticed Socrates' approach. Tony turned around following her gaze. The look in his eye reminded Socrates of Stony's.

Stony and Tony he thought. The rhyme didn't make him smile.

"Hey, Tony," Socrates said. "I."

Tony was of medium height and had dusky skin. His features were half the way between Negro and white. His most noticeable features were his eyes, which were both small and flat. Instead of responding he rose, kissing Iula on the cheek before walking off.

Socrates had never known Tony to be rude. He'd never seen him kiss Iula either. But he took the empty stool and slapped his hands together a couple of times to indicate that he had something to say.

"Meat loaf plate?" Iula asked.

This was also new. Iula always asked how he was doing before plying her trade.

"I wanted to ask you sumpin'," the big man grumbled.

"Well you know I'm pretty busy. This here is rush hour for the restaurant business."

"Okay." Socrates moved to leave but Iula put out her hand. She touched his hard forearm with three fingers. His muscles bunched together and bulged under the gentle pressure.

"Tony want me to get back together wit' him," she said in a flat, accusing tone.

"He wanna get married again?"

"That's what he said."

The noise in the room became an irritating buzz in Socrates' ears. He flicked his powerful fingers at the side of his head and grimaced.

"You want that?" he asked.

"Ain't nobody else askin' me nuthin'," Iula said.

"That what you want? You want somebody t'ask you sumpin'?"

"What I want don't matter."

Looking at those hard lips Socrates knew he wasn't going to get kissed. He knew that she wasn't going to come over and help him plant Levering's tree.

"Well?" Iula's question was a concession to the passion she felt for the ex-con. He knew that. He knew what she wanted. He knew what he should say.

"You know how they say some folks ain't got a pot to piss in?" Socrates asked.

"Uh-huh."

"Well I got me a pot okay," he said. "But it's old an' it's rusty an' it done sprung more'n one leak."

"What you talkin' 'bout, Socrates Fortlow?"

The diner didn't seem noisy any more. Now it felt as if they had all gone quiet to hear his sad excuse.

"You got a business here, I," Socrates whispered. He glanced over his shoulder but no one was looking his way. They were all still talking

42

and eating, minding their own affairs.

"Yeah," Iula said. "An' it's a good business too."

"I know it is," Socrates responded. "Tony's always workin' too. You got that sour boy doin' dishes in the back. Tony got a four-legged German shepherd an' here my own dog only got two front legs to drag around wit'."

"You have a job, Socrates."

"I put groceries in bags, I. I live in a house that nobody knows is there. You know I been workin' for a year an' I'm still savin' up for the deposit on a phone."

Socrates was looking at the three big freckles on Iula's face. There were seven more on her back. He remembered kissing all ten of those dark beauty marks. The last one was in the middle of her left buttock. When he got there Iula let out such a sigh of pleasure that he could have gone home right then sure of her satisfaction. He could see that Iula was thinking about those kisses. But this time there was ice instead of fire in her eyes.

"Maybe you can wait forever, Mr. Fortlow," she said. "But you know this black woman got to get on with her life."

She stood up and walked toward the kitchen. He didn't reach out to stop her. He didn't even have his Tuesday meat loaf plate.

◪ ◪ ◪ ◪

Antoine and Joseph stood so close to one another that Socrates thought they might have

43

been frightened of him. Slender Joseph was a few inches taller than his nursery friend.

"Antoine says that you were here for the ebony tree already," Joseph said. He extended his skinny neck and gave Socrates a gawking grin. "That's sweet."

"You said that you might could get it," Socrates answered.

"I was wrong," Joseph said with his head nodding forward and back as if he were following some complex melody. "The ebony, real or not, cannot thrive in this climate. Maybe if you had a hot house environment . . ."

"Naw, man. All I got is a yard. And it don't get sun but half the day."

The men were both beaming with pride. Antoine was barely suppressing a grin.

"I was sorry to be so rude the other day, Mr. Fortlow," Antoine began. "Joseph and I talked about it at home last night and we came up with an idea you might like. Come on."

The men turned in unison beckoning the big man to follow. They walked through the entrance of the shelter they used as their office. It was just an arched tunnel of heavy plastic fabric supported by thick bamboo poles. On the left were bird of paradise, dwarf avocado trees, rosebushes, and other potted plants for the yard. On the right were cut flowers in rubber vases of various heights waiting for young men to buy in the early evening before going out with their girlfriends. It flashed through Socrates' mind that he could get a big sunflower for Iula. But the idea receded when he remembered how hard she had looked on Tuesday night.

They went out through the back end of the shelter into a large yard of potted trees. They came to a small green rubber tub with a small white tree in it.

"Isn't it beautiful?" Joseph asked.

"It sure is," Antoine said. For the first time Socrates noticed a slight southern drawl in Antoine's words.

"What is it?" asked Socrates.

"Coral tree," Joseph informed him. "Very exotic, from Japan. And expensive if it's full grown. But this sapling's only forty dollars."

Socrates wondered if these men were trying to fool him out of his money; if they were trying to sell him some apple seed that fell in a barrel full of dirt. How did he know what this twig was?

"Have you seen those beautiful white trees with the crimson flowers down the middle of Olympic Boulevard out in Santa Monica?" Antoine asked.

"The ones that's mostly bare?" Socrates could see the tall trees with the orange-red flowers in his mind, their brawny white limbs circled with black seams. He remembered how they spread out over the street and found himself smiling, no longer worried about being cheated.

"They grow pretty fast," Joseph said.

"How do I plant it?" Socrates asked.

45

Socrates carried the tub from the bus stop to a phone booth on Central. He took a slip of paper from his pocket. On it he had written a phone number given to him by Bernie at Harold's Liquors the night before.

The phone only rang once.

"Hello," she said.

"Charlene?"

"Is that Socrates Fortlow?"

"You recognized me, that's pretty good."

"Stony's at home with his wife and kids," she said.

"I really wanted to talk to you, Charry."

"Oh?"

Socrates could feel his heart beating. He took in a deep breath through his nostrils and exhaled through his mouth.

"Yeah, Charlene. I bought me a tree and I plan to plant it in my li'l yard here. An' . . . well, it's kinda special."

"Special how?"

"It's for a friend. A friend that died. He died a long time ago but still I should, I mean I want to do this for him."

"Uh-huh, I see," Charlene said. "But what you want from me? You wanna borrah a shovel or somethin'?"

"Levering, that was my friend's name, he was a ladies' man but they had him in prison and he died there. Anyway he asked me to invite a beautiful woman over when I plant the tree and say some words. He wanted to know that a pretty girl was there for his last request."

The phone was silent for a moment and then a moment more.

"Charlene, you there?"

"Uh-huh," she whispered.

"I don't mean to disrespect you now, sister. It's just that's what Levering . . ."

"You couldn't be disrespectful if you tried, Mr. Fortlow. No I don't believe that you could."

Socrates' chest filled with air. The growing erection made him shift his position at the pay phone.

"I just meant that it would be a favor to me if you could come watch and then maybe drink a toast."

"What time you want me?"

"Tomorrah afternoon 'bout five'd be good. I mean if you ain't busy."

"I'll be there at five."

"I live at . . ."

"I know where you live at. In that alley offa Central where them old boarded-up stores is, right?"

"Yeah. How'd you know?"

"Stony showed me once. He said how you was so poor that you just lived in a crack between two buildin's. He was makin' fun but I remembered just in case I had to come by one day."

Socrates shifted his stance once more.

"So I'll see ya tomorrah?" he asked.

"At five. Bye now, baby."

On the way home Socrates was glad that he had the tub to hold in front of his pants. He was relieved to get home but he wasn't relaxed.

Socrates' dick stayed hard, off and on, all night. He had to take off his pants to ease the discomfort. But he was just as miserable naked. There he was walking around the place like a teenage boy after his first kiss. He was almost sixty. It was a shame and indicated weakness, that's what Socrates felt.

He didn't want to lose control because of a woman. He cursed himself for inviting her. What did Levering care or know about who came to his tree planting and who didn't?

The erection was persistent. Sometimes it would deflate a little but as soon as he remembered Charlene's words, and the huskiness that accompanied them, he was back to full mast and angry.

His dreams didn't help. All the prison dreams about women came on him in a rush. It wasn't one dream or one woman but all of the women he had known or dreamed about. Even Muriel, the woman he'd murdered, was there stroking his brow and begging for more.

In the middle of the night when he got up to go to the toilet he was hard. He wondered if something had broken, a blood vessel or something. But he knew that it was a dam that had burst, a dam that he had built in his heart many years before. Somewhere between Iula's angry lips

48

and Charlene's eager willingness, somewhere between his promise to Levering Jones and his job, Socrates had allowed himself to want. But the wanting scared him. Charlene scared him.

He decided that he would meet her in the yard and stay there. If she wanted to go to the toilet he'd point the way but stay outside.

If she said she was hungry he'd take her to Bolger's for short ribs and corn bread.

That way he wouldn't have to do something that might get out of hand. That way he could honor Levering without going crazy and doing something wrong.

Socrates spent the morning excavating a hole for the coral tree. After that he went down to the nursery on Hooper to get fertilizer for the soil. He read the newspaper and ate canned chili for lunch. Then he went down to Harold's to buy a bottle of Old Grand-Dad just in case Charlene wanted a drink.

"Old Grand-Dad?" Bernie asked with a sly grin.

"Yeah, what of it?" Socrates said.

"Nuthin', man. Nuthin'," Bernie said. "It's just that Old Grand-Dad is Charlene's favorite whiskey and you just axed me for her number the other day . . ."

In his mind Socrates was afraid. Deeply afraid, but not for his physical safety. He knew a hundred ways to kill a man. He knew how to disappear and show up when you least expected it.

He wasn't afraid of Stony Wile's jealousy and neither was he afraid to die.

But there he was again, still doing the same thing, making the same mistake after thirty-six years of prison and poverty. His fear was that he couldn't stop making the same mistake. He didn't want to kill another man over a woman who smiled his way. That's what frightened Socrates: he was afraid that he couldn't control his own urges and that those urges would wipe out all the good he had tried to do.

But the fear was on the inside of Socrates' mind. His face was, to judge by Bernie's reaction, a visage of black rage.

"Hey, Socco. Hey, man. I was just jokin'," Bernie stammered. "I didn't mean nuthin', man. You know what you do is your business an' you better bet I ain't gonna get in that. Here, take this fifth. It's on me, brother. On me."

Socrates accepted the gift because he knew that he couldn't talk without throwing his fists. He gritted his teeth and shoved the paper bag under his arm then he nodded to Bernie and walked out holding his breath.

For a long time after he got home Socrates rehearsed how he'd plant the tree and drink a toast and then tell Charlene that he had to go to work to do an overnight inventory at Bounty.

But then four-thirty rolled around and he got hard again. He went out into the yard and began playing with Killer. Socrates had set up two seven-foot steel poles at diagonal opposites across his small yard. He attached them with thick nylon cord. He took another cord, nine inches shy of six feet, attaching one end to the high wire and the other end to a leather harness that supported Killer's backside. That way Killer had the run of the yard and Socrates could take down the short cord and use it as a kind of leash to take his dog for walks. It was good exercise for the ex-con because even without his hind legs Killer was seventy pounds of jet-black mutt.

By five thirty Socrates could hear his heart beating. By six he was sure she wouldn't show.

When she finally appeared at six fifteen he didn't know what he was feeling.

She was wearing a black dress that you would have said, if you saw it on a wire hanger, belonged on a woman half a foot shorter and twenty pounds lighter. But Socrates didn't complain about the deep brown cleavage or the flesh of her thighs. He didn't ask why she was late. He didn't even remember that she was late. He said no more to Charlene than he had to Bernie but his face was an open book.

She said, "Hi," and he opened the gate to the alley. She held out her hand and he took it to lead her across the threshold. They walked past the hole he'd dug and the tree next to it. Killer shoved his friendly snout up under the short dress. Charlene giggled and scratched his ear.

In the kitchen Socrates took Charlene by her waist and guided her to sit in his one good wood chair. He took off her flat-heeled black suede shoes and caressed her calf with a hand that knew a hundred ways to kill.

Charlene sighed and he said, "Stand up."

He pulled the black straps off her shoulders and then went down on his knees again as he pulled the dress toward her ankles. He swung around to sit in the chair. Using his hands he turned her slowly around to look at the body that had lived in his dreams.

"Baby," Charlene said in a voice that was almost pleading.

Socrates could see that she was getting shy from his deep scrutiny and his powerful hands.

"What?" he asked her.

"I don't know," she said.

They played love until nearly midnight. It wasn't until then that Socrates broke the seal on his whiskey. They had only one drink before going back to bed.

"What you thinkin'?" Charlene asked him in the darkness of his sleeping room.

"That it's always about me," Socrates said.

"What you mean?"

"Here I am sayin' that I did this for Levering. But Levering is gone and I'm here with you. You know I think I woulda bust if you didn't come over. It was me had to sleep with you. Even though I knew it was wrong."

"What's wrong with it? I ain't married. You ain't neither. Are you?"

52

"Maybe it ain't. I don't know. At least nobody died over it."

"I almost did," Charlene sighed.

They fell asleep in each other's arms.

◪ ◪ ◪ ◪

At four o'clock the next afternoon Socrates went to Iula's diner. Before he climbed the aluminum ladder he saw Tony working in the machine shop below the restaurant. Socrates waved at Tony who had a blowtorch in his hand. The mechanic made some kind of gesture and Socrates continued his climb.

Iula was alone behind the counter. Charles Rinnet was in the kitchen bus behind.

"Hello," Iula said in a neutral tone.

"I," Socrates said.

"Not quite ready yet but if you give us ten minutes you could have somethin'."

"I just had to say somethin'." Socrates' voice was full of the love that Charlene gave him. It arrested his ex-girlfriend and she gave him a nod.

"I ain't stayin'," Socrates said. "I just wanted to say that you mean somethin' to me and I care a lot about you. You a good woman. You got a lot goin' for you that any man would like to share. If you need a man today you should have that. And I'm sorry it ain't me. But you know I got business t'take care of before I could saddle a woman with this here heart I got. You know sometimes I feel like I'm gonna explode. An' you cain't blow up on someone you love, baby. No."

Iula said nothing but she didn't seem angry.

53

She just nodded and looked at him.

He kissed her on the cheek and left.

That night he sat outside with the black dog's head in his lap drinking toasts to Levering's coral tree. At some point he fell asleep. Hours later he came awake. The stars were shining and his neighborhood was quiet and peaceful. He felt safe even though he was outside because there was no light stronger than a star shining on him or his promise.

shift, shift, shift

"But I ain't did nuthin'," Darryl said in a voice that was sometimes husky and sometimes high.

"If you ain't did nuthin' then why they kick you outta school?" The ex-convict asked. They were facing each other in Socrates' apartment.

"It wasn't my fault," the skinny boy said. He had shot up in the last year. Almost as tall as Socrates, the boy slouched under the angry glare.

"Then whose fault is it?"

"It was Cassandra. If she wasn't always messin' wit' me everythin' woulda been okay. But she always wanna be makin' fun."

"So you hit her?"

Darryl's head bowed even lower.

"You hit a girl on the school yard but it wasn't your fault? Somebody threw your fist for you?" Socrates brought his knuckle underneath Darryl's chin and pulled him up straight. "Huh?"

"I didn't hit her wit' no fists. I just pushed her an' she fell. I'idn't mean it."

What Darryl saw in Socrates' eyes had meant death for some unlucky men in the past. Darryl knew all those men's names and the exact time of each death. He was the closest living being on earth to the ex-convict/murderer turned boxboy. Darryl had also killed once and confessed to Socrates. There were no secrets between man and boy.

"Ain't you learned nuthin', Darryl? Ain't you listened t'me at all?"

"She was makin' fun'a my clothes. I asked her to go out wit' me an' she run to her friends an' started talkin' to them 'bout how I was dirty an' dressed bad." Darryl was shaking with rage even while he cowered under Socrates' stare.

"What the MacDaniels said about this?" Socrates asked.

"Nuthin'."

"You told 'em?"

"Yeah," Darryl complained. "They just said not to do that no more and that I better just go to Bounty for the day I was suspended so I don't get in no trouble while they at work."

"They didn't make you do nuthin' else?"

"No."

Darryl slumped away from the big hand. The ex-convict could see by the way the boy held his shoulders that he expected to get hit. He'd been standing in that posture ever since Socrates came up and asked him why he was at work when it was a school day.

"I'm not gonna hit you, li'l brother," the man said. "Somethin's wrong here but hittin' ain't gonna make it right."

"What then?" Darryl asked.

Before Socrates could answer, Killer started

barking in the yard. Then a hard knock came on the door.

Socrates hesitated a moment. Maybe, if Darryl wasn't there, he would have fished his .38 from behind the loose board in his kitchen wall.

Instead he called out, "Who's out there bangin' like that?"

"Police!"

■ ■ ■ ■

There were three white men standing at Socrates' only door. Two of them were in uniform and one sported a well-worn brown suit. Socrates cursed himself silently for never putting in the escape door he'd always thought about.

"Socrates Fortlow?" the man in the suit asked.

"You got a badge, man?" Socrates said in a voice that didn't give away his fast-pumping heart.

"Don't fuck with me, jailbird," the man in the brown suit said.

He was short and well built for a middle-aged man. His face was flat and oval. He had squinty eyes and tight skin but he was still a white man, confident with the tall and athletic-looking cops at his back.

Confident but no fool. He made sure that Socrates' hands were in sight. They were big hands. A giant's hands really.

"Inspector Beryl," the plainclothes cop said as he displayed a badge and identity card in a leather fold. "Homicide."

The spasm that went through Socrates' neck and shoulders was one tick away from attempted murder.

"Are you Socrates Fortlow?" Inspector Beryl asked again.

"Yeah. What you want?"

"Put your hands against the wall behind you and spread your legs."

Again Socrates' mind went to violence. The policemen were standing close to each other. None of the three had weapon drawn. Socrates was almost sixty and they weren't afraid of him. He could have easily bowled them over. There was a spade propped up against the outside wall that he could grab after bringing them down with his weight. The chances were good that he'd get away. But almost definitely somebody would die.

A second had elapsed.

"Put your hands on the wall . . . ," Beryl began the command anew.

It would have to be then that Socrates moved. Those men were all younger than him. He'd have to use surprise to the hilt.

He turned his head, pretending that he was going to comply. Darryl was standing there trying not to look scared. Socrates felt Beryl's hand against his shoulder.

The moment for escape passed. Maybe if he had been alone. Socrates chuckled.

"What you say?" the plainclothes cop asked.

"I said, you're welcome, officer."

At the station they took his green army belt, folding knife and shoelaces. Then he was led to an interrogation room and made to sit down on a metal chair that was bolted to the floor. They attached his handcuffs to two thick metal rings screwed into the floor and then left him alone.

The only thing that showed how fast Socrates' heart was working was the sweat that glistened on his bald black head. Otherwise the ex-con could have been a dark statue placed in the center of that small room by some sculptor who knew that the truth could only be told in secret.

After some time the door to the room opened again and Beryl appeared with two other men in suits. One was white and the other a milky brown. The colored man had a thick mustache. The white one had a big belly hanging down. They were about the same height, not over six feet.

"Socrates Fortlow?" the big-bellied cop said.

"You gonna charge me or what?"

"My name is Kirkshaw," the big white cop continued. "Captain Kirkshaw. Tell us what you know about Minnie Dawn Lee."

There was a mechanical hum somewhere in the wall. Socrates wondered where it came from.

"Do you understand me?" the policeman asked.

"Do I get a lawyer?"

"Do you need a lawyer?" the milky brown cop asked.

59

Socrates turned toward his fellow black man but he didn't say anything.

"The key to those chains is the truth." Inspector Beryl spoke for the first time.

He almost cursed them but Socrates knew that any show of feeling would bring on some sort of assault. They'd wait until he opened up a crack and then they'd concentrate on that chink until he was either dead or guilty.

But Socrates could outwait any man who had a home to go to. From the moment those policemen showed up at his door he was a convict again. And a convict could wait his whole life without cracking a smile or shedding a tear.

"You killed a woman in Indiana," Biggers, the Negro cop, said. "Did you shoot her too?"

Socrates' nose itched but he wouldn't have scratched it even if his hands were free. Just that small gesture would have given up too much to the thugs who called themselves law.

It had already been over two hours. All Socrates had asked for was a lawyer or some kind of charge. He was thirsty and thinking about the woman he'd murdered thirty-six years before, Muriel. He could feel the husky gust of her last breath against his face. He didn't remember the night of the murder at first but this last gasp had returned to him in a dream he had in prison many years later.

"Tell us about it, Fortlow," Kirkshaw said. "What happened with Minnie? You wanted a blow job for free? Is that it?"

The easiest time in a black man's life is when he cain't fight at all. The words were from his aunt Bellandra after the first time Socrates had been brought home for fighting in the street. *He don't care about winnin'. No. He know he ain't never gonna win. But as long as he can swing his fists he thinks at least he could hurt somebody else. But once he cain't fight at all, even if that mean he gonna die, the black man don't have to worry. He give it his one shot an' now he can take his medicine.*

Socrates let his shoulders slump down when he remembered the words of his crazy auntie and Muriel's dying sigh. The men hovering about him were in charge. They could do whatever they wanted and so he wasn't responsible for a thing.

"You worried, huh?" Kirkshaw said, mistaking Socrates' relaxed shoulders for defeat.

Socrates looked at the man's shoes thinking that it wasn't the first time he'd been kicked.

The questioning went on for about five hours. Finally the shift was up and the overtime was no longer worth it. They hit him with rolled-up newspapers and open-hand slaps. The only blood was on the inside of his mouth. Bruises didn't show on black skin unless there was swelling.

When they brought Socrates to his cell, he was tired. He'd learned that the girl in the silver miniskirt, the one found in his alley a month earlier, was Minnie Dawn Lee, a party girl. The police were investigating but they had no leads until someone said something about the ex-con who lived in that alley. They got his records from the prison authority and figured they could close the case before Friday.

He wasn't a suspect, they said, and so he didn't get read his rights or given a lawyer. All he got was some questions, that's what they said.

▰ ▰ ▰ ▰

Socrates was put in a holding cell with another man, Tiny Jones.

"He was the kinda man," Socrates told Darryl a few days later, "scare the panties offa some white woman at Bounty. Nineteen years old an' about three hundred fifty pounds. He come up to me not one minute after I was there an' say, 'You got some fuckin' cigarettes on you, old man?'"

"What you say?" Darryl asked.

"I pushed him wit' one hand an' he fount himself up against the wall. After that he just went back to his cot an' stayed quiet."

"Fortlow." The voice came from far away. Socrates imagined a black giant that sometimes appeared in his dreams. A big man with powerful limbs who came to remind Socrates, now and then, that there was a lot of work left for him to do.

"Fortlow." But it was only a policeman, a guard really. "Your lawyer's here."

"Have I been charged?"

"Come on," the uniformed guard said. "I don't have time to waste on you."

"Ernesto Chavez," the lawyer said to Socrates. He was slender and sharp with a razor thin mustache and eyebrows that might have been plucked. His skin was olive and his eyes were the sleek color of a black widow spider's skin.

"Who sent you?" Socrates asked.

"Marty Gonzalez asked me to represent you."

"Shit," Socrates said through the mouthpiece in the wire-reinforced plate glass. "Man, I couldn't even buy you pomade."

Ernesto Chavez had perfect white teeth and a good sense of humor to show them off.

"You got that right, bro," he said. "But this is free."

"Free?"

"Marty used to bring me a care package from the store every week when I was in law school. You know . . ." Chavez finished the sentence by rubbing his hands together indicating how one washed the other.

Socrates understood.

"So," Ernesto continued. "You got a problem here."

"Somebody killed a girl and dumped her in the alley not too far from my door. I was in for a murder in sixty-one. They think it's in my blood."

"Did you tell them anything?"

"Nuthin' to tell."

"But maybe they made something up," Ernesto suggested. "Your eye's kinda swollen."

"I asked 'em for a lawyer. They said that there wasn't no charge."

The young man's eyes rolled and a smile flitted underneath his mustache.

"You have some good friends, Mr. Fortlow. They came down here with the money to get you out but I think a quick call to the court will work just as well. You didn't tell 'em anything, right?"

Socrates stood up and gestured to the guard that he was ready to leave.

◪ ◪ ◪ ◪

Outside the police station that morning Socrates found Marty Gonzalez, his friend Howard Shakur and Darryl, along with the lawyer, Ernie Chavez. Howard was by far the largest of the men and Socrates was most surprised to see him there.

"Darryl called me," triple-chinned Howard said. "He got my number from Luvia and called out to Venice."

"Are you okay, Socco?" Marty Gonzalez asked. "Did they do that to your eye?"

Socrates didn't answer Marty's question. There were too many things going through his head. It was early in the morning. Each man there was missing something, work or sleep or a paycheck or school.

64

"You okay, Mr. Fortlow?" Ernesto Chavez asked.

"Man, I don't even know you," Socrates said.

"He's my cousin," Marty Gonzalez said.

All Socrates could do was stare. His friends looked at each other.

"Well," big Howard said. "I got to go home and get to bed. You know I just did the graveyard shift. You wanna ride to school, Darryl?"

The boy looked at Socrates.

"Try to stay in it this time," Socrates said.

"You wanna ride to work?" Marty asked.

"No." Socrates was curt. "I got to do some things at home first. I'll be in at about noon."

"You wanna a ride home before I take Darryl?" Howard wanted to know.

"Just lea'me alone, all right?"

They left him standing on the street in front of the police station. Again he was like a statue; a slightly larger than life-size image of a black man against white stone. His khaki pants and black T-shirt were tight over arms and legs that bulged with angry strength. His head tilted up slightly.

The assistant manager Jason Fulbright looked at the clock when he saw Socrates coming through the sliding glass doors of Bounty. Socrates followed his immediate boss's eyes to see that it was two fifteen.

Socrates stifled the urge to go up to the younger black man and say, "I have a good excuse, boss man. I had to wipe the prints offa my thirty-eight and go hide it under a wreck in the empty lot down the alley from my place. 'Cause you know a ex-con been down for double murder and rape cain't own no pistol to protect himself in this country. In this country they got to protect niggahs like you."

Socrates realized that he was speaking under his breath, saying what he was thinking and building into a fury. So he turned away and went to the back of the store where he could find some hard work for his hands to do.

"The police came to see me today before you got here," Marty Gonzalez, the store manager, told Socrates.

It was ten fifteen that night and the last customer had been let out of the front door with a key by Sarah Shulberg and her best friend, the black girl Robyn Craig.

"Oh yeah?"

"They said that you killed two people, that you raped the woman, and that you were labeled incorrigible at a prison in the Midwest."

They were standing next to a bin of pink grapefruits that were piled in a pyramid.

"Oh yeah? What you say?"

"I said that to begin with I knew about your record and that Bounty had a policy of giving people a chance to reform. And then I told them that midwestern prisons must be pretty strange to release incorrigibles and let them move out of state."

"I ain't told you 'bout my record," Socrates said.

"It's not any of my business and those cops were wrong to tell me."

Socrates wanted to hit Marty. He wanted to pick up a grapefruit and squeeze it until all of the bitter juice was wasted on the floor. His distress was physical. His head ached and his stomach was ready to roll over. Socrates' mouth was filling up with saliva when he said, "I got to get outta here, Marty."

The shorter supervisor put his hand on Socrates' right biceps.

"I still want you for my produce man, Socco."

"I gotta go" was the only answer he could give.

◢ ◢ ◢ ◢

Weakness was the convict's worst enemy. Soft muscles, bad eyesight, poor mental faculties or just plain tired — all of these were life threatening conditions in the state pen.

Socrates couldn't rise out of bed for twenty minutes after he woke up the next morning. The room was spinning. He hadn't eaten since the afternoon of the day before. In the slam the guards would have beaten him to his feet, or to the floor.

Because of the dizziness he had to sit down to urinate. He was still on the toilet when the knocking started.

They knocked for a long time. Long enough for Socrates to drag himself to the door.

Beryl and Biggers stood side by side.

"Can we come in?" the milk chocolate man asked.

Socrates slumped in his good chair while the two cops leaned up against the wall.

"You know we got a quota down at the station, Fortlow," Beryl was explaining. "They expect us to solve one out of three murders and they expect one out of five of the perps to be put in jail. It's not as bad as it sounds. Because you see if you killed once you probably will again. I mean it's like a habit with you people."

Socrates looked at Biggers but the black cop didn't seem to think his partner meant any insult to *his* race or kind.

"One out of five is more like three or four outta five because the one you get's prob'ly done a couple'a others." Beryl smiled. "Like those three Mexican kids killed up on MLK last March. Girl was raped and shot just like this Minnie Lee. Would you submit to a blood test, Mr. Fortlow?"

Whatever it was they expected from Socrates, it wasn't laughter.

"Shit, man," the big friendly killer replied. He took a deep breath and then sat up straight. "I ain't never bled for nobody wasn't willin' t'give up sumpin' too. Shit."

"We know you killed her, Socrates." Biggers spoke so softly it was almost a whisper. "And we intend to bust you for it, don't make any mistake about that."

"Tell me, Detective Biggers," Socrates said.

"What's your first name?"

"We're asking the questions here," Beryl answered for his partner.

"Listen t'me, motherfucker." Socrates stood up from his chair. "I ain't afraid of you. You get that? You ain't gonna scare me into pleadin'. An' if you think you could hurt me then you don't know what pain is." Socrates thumped a heavy point finger against his own chest. "*I* am pain. Me. I ain't killed nobody in a lotta years. So you could forget a confession. Ain't nuthin' that the cop squad gonna get outta me. You sure cain't hurt me. You could kill me. You could set me up. You can put chains on my arms and legs but you sure the fuck cain't make me lie on myself."

The policemen stood straight and made subtle defensive motions with their hands. Socrates laughed again.

He looked into Bigger's face and said, "Listen, brother. You one'a them, I know that, but you one'a us too. You know what it's like out here. You know what it's like. Read up on me, brother. Read about how when I woke up and found I had killed my friends I just wandered off to a bar somewhere, I didn't even know where I was. When the cops come and th'ew down on me I gave up. They asked if I knew why I was bein' arrested. I said yeah. I knew. I knew. I ain't no gangster, man. I ain't no thief or hired muscle. I'm just mad, mothahfuckah. Now take this white man an' get outta my house."

The veins on Socrates' neck writhed as if some

unnatural evil threatened to burst through his skin.

Beryl stepped in front of his partner but there was no need. Neither man would have stood up to Socrates, not in the mood he was in, not if he was eighty.

"We're gonna take you down on this one, Fortlow. You'll be back in prison soon enough. And this time there won't be any parole for you."

Socrates went in to work. He was only half an hour late. He avoided Marty most of the day. Even when they had to talk, Socrates kept it short and gave away nothing of what was going on.

"How's it going?" Marty asked after the lunch break.

"Fine."

"The police come to see you any more?"

"Naw. They just want somebody t'pin it on. I woulda been the one if you hadn't put your cousin on the case. Thanks, Marty. I owe you."

"Have you —" the manager began.

"I got to get to work, Marty," Socrates said. "Talk to you later."

Socrates was sure that the knock on the door at six thirty that evening was the police again. He looked forward to their visit more than any friends. Enemies brought out his strength. Somebody to go up against where you knew the trouble and were ready for war. That's what

70

Socrates knew best.

He put away his evil grin before pulling the door open but the men standing there were not official.

"Darryl. Howard. How you boys doin'?"

"You gonna stand outta the way an' let us in?" Howard asked.

"I'm tired, man. Been workin' all day. What you want?"

"We done drove all the way out here," Howard said. "You know I picked up Darryl 'cause he was worried about you."

"Well I'm fine. Just fine. You don't have to worry 'bout me." Socrates shifted from one foot to the other as if he wanted to close the door but didn't want to be rude. Howard put three hundred and some odd pounds across the threshold to make sure that the door stayed open.

"What's wrong with you, Howard?" Socrates said. "You wanna get hurt?"

"What's wrong wit' *you*, man? Here we come on down to the jail wit' our piggy banks and lawyers an' all you got to say is you tired and please step out the way."

Socrates looked hard at his friend. Howard was one of the few men that Socrates was jealous of. He had a beautiful wife who had a job, he had kids that were just like butter and brown sugar. He had a job working with computers and lived in Venice down near the beach. Howard had more than Socrates could ever hope for but he didn't seem thankful or even proud.

71

"Let us in, Socco," the big man said. "We got stuff to talk about."

". . . so I went over to the MacDaniels' an' told 'em that me an' Corina would be happy to take Darryl in," Howard was saying. He and Darryl were sitting on folding chairs in Socrates' sleeping room. Socrates only had two rooms. One was the kitchen, where he ate, and one was for sleeping and talking to his guests.

Darryl was quiet and so was Socrates. Howard explained how when he drove Darryl to school they talked about how he had been suspended for hitting a girl.

"I told 'em that maybe Darryl needed a little more supervision from somebody who come from down where he was from," Howard said. " 'Cause you know old Mr. MacDaniels is okay but he don't know how to thump a boy upside his head when he get fresh or sullen."

Howard playfully flicked a finger at Darryl's ear. Socrates saw the pain on the boy's face but Darryl didn't complain.

"When they took him in they thought he'd be just like their son that died, like he'd know all the rules. But I told'em that Darryl's a hardheaded boy from the hood an' he needed somebody like me t'keep him straight."

"What they say?" Socrates asked Howard.

"They were scared, man. Scared 'cause 'a how their son died in that drive-by. You know they worried that Darryl be arguin' 'bout goin' t'bed at night. They think that might lead to crack." Howard laughed at his own joke while Socrates and Darryl watched. "Naw, man, they want somebody t'take Darryl."

"They said that?"

"I'ma bring the papers down to social welfare next week."

Dizziness assailed Socrates again. He felt like a boxer sucker-punched after the bell.

" 'Cause you know, Socco," Howard said, not yet tired of his own voice. "You done me some good turns. You helped me out an' ain't never axed me for nuthin'. Corina said that I owed you, man. An' I know that you an' the MacDaniels don't get along so good. But you know Darryl could come down here wit' you whenever you want. I mean me an' Corina'll have custody through the foster service but you could be like his uncle."

Darryl rubbed his hand over the top of his head and stared at Howard the mountain, as Socrates' friend Right Burke used to call Howard Shakur.

"Well?" Howard asked Socrates.

Socrates was still reeling, looking for a reason to get mad. He wanted Howard to go away. He wanted Darryl to go away too, but then he didn't. He never felt like an old man before he walked out of that jail. But now just standing up seemed like a heavy chore.

"What you want, Howard, a medal?"

"At least a thank you."

"An' if I was so sick that I was laid up in a hospital an' a nurse had to wipe my ass would I have to say thank you to her too?" Socrates watched Howard's back get straight. Howard was strong, and tough too. But for all his weight and youth he wouldn't have been able to prevail over twenty-seven years of studied violence.

Socrates could feel the fight gathering in his shoulders. The tick down along his spine that had almost set him against the police was throbbing again. There was no dizziness or weakness now. All Socrates had to do was straighten up like Howard had and there wouldn't be any question anymore about who was right or who was in charge.

"Hey, man," the ex-con said instead of altering his posture. "I'm sorry. It's just that I don't know how to act when people get all in my business."

"We were tryin' t'help."

"I know. I know. An' I appreciate it. But you know when the shit come down I only know one way to be."

It wasn't much of a thank you but it was enough to smooth out Howard's feathers. The fat man nodded, considered the ex-con's words and then shrugged his acceptance.

"Leave Darryl wit' me, Howard. I'll bring him out over to there tomorrow."

The big man nodded and rose to leave. He rubbed the boy's head and walked out through the kitchen. Socrates followed him to the threshold and watched him walk to his old

Impala. At the last moment Socrates went out to his gate and waved as the Impala drove off.

◪ ◪ ◪ ◪

"Why you wanna be tellin' my business all over the place, Darryl?"

"Huh?"

"Howard. Marty. Why you wanna tell them I was in jail?"

"I told the MacDaniels too but they said that they couldn't stand in the way of the law," the boy said. "That's why I asked Howard if I could go live wit' them."

"But why you wanna go tell Marty, man?" Socrates asked.

"They killed my daddy up in jail," Darryl said. "I didn't try an' get him out. I didn't know."

Cassandra Tuthill and her family lived at Stanley and Airdrome. Darryl and Socrates left home early and got to her house at just a little after seven in the morning.

"Yes?" Mr. Tuthill, a grayish looking Negro, asked at the door.

Socrates, his big hands on Darryl's shoulders, said, "Mr. Tuthill? My name is Socrates Fortlow. I'm Darryl's, um, Darryl's uncle."

"I don't know Darryl." Mr. Tuthill was small with sloped shoulders. He was wearing a brown suit with a vest and tie. He'd missed a small patch of hair in his morning shave and he was squinting.

"Darryl pushed your daughter at school," Soc-

75

rates said. "He got punished but I brought him over here to apologize. Because you got to answer for what you did wrong. That's what I know."

Tuthill blinked twice and then took a pair of glasses from his breast pocket. He looked closer at the skinny boy and closer still at the man with the philosopher's name.

"Cassandra," the gray father called without taking his eyes off of the man and boy standing at the front door.

The girl was a study in round and brown. She wasn't at all heavy but her dark eyes were like big marbles and her head was a pretty ball. The blue dress and yellow sweater set off her dark skin. Her cheeks were apples. Socrates couldn't help but smile.

"Yes, Daddy?" she said. Her eyes turned sullen when she caught sight of Darryl.

"This boy has something to say to you, honey."

"I'm sorry, Cassandra," the boy said immediately. "I'm sorry I pushed you. I didn't mean to hurt you or nuthin' an' it won't happen no mo'."

"Uh-huh," the girl said. She was just about to turn away when her father stopped her.

"Cassie," he said.

"What?"

"This boy just came all the way to your house in the morning to say he was sorry."

"I said all right."

"You shake his hand and tell him that you accept his apology."

76

The girl did as she was told. Both children were somber while the men smiled on them.

"Have you had breakfast, Mr. Fortlow?"

"We got to go," the ex-convict said.

Officer Biggers was waiting for Socrates that evening when he got home. He was standing at the back gate smoking a cigarette and staring off into the distance.

"Officer," Socrates said.

"Socrates," Biggers replied.

"Am I under arrest again?"

"Not this time."

"You got a question I ain't answered?"

It was time for the policeman to laugh.

"Sumpin' funny?" Socrates wanted to know.

"I don't think that you'd ever answer a question of mine straight."

"So what you want?"

"I read the police reports from Indiana," Biggers said. "What you said was true. Even the arresting officer said that you were more in shock than unrepentant."

Socrates had never heard that. He wanted to know more but didn't ask.

"So as far Minnie Lee is concerned, well, it don't mean you did an' it don't mean you didn't. I wouldn't bet one way or the other on that."

"So you gonna let up on me?"

Biggers shook his head. Maybe he was even sorry.

"No," he said. "Beryl and the captain got a

hard-on for you now. They gonna be down on you every time there's a crime within six blocks of here."

"Shit. That's every other day."

"Maybe you should move. You know if you leave the district they'll forget about you."

Socrates felt a moment of dizziness but that passed quickly.

"Naw, man," he said. "They know where they can come get me. I'll be right here they need to play around."

what would you do?

"What would you do if you seen a dude stand up at that park bench over there an' then you see that his wallet done falled to the ground behind?" Little Willie Ryan asked.

"Gimme fifteen," Socrates Fortlow commanded. He slapped down a four/six domino, placing it off of a double four branch in the long line of *bones*.

"Was it a fat, brown, real leather wallet?" big-boned Brad Godine asked as if the event had actually occurred. "Or just one'a them paper jobs made up to look like it was leather?"

Young Tito Young, a man in his fifties, wrote down Socrates' score on his yellow legal pad, three vertical lines to start a new batch of twenty-five points. The five men were sitting at a picnic table in South Park playing dominoes for a penny a point. Lydell Samuels was searching his tiles for a good play.

"Man," Little Willie complained. "It's a wallet. Don't matter if it cost a lotta money. What matters is if they's any money in it."

"Yeah," Young T Young said. "A man got a good wallet might be too smart to be carryin' a lotta money in it. It's a fool an' his cheap wallet more likely to have a fifty-dollar bill up in there."

"You gonna play that bone, Lydell?" Socrates asked the carpenter.

"Yeah," chimed Brad Godine. His face was like an African mask. The bones around his eyes were big and protruding, making the eyes seem like glass orbs in twin caves. His nose was broad and broken in at least three places. The triangle of his face was long and sharp. All in all Brad was the visage of a minor demon. Children loved him, which was lucky because, by his count, he was the father of fifteen by almost as many mothers.

"Hold on," Lydell said. "I'm lookin'."

"But maybe a good wallet have some credit cards in it," Young T postulated. "Smart man gots to have a credit card. That's the way of the future."

"An' what you gonna do with another man's credit card?" Socrates Fortlow, the deadliest man in sight, asked.

"Sell it down at Blackbird's bar. You know since Craig Hatter took over they give you fifty bucks for a credit card down there," Willie Ryan said. He was a smallish man with rounded features. His hair was short cropped and dark except for his mustache, which had light red highlights. Women loved his perfectly sculpted lips.

"What would you do wit' that fifty dollars, Willie?" Socrates asked his park friend.

Quietly Lydell put down a three/four domino

against one side of a three/three tile which had branched out along a tributary from the main stalk of the game.

"Hah!" Young T cried slapping down his bone. "Twenty points!"

The men went silent momentarily to check out the math on Tito's claim.

"What you axed me, Socco?" Willie Ryan asked.

"What would you do with the fifty dollars you got from that credit card?" Socrates gestured toward the bench where the phantom wallet had been lost.

"Shit, man. I'd get me some'a that good whiskey an' then I'd be down at Linda Harris's place. You know she let up on some leg if you buy her dinner an' fill her glass."

"So you gonna mess up some man's credit and put him all out with his business so that you could have a hangover and a dose of the clap?" Socrates was smiling but Willie still cowered under his gaze.

"You gonna play, Willie?" Young T asked, still smug over his twenty-point coup.

"Yeah," Lydell added. "Maybe if you pointed out that the man dropped his billfold he might give you sumpin' for that. Maybe if you did the right thing everything'd be better."

"Well," Young T said. "Maybe if you went after him and picked his wallet up. If you did that an' handed it to'im. But if you just said, 'Hey, you dropped sumpin',' he'd just give you the nod an' be on his way. You got to touch a man you wanna get touched. Uh-huh."

Lydell frowned without responding. Willie played a three/two tile, making the board score twenty-two.

Brad Godine lost interest in the conversation for a moment as he studied the seven dominoes that he'd lined down the center of his large hand. Brad had big hands and black/brown skin except where his face bones protruded. Along these ridges Brad's skin was a lighter, almost reddish, brown.

Socrates was looking at Brad's hand. It was big and powerful but nothing compared to the *rock breakers* that Socrates had.

"What would you do if you found out that somebody sold your wallet to Hatter?" Socrates asked Willie.

"If I'd find the motherfucker," Young T interrupted. "I'd make him wish that he'da left it alone."

"Man, how the fuck you gonna do that?" Brad asked.

"I got me somethin' right here in my pocket for big-assed ugly niggers think they can weight lift you to death," Young T replied. He slapped his windbreaker pocket and sneered.

"Oh yeah?" The dominoes folded into Brad's big fist.

"Yeah."

" 'Cause you know I'm half ready to whip yo' ass an' then plug it up wit' whatever it is you think you got in that pocket."

"Hey, man," Lydell said. "Cool it. There ain't nuthin' t'fight about here."

Socrates wondered for a second, maybe even less, at the look on Lydell's face. He wasn't scared or even concerned, it was more like he was heartbroken. Heartbroken over two fools.

"Kill each other if you want," Socrates said. "But you mess up the bones and you will answer to me."

Whatever weapons Young T and Brad had, they weren't brave enough to use them against Socrates.

Brad carelessly played a two/six, bumping the table score up to twenty-eight.

Young T took a sealed half-pint of Jack Daniel's and a short stack of five plastic cups from the pocket that supposedly held a weapon. He poured everyone a shot and passed them around. Then he put the bottle back in his pocket just in case the police happened by.

Brad laughed when he got his shot. Young T nodded, agreeing that they were both fools.

"But if you did have a gun," Socrates began. "You'd shoot'im?"

"Damn straight," Young T said.

Brad and Willie agreed.

"So then you think it's wrong to take a man's wallet if he drop it."

"It's wrong if you get caught," Little Willie Ryan chirped.

Everyone, even Socrates and Lydell, laughed.

"Shit," Little Willie continued. "You an' me would be best friends, until you find out I been doin' it wit' yo' ole lady."

Socrates played a six/one, bringing the score back down to twenty-three. When you can't score the best thing to do is to limit the potential of the bones.

"And when I find out about it you dead," Socrates said in a voice so clear that the men stopped and looked at each other like a room full of strangers who just heard a loud sound from outside.

Willie half rose from the table, looking quickly over his shoulder for a clear avenue of retreat.

Socrates stared at the little man. The look was in no way benign.

Lydell had forgotten it was his turn. His face was a study in grief.

"Hey, Socco," Wille said through a nervous laugh. "Hey, man, I was just talkin'. Talkin' you know."

"But if I come in my house an' see you stickin' it to my woman then you dead. Shit. If Young T right here pull me to the side an' say that he heard it from Brad who got it straight from Lydell who was told by his wife's girlfriend — just if that I'd prob'ly cut yo' throat right here. Don't give a fuck what the police say."

A drop of sweat went down the right side of Willie's nose and into the cleft of his perfect lips.

"Now tell me somethin', Willie."

"What, Socco, what?"

"When I come in on you with my butcherin' knife an' I knock you to the floor. When I let my knee down your chest wit' my full weight an' you feel your breast bone crack open. When I put that knife to your throat an' you feel it tearin' through your flesh and the blood goin' all down your chest. What would you do then?"

"Say what, man?" Willie managed to keep his shaking down to a fidget.

"If you could go back an' fix it. If you could go back an' when that woman smiled at you you just smiled back an' walked away. What if you could go back before I ripped your flesh open like that? What would you do then? That's what I'm askin' you, Willie."

"You cain't go back, man," Lydell said. "That shit is over. Nuthin' you could do."

Brad Godine sat back and shook his head. "We gonna play dominoes or what?"

"It ain't ovah till it's ovah, man," Socrates said. He was looking at Willie but talking to Lydell.

He knew what he was saying, he was sure of his words, more sure, maybe, than he had ever been. But still Socrates was confused. It was as if he had just come alive when Willie started joking about getting away with his little crimes against his best friends and brothers. He could feel his heart beating and his breath coming in and out. But he wasn't breathing hard. He felt the breeze over his bald head and an ache on the inner side of his right knee.

Socrates felt big and angry. He was like an

85

animal who just caught a whiff of something. Like Killer, his two-legged dog, who for no reason sometimes in the middle of the night sat back on his legless haunches and cried for all he was worth.

All of that was clear to the ex-con. But what he wondered was where was he before Willie called him to life? What was he thinking? Was he just like a dog? Waiting for food or foe or sex to wake him from slumber?

He wanted to say something about all that but didn't know how.

"Socco," Young Tito Young said. Maybe he'd said it more than once.

"What?"

"You okay, man?"

"I gotta go, Young T," Socrates said. He fished three dollars out of his jeans pocket and handed them to the potbellied man. "Pay me up at the end an' gimme my change next week."

Socrates left the unfinished game asking himself the same questions, questions that he could ask only himself.

◪ ◪ ◪ ◪

Three days later Socrates had forgotten the game, the arguments, and the questions he had about himself. If anyone was privy to his inner thoughts and questioned why he had forgotten, he would have answered, "Man, I got a job, a dog who needs care, a boy I look after, and streets where you got to watch where you're steppin' elsewise you might just walk off a cliff."

Socrates had learned how to survive in prison and you couldn't make many missteps among the convict population. He carried prison around in his pockets like a passport or a small Bible. Sometimes at night he'd wake realizing that even in his sleep he'd been listening to the noises, and silences, on the street just beyond the thin plasterboard wall.

His days were spent watching out of the corner of his eye while working or having conversation. He didn't remember faces so much as hand movements and body size. If two or more big men were walking down the street behind him, even a block away, he'd turn off into an alley or store and watch to see what they did when they passed by.

Socrates didn't have time to think about how his mind worked or how lonely his thoughts were for company. He didn't have much time to think at all.

"It's like in a fight," Peter David, a heist man serving five years, once said to Socrates in the Indiana state penitentiary. "If you hesitate you're dead. If you think or wonder or ask why you might as well just put the gun to your head. Because there's no time for thinking on the job and a poor man is on the job twenty-four hours a day."

Socrates was coming home from Bounty Supermarket. He'd been staring out of the bus window only barely aware of how the sights slowly changed from the west side to Watts, from lush green streets that sometimes seemed more like botanical gardens than neighborhoods, to hard cracked sidewalks where a choked palm tree could be found every quarter mile or so. From bustling shops, catering to women who had worked on their outfits and makeup for hours before leaving the house, to burnt out and abandoned businesses standing like barricades against gangs of laughing children watched over by tired mothers, sisters and friends.

Socrates got off the bus twelve blocks from his house. There was a closer stop but he wanted to walk down the street he'd been observing.

"Hey, Socco," a man called.

Socrates had seen the man's white overalls when he'd scanned the street but dismissed them as being no threat.

"Hey, Lydell. What's happenin'?"

"Hey, Socco," the slender carpenter repeated. His dark face was long and his features were fine. Again Socrates noticed the grief in that face.

"What's wrong, man?" the ex-convict asked.

"Nuthin'. Nuthin' at all. I just seen you. Thought I'd say hey."

"Hey," Socrates said.

"Hey." Lydell smiled and winced at the same time.

The men stood in the street surrounded by children and old men. Standing still, Socrates became momentarily aware of laughter. It struck him as odd but he didn't think any more about it.

"Well," he said. "I better be goin'. See ya, Lydell."

"See ya, Socco," Lydell said but he kept a steady gaze in Socrates' eye.

"Well, okay," Socrates said. "I better be goin'."

"You was up in prison, right, Socrates?" Lydell asked.

Socrates gave the carpenter a hard look but it was wasted on the deep sadness of the man.

"Yeah," Socrates answered. "Yeah I was up there. Way up in there."

"Me too," Lydell said. "I killed a man an' they send me up there. Send me up there. Yeah, you know. For manslaughter."

The street was full of people but there were no witnesses to Lydell's confession. No one but Socrates was listening to the anguished carpenter.

"You wanna go get a drink?" Socrates asked his newfound friend.

Bebe's bar was run by a black Chicano named Paolo Herrera who everybody called Chico. He got that name because of the hat he wore, which was reminiscent of the Marx brother's. Bebe's was one of the few places where the Latino and Negro races mingled around Socrates' neighborhood. That was because of Chico's appearance which he inherited from his mother, a descendent of a Brazilian woman from Bahía.

Socrates went into Bebe's place now and then because it reminded him of prison. Only men patronized the bar. They played chess but there was no jukebox. They talked in low voices keeping secrets that no one cared about. And everyone was always watching, on the lookout for any trouble. Socrates felt safe among the denizens of Bebe's bar because he could relax a little surrounded, as he was, by sentries who he could trust to sound the alarm.

Socrates knew from the minute they went into Bebe's that Lydell had told the truth when he said that he was an ex-con. The carpenter shot glances in all directions, sizing up men and groups with immediate certainty. He looked around for a table against a wall but they were all taken.

"We could sit at that table over there," Socrates told his companion. "Bebe's is cool."

He pointed to a spindly legged wooden table that was almost black from cigarette burns and stains.

"Two beers, Chico," Socrates said to the owner who stood behind the oak-stained pine bar.

"It's just beer and whiskey," Socrates said to Lydell. "Scotch and gin. No brand names or special drinks. Chico got soda water but no tonic. And if you wanna sandwich you gotta bring it in yourself."

The room was well lit. The pale linoleum floor was clean and swept. Lydell swiveled his head from side to side taking in the corners, but there were no hiding places at Bebe's.

"Where'd you do your time?" Socrates asked.

"Soledad. You?"

"Back east." This wasn't Socrates' confession. He didn't feel the need to unburden himself.

The beers came with Chico, who sat down for a little while to say hello to Socrates and to check out the new man. Lydell passed the test because all he said was "Hello."

"A man with no questions," Socrates said to Lydell when Chico went away, "is a man you could almost trust."

It was the first friendly smile to cross Lydell's lips that Socrates could remember. But the grin was followed by that pained grimace. Socrates could remember when happiness brought him pain. He was considering asking the carpenter what had he done but Lydell beat him to it.

"I killed my friend. My wife's boyfriend. Henry Wentworth." Lydell looked at Socrates who held up his empty glass for Chico to see. "He was with my wife. In the bed. In my own damn bed. An' I killed him with a knife. Stabbed the motherfucker. Forty-two times they said."

You got your crazies, your criminals, your slackards and your good men, Cap Richmond, the seventy-year-old lifer, used to say. *Good man kill ya 'cause he just couldn't live knowin' you did him like that an' didn't pay for it.*

"Henry was always hangin' 'round us. He used to always say how if I didn't marry Geraldine he

91

would have. She liked him and I worked the night shift. Lotta times I'd come home and he'd be there watchin' TV or eatin'. I even liked it that he looked in on her. So you see," Lydell said like some kind of law student, "it really was my fault in a way. You cain't be havin' no man comin' up in your house lookin' after your woman. Man starts to feel like he own a woman he's protectin'. She cain't help but to take on his scent too."

"How many years?" Socrates asked when he realized that there was nothing he could tell Lydell.

"Sentenced to twelve but I got out in eight."

Socrates figured that his drinking partner was mid-thirties, not much more. "How long you been out?"

"Six years, seven months, five days," Lydell answered. "I went in when I was nineteen. My mother died the next year."

"You done did all right, man," Socrates said. "I mean you run that carpentry business, right?"

"What you mean when you say it ain't over till it's over?" Lydell asked.

"Huh?"

"That's what you said in the park this weekend."

"I'idn't mean nuthin'." Socrates was trying to remember exactly what he had said and why. "That was just some talk."

"You said what would you do if you could go back. That's what you said to Willie Ryan. You

92

said it like you was givin' him a chance, like there was somethin' he could do right now."

Chico came with more beer. Socrates nodded and made a sign to keep them coming.

"What you askin' me, Lydell?" Socrates asked. "What you really wanna know?"

"They told me about you bein' in prison, man." The carpenter rubbed his face pushing his jaw impossibly far to the right. "They said that you was all hard and mean when you got out but then you started doin' stuff. You know. How you help people and talk about what's right an' what's wrong. They said it was like you learned somethin'. Like, like you . . . I don't know. Like you know you wrong and you figured out how to be right anyway."

"That's just some talk, man. I ain't got nuthin' on nobody. You know. Shoot. I got a job as a boxboy an' my head don't feel right less I'm sleepin' or drunk." The words came easily. They were all true but he was barely aware of a truth that lay just under their meaning.

Lydell felt that truth too.

"I don't sleep at all. Not really." The thin black man started rocking gently in the chair. "I close my eyes. But you know you cain't block out that shit. It get worser every day. Every day that I'm up here an' Henry's in the ground. I try not to think about how it was my fault. And then I try an' do what you said to Willie. I try an' go back. In my mind I go back there tellin' myself that I set Henry up for that shit. I tell myself that he

93

didn't deserve to die." Lydell looked at Socrates with those ruined, heartbroken eyes.

Chico came around with two more beers. The ex-cons waited for the bartender to leave.

". . . but when I get there," Lydell continued, "an' I hear that noise she makes. I tell myself, 'You could just hit him,' but then the knife is in my hand again. Here I am tryin' to make it better in my mind but I just kill'im again. Kill'im again."

Socrates jerked his head back because he felt something strange at his mouth. But when he looked it was just the forgotten beer glass in his hand grazing his lower lip. Again he wondered where he'd been.

"It's like I done killed ten thousand Henrys," Lydell Samuels said. "You asked Little Willie what he'd do? Well I could tell ya: the same thing. That's what he'd do. No matter what you showed him or how hard he tried he'd'a been on the same killin' floor. 'Cause even though Willie don't want you to kill'im he still want that girl and that wallet."

Socrates remembered the conversation clearly then. The domino game where they had argued over right and wrong. He could see that Lydell had turned it over in his mind again and again over and over until it was like a worn page in a condemned man's bible.

"You got to let it go, man," Socrates said.

"Willie don't even want to do right except that he's scared," Lydell said as if he hadn't heard.

"Here I want it but I cain't help it but to do wrong."

"He's dead, Lydell. He only died one time. It was wrong. All of it. Your wife, you, and him too. But it's over an' you got to let it go. I don't mean forget it. I don't mean you got to smile like they baptized your sin away."

Lydell looked up at Socrates with fever glazing his eyes. He was jittery like Willie had been on the weekend but he wasn't afraid.

"I try to do right, man," Lydell said. "I try but they don't let me."

"Who?"

"I try to do right. I try to do like you told Willie."

"I said that to Willie 'cause he ain't been on that floor yet. He just dreamin' 'bout another man's wallet and another man's wife." Socrates felt, again, like he was back in prison, trapped in his own mistakes. "You'n me been there. You'n me got to take all we've seen and make somethin' new about it. It's not what would you do for men like us. It's what *will* you do that we have to worry about. For us it ain't no game. We got to see past bein' guilty. We already been there."

"Like you mean we still got some place to go?" Lydell asked.

"This is life, Lydell. Life. What's done is done. You still responsible, you cain't never make it up, but you got to try."

Lydell smiled again. This time the smile lingered. There was a question in his face and then a certainty. He nodded and grinned and ordered another drink.

◢ ◢ ◢ ◢

Two weeks passed before Detective Biggers, the black cop assigned to keep tabs on Socrates, dropped by for one of his irregular visits. Socrates knew the policeman's knock and took his time getting to the door. Sometimes when Detective Biggers came by Socrates didn't even answer. Sometimes he'd just sit on his foldout bed reading the newspaper until he heard the gate to his yard open and close again.

But that day Socrates wanted company. He pulled the door open and said, "Afternoon, Albert."

The burly cop always paused a moment in silent protest when Socrates used his first name. But he couldn't complain when he didn't have a warrant or a pressing reason to be at Socrates' door.

"You know a man named Samuels?" Biggers asked.

Just that quickly Socrates wanted to be alone again. He didn't want to answer any questions — or ask any.

"Do you?"

"What you want, man? I ain't had dinner yet."

"Geraldine Samuels said that you and her husband had been friendly lately. She said that you and he were regulars over at Bebe's bar. She said that Lydell had been saying how you were so smart and wise and that you were helping him to figure out how he could live with what he had done." Albert Biggers seemed to know that his questions would hurt Socrates, that the hurt would linger and blossom over time. "He was like you, you know, a murderer."

"Did you say Geraldine?" Socrates asked.

"His wife," Biggers said, nodding. "Didn't you know he was married?"

"Uh-uh. He never said a thing about that. I mean he said that he was married before, that he killed his wife's boyfriend. Her name was Geraldine too."

"Same." Biggers smiled. "She got sick after he went to prison. I guess she was pretty bad off when he got out. Some kind of nerve disorder. She's the one that found him. They slept separately. Cut his own throat in his own bed. I don't think Geraldine liked him much but he did pay the rent. Cut his own throat. You know that takes guts."

Killer, the two-legged dog, jumped up buoyed by the harness attached to the line strung across Socrates' small yard. The dog padded his way to the door and pressed his snout against the ex-con's hand.

"What you want, Albert?"

"Was Samuels distressed? Was he depressed?"

The laugh that issued from Socrates' deep chest was hard earned. "You the one said he was livin' with a woman hated him. What do you think?"

"But you said you didn't know about his wife," Biggers argued uselessly.

"You ever hate anybody, officer?"

"I asked you a question, Mr. Fortlow."

" 'Cause you see Lydell hated somebody. He hated a man and he killed him. He couldn't help himself. And if you put that man in front'a him today he'd kill him again. All he wanted was to wipe that man from his mind. That's what he talked about."

"So he killed himself because he couldn't kill his wife's boyfriend again?" Biggers asked.

"I don't have no idea, man. I wasn't in his head. We just got drunk together."

"So he didn't give you any indication that he intended suicide?"

"There weren't no play in Lydell, officer. No play at all."

"What is that supposed to mean?" the policeman wanted to know.

"It means what it means, man."

Socrates turned on his radio that night. There was jazz playing on the university station. Fats Waller. The image of a smiling fat black man came up in Socrates' mind. He was laughing and playing those ivories. He was cooing and wooing. Socrates knew that there must have been tears behind all of those funny lines. And then the announcer said, *Waller suffered a diabetic attack on tour and the all-white hospital turned him away. He died from the disease of racism and he left us his legacy like the smile an undertaker draws on his corpse.*

Socrates wondered who he could blame for Lydell's death. He wondered that until he drifted off to sleep.

a day in the park

Socrates got to the front stairs of the house on Marvane Street at six fifteen that Sunday morning. The block was lined with a few large homes left over from the more prosperous days of South Central L.A. Most had been subdivided into rooms for let or knocked down and replaced by large stucco apartment buildings. There was the big brick house a few lots down, the one that the radical college students called the New Africans once occupied. It was vacant. The young college radicals had splintered into two smaller organizations, Socrates had heard, neither of which could afford the rent.

The police surveillance house across the street was empty now too. Without potential revolutionaries to spy on the police saw no reason to maintain their presence on the block.

The only industries left were Luvia's private retirement home and the crack house down toward the end of the block. Even at that hour there was a fat man in a cheap suit who had driven by for a quick blow job in the deep lawn. Socrates couldn't tell if it was a man or a woman down on one knee before the fat man.

Socrates was remembering the days when he

and Right Burke sat out on the front porch of Luvia's and watched the cops sneak in and out of their nest. Right Burke had been Socrates' best friend but now he was dead.

It had been almost a year. Socrates wasn't invited to the service. Right's sister had come down from Richmond in the Bay Area and organized the funeral with Luvia Prine. The women had blamed Socrates for Right's death. They were angry because Right had gone out with Socrates one night and the next morning he was found at a bus stop, dead from an overdose of morphine complicated by a large quantity of alcohol.

He didn't blame them but still he'd gotten himself up and out of bed at five in the morning to come down to Luvia's retirement home.

She the onliest person I ever met who might be able to stare you down, Socco, Burke had once said to his friend. *You know she ain't afraid of nuthin' but Jesus and I do believe that even he would say 'yes ma'am' to her.*

Socrates remembered the suicide of his friend with no guilt or even remorse. He was dying to begin with. All those pills he took did what they were supposed to do — they stopped the pain.

Three young girls walked past the big man, looking frightened and beautiful in calf length pastel dresses that set off their dark skins like three flames. The smallest child, who must have been about ten, smiled at Socrates and waved as they walked past.

They got to walk through hell, he thought, just to get to Sunday school.

When the girls got past Socrates they began to run, giggling and laughing as they went. They looked back over their shoulders at Socrates and screamed as if he were a monster.

A car door slammed. The fat man had finished his business. He turned over the engine on his old Buick and cruised past Luvia's home looking straight ahead.

◪ ◪ ◪ ◪

"Socrates Fortlow, what you doin' at my door?" She was at least five eight but weighed no more than a hundred pounds fully dressed. Luvia Prine had the stare of a heavyweight though.

"Miss Prine," Socrates said as a greeting.

"Well?" She held a bunch of freshly picked dahlias.

"I heard that somebody picks you up here at six forty-five an' takes you to Right's grave on the first Sunday of every month. Topper Saint-Paul told me he heard that."

The flesh around Luvia's watery eyes hardened into two tight squares. "What I do and where I go and who I go with ain't got nuthin' to do with you."

"An' Right told me that you were a Christian woman." Socrates fought to keep the humor he felt out of his voice. He enjoyed the vehemence of Luvia's hatred. He *was* a bad man. He had done awful things. And even if Luvia didn't know exactly what crimes he had committed, she could feel that he had done something. That intimacy, even though it was shown in distaste, made Socrates feel kinship toward the hard, churchgoing woman.

"And what do you mean by that?"

"I mean that a Christian woman, on a Sunday too, would not keep a man from paying his respects to his dead friend," Socrates said.

"I ain't keepin' you from nuthin'," Luvia said angrily.

"You didn't let me come to my friend's funeral. You didn't even let me know where I could send no flowers or even a card to say I was sorry and sad."

"You don't deserve to be invited with decent folk, Socrates. It's your fault he's dead. He was alive when he left wit' you and then the police called to say that they found him cold on a bus stop bench. And where were you? You don't deserve to stand at his grave. You ain't earned a place to pray."

Socrates could tell by the waver in Luvia's voice that she felt deeply about his crime. He almost lost heart then and turned away, allowing her her victory over Satan.

Almost.

"You see?" he said instead of leaving. "What kind of real Christian woman would put herself in the place to make a judgment on a man's soul? It's a blasphemy for somebody to say that another man is unworthy in God's eyes. But here you go sayin' that I cain't pay my respects to my friend. Here you go actin' like the Lord give you the power to judge."

The squares screwed themselves down to pinpoints. Luvia actually shook in her loose Sunday dress suit. Her fist grasped so tightly on the bunch of hand-picked flowers that he heard the stems cracking.

"You tell me that I killed Right but the truth is I saved him," Socrates added.

"Saved him!"

"That's right. You had him up in that room moanin' from all the pain that that cancer could make. Your doctor couldn't get him the kinda medicine he needed to kill the pain. All you could do was leave him upstairs to wither and die. No dignity, no manhood. Just four walls and a Bible on his nightstand. You ain't never asked me about what happened, Luvia. You think you know but you wasn't there. You didn't see him in his final suit tellin' stories and laughin' about the short skirts some'a these girls wear out in the street. You didn't hear him say good-bye to Charla and then tell me t'leave him on the bench. He said that he wanted to stay and watch the lights, Luvia. What business did I have to tell him no?"

Socrates had lost his sense of humor. Luvia, from his experience, never had one to begin with. Socrates was wondering how far he'd have to go to look for a smile when a long, gold-colored Lincoln drove up behind him.

"Damn you, Socrates Fortlow," Luvia said. "Come on."

▟ ▟ ▟ ▟

Luvia Prine whisked past the big ex-con and he turned around to see a dapper man standing at the open door of his car. He was about Socrates' age with a mustache and no beard. He was wearing a light brown sports jacket and dark brown pants but his red, yellow and green shirt was an African cut, as was his brimless and beaded hat.

"Luvia," the man said. When he smiled Socrates could see that one of his bottom teeth was gold.

"This here is Socrates Fortlow, Milton," Luvia said. "If you have any room he wants to go out and pay his respects, I guess."

"Hey, my man," Milton said extending a hand. "All I got is room in this boat. Ride on up front with me. You know Miss Prine always take the backseat."

With that Milton pulled open the back door for Luvia. Socrates made his way around to the passenger's side and let himself in.

"Strap yourself down, brother," Milton said as he turned the ignition key.

"Say what?"

Milton, who was the color of coffee mixed in with an equal amount of cream, turned and smiled brightly at Socrates. "Between alcohol and cigarettes, guns and blunt objects, between high blood pressure and low test scores in these piss-poor schools they —"

"Milton!" Luvia cried.

"Sorry about the language, Miss Prine," Milton said and then he continued, ". . . caught in between all that I'm as cautious as butterfly in a hurricane."

Socrates buckled his belt feeling a little foolish and not knowing exactly why.

They drove down Central for a long while, cruising, stopping at every third traffic light. Every now and then Milton would beep his horn at someone making their way to early service. He seemed to know a lot of people.

"Car's in good shape," Socrates said. He knew that the compliment would get the driver to smile.

"Bought it new twenty-five years ago when I was a letter carrier with nuthin' but a room, a bed and this here car. I hate to let anything go. This the fourth engine on this sucker but you know I'd really be sad if I ever had to give'er up."

Socrates turned away and looked out of his window. Luvia had moved to the seat behind him. She was staring out at the same street that Socrates was watching but he still wondered what it was that she saw. He knew that Luvia lived in a completely different world than he did. Maybe the world she saw had different colors; maybe there were truths revealed to her scrutiny that Socrates missed.

"You just like me, eh, my man?" Milton words

were wrapped in the rhythms of sixties jazz.

"What you mean?"

"The name. Some old dead white man wrote a book an' our mommas hoped the name'd rub off on us. They didn't think that a famous black man is usually dead before his time." The driver's laughter sounded hollow to Socrates.

"I don't know 'bout all that," Socrates said.

"All what?"

"How you know that somebody's a white man? I mean Augustine was a African. Socrates come up around the Mediterranean, you know that's spittin' distance from the Arab world. Maybe your name is really a black man's name too."

"Will you please keep it down," Luvia said. "This *is* Sunday."

"Sorry, Miss Prine," Milton said. But he was thinking about Socrates then, casting sidelong glances at the man.

By then they were headed north on Highland up toward Barhum. The car *did* feel like a boat to Socrates. It almost floated on the streets of L.A., banking instead of turning, never jolting at a stop.

"Where'd you hear that about Saint Augustine?" Luvia Prine asked. Socrates was expecting the question but not from her.

"I got that at the Capricorn Bookstore. I used to go there before it got burnt down in the riots."

"You knew the Minettes?" Luvia asked.

"Enough to eat at their apartment over here

offa Forty-seventh Street."

In the rearview mirror Socrates could see his words register on Luvia. He felt a childish glee that she had something close to respect for him if only just for a moment or two.

"I never heard'a that place," Milton said.

"It was a black bookstore where anybody could go an' read and talk," Socrates said. "They had art shows and poetry readin's but I didn't go in too much for that. I liked to read about all the history that we got an' we don't even know about. About alla the lies we tell each other but here we go thinkin' we tellin' the truth."

"What's that supposed to mean?" Milton wanted to know.

"Like Luvia."

"What you mean like me?" the landlady said angrily.

"You didn't know that Augustine was African and you in church every minute you can find. Maybe your minister don't know it. All kinda stuff they teach us and then we go passin' it around like it was gospel. All up and down the street you got people believin' lies about each other and tellin' them lies like they was the Lord themselves."

"I didn't tell you that I didn't know Augustine was an African," Luvia said. "And why should I believe you anyway?"

"Oscar Minette was the one told me, Miss Prine. But that's okay. I didn't mean to insult you. I was just sayin'."

The car went quiet after that. The gold Lincoln climbed up Forest Lawn Drive toward the cemetery.

◪ ◪ ◪ ◪

They had to walk up a hill to get to the grave site. Luvia found it hard going. Socrates put his hand under her elbow for support. She almost balked but then she relaxed into the strength of his hand.

It was just a plaque of granite lying flat in the grass. EUGENE BURKE, 1923–1997. No poetry or catchy remembrances.

"Looks like a dinner plate," Socrates said. "Seems like Right deserved something better."

"He left all his wealth behind him," Luvia said. "A bronze coffin and a fancy headstone won't get you into the Kingdom."

"You sure cain't take it with ya," Socrates agreed.

Luvia put down her injured flowers. Socrates took a crystal teardrop, the kind used in chandeliers, from his pocket and placed it next to the poor bouquet.

"What's that piece of glass supposed to be?" Luvia asked.

"Darryl give it to me to leave. It's his favorite thing. When I told him that I was gonna try an' find Right's grave he gimme that to leave."

At first Socrates thought that Luvia was nodding, somehow agreeing that leaving the crystal was the right thing to do. And maybe that's how it began. But somewhere along the way the nod became crying. The quiet, tearless crying of a woman who had given up everything and never looked back.

Socrates watched her clutching her gloved hands and shaking like someone suffering from palsy. He reached out but she put up a tremulous hand.

"I don't need your help," she said. "Just let me have my cry alone."

Socrates walked down to the car where Milton waited leaning up against the hood. He was smoking a cigarette and staring peacefully at the wispy clouds snaking their way through the blues skies.

"Hey," Milton said.

Socrates nodded.

"She usually spends a while up there. And when she comes down she's all quiet and smaller, you know? Like she got the weight of the whole world on'er."

Socrates nodded again.

"I think she was in love with him. That's what Dottie Monroe told me. Dottie said that when Luvia talks about Right she just loses it. Even now he been dead almost a year all you got to do is ask her about him and she can't get out but a few sentences 'fore she choke up."

"Yeah, well," Socrates said. "Right was a good man. He never let the world break him down. He was old and crippled but he'd still stand up to anyone'a these young cowards you got runnin' around out here. I'm just surprised that he made it as long as he did."

"You gonna pay half?" Milton asked.

"Half'a what?"

"I charge fifteen dollars for the ride up here an' back to ten o'clock service. I figure wit' you here she could save a little."

◢ ◢ ◢ ◢

Luvia's church was on Sixty-third Place near Hooper. It was a large salmon pink building with a white cross, almost three stories high, rising from its roof.

The congregation was coming from all over the street into the three double doors that stood atop the building's wide stone staircase. There was the flowery smell of women's perfume in the air. Socrates and Milton both got out of the car to help Luvia but she pushed them away.

Many well-dressed parishioners took a second look at the big ex-convict in his army fatigue pants and tight black T-shirt. His big hands and stern features marked him out from that God-fearing crowd.

"See ya in a few weeks, Miss Prine," Milton said. He gestured as if he were doffing his hat but he did not do so.

"You're welcome to come into church, Milton Langonier," Luvia said.

"I got to get another fare, Miss Prine. Maybe next week."

Luvia turned quickly toward Socrates, almost, he thought, like a frightened leaf eater who suspected a predator stalking from behind.

"You could come to church too, Mr. Fortlow. They made church for sinners. And it's only God can tell them no." Her left eye shut for a moment and her gloved hands made themselves into fists.

"Thank you, Miss Prine, but not today. I appreciate it though."

Luvia actually sighed in relief. For the first time Socrates saw gratefulness in her eyes.

◪ ◪ ◪ ◪

"Wanna go down to MacArthur Park?" Milton asked when they were driving again.

"How much that gonna cost me?"

"I'm off duty now, boy. You know I only do one ride on a Sunday and the rest I take off."

They sat together on an iron bench that was painted pink. Milton brought out a pint bottle of peach-flavored schnapps and they passed it back and forth taking small swigs and gasping from the alcohol burn.

"She used to sit right over there on that bench," Milton said, pointing to a tall pine tree.

"What bench?" asked Socrates.

"It ain't there no more. That was thirty-five years ago when I was a mail carrier and I used to come here on Fridays with my boss Moses Goldstein. Jewish man."

Socrates took another drink and remembered that he hadn't eaten that morning. A warm fuzzy feeling nuzzled in around his ears.

"But who was sitting on the bench?" he asked.

"Cherry Winters," Milton said. He took a

drink and then lit a cigarette.

It was a sunny day and there were more than a few people out strolling in the downtown park. Pedal-boats were gliding across the man-made pond. Two young men were throwing each other long passes with a football. Socrates thought that they were imagining playing in the big game on TV, dreaming that they were sports stars running and passing to the shouts of a whole stadium full of fans. He could almost hear the cheers himself.

"Yep," Milton said. "She used to sit right under that pine tree. It was smaller back then."

"Who was she?"

"Black girl. Real real black and ugly from the way I looked at things. She used to sit right over there every Friday and me and Moses used to sit down at a redwood bench near the pond." Milton smiled at the memory. "Yeah, yeah. We'd sit down on the bench and he'd bring peach schnapps and we'd pour it in these little Dixie cups. I was just a kid really. Moses was more than fifty. It took me a long time realize it but he had a reason to come down here with me. It was that Cherry."

"What about her?"

"Moses was married. Had three kids and one grandchild. And here that fool falls in love with the ugliest black girl I could imagine. You know the kinda girl don't even style her hair but just comb it straight back and tie it up with a rubber band. Skinny and big lipped. You know back then I thought beauty was Sarah Vaughan or Dorothy Dandridge. That child just wore a one-piece dress and brown shoes that laced up like a man's shoes."

"An' she would eat here on Fridays while you an' Moses was drinkin'?" Socrates asked. He was enjoying the way that Milton's story unfolded.

"Yeah. One day I figured out that it was because'a that girl that Moses brought me out here," Milton said with wonder in his voice. "You see I was one of the few blacks they had workin' in his area. He'd been comin' down here for over a year already, watchin' that child."

Socrates felt his mouth come open the way that it did when he was on the way to drunk. He smiled and looked up at the false horizon line of the trees, that jagged line of pines underscoring blue.

"He was in love," Milton said.

"Love?"

"Crazy. That's what I said. Crazy. Here you got a old big-bellied Jewish man in his fifties actin' like a school kid over a black girl he ain't ever even been within arm's distance of. But that's what he said. After we been comin' to the park about two months. I guess he had a little too much peach schnapps that Friday an' he told me how much in love he was. I said, 'Moses, why'ont you go ovah there an' say hey.' You know I wasn't a day over twenty-five and arrogant the way young men can be. Moses just shook his head and blushed. Blushed!"

It was that last word that made Socrates understand that this long-ago talk had stayed with him, like that Lincoln Continental.

"I yelled over to the girl. Moses said not to but he really wanted me to call her. Why else did he bring me here? I yelled over for the girl to come to our bench. She was a little shy but I guess she figured what could we do in broad daylight in the park?"

Socrates was watching two young lovers, a dark-skinned Hispanic man and his fair Asian girlfriend. He didn't want to hear any sad story right then. The schnapps working its way through his brain only wanted candy colors and a pleasant nap.

"I told her that my friend liked her and she said go on but she sat down anyway. When I left Moses was still on the bench with that girl. I had to lie back at work and say that he ate something bad and went home." Milton stopped there to take the final drink from the bottle. He lost the thread of his story with that last smacking swallow and sat still staring at the boats gliding across the lake.

"Right Burke was my best friend," Socrates said. "It feels good to say that. You know? That somebody is your friend. Your best friend. Even though he's dead it's like he was here."

Milton nodded.

A pair of policemen wandered by on horseback.

"It's nice here in the park, man," Socrates said.

For a long while after that the two men sat in silence.

"So what happened?" Socrates asked.

"What?"

"With your boss and that girl?"

"Oh. Moses and his girl on the side." Milton squinted his eyes, trying to remember. "Yeah. He set her up. Got her a little place down offa Adams. Went to see'er every day almost. She had a baby. Named him Moses. And you know I had it made after alla that. I mean Moses loved me almost as much as he did Cherry. After all it was me broke the ice. Every time a promotion was due I got it. I was his second in command after only three years. That way I could cover for him when he was spendin' the afternoon over with her.

"Oh yeah that was real love there. Even before she proved it I knew that Cherry loved that man. You know he couldn't leave his wife. All them kids and the grandkids kept comin'. Nobody would'a had no sympathy for him so they kept it quiet. Cherry didn't care though. She used to make his lunches and send 'em through me. She knit him sweaters, never complained as far as I knew. And when he got sick with the heart disease and he couldn't even get up outta the bed Cherry used to bring me little notes that I'd take up to his house on Fridays an' show'im. And every time he'd tell me to tell her that he loved her and that when he was better that he'd leave Sophie and come be her husband."

Socrates noted the heaviness in Milton's voice.

"You know I don't think that they never knew each other at all," Milton said. "I mean they was in love but the worlds they lived in was so different. It was just somethin' about the way she ate her lunch and the way that man loved her even though he had a whole world someplace else."

"Did they ever get married?" Socrates asked.

"Naw," Milton replied. "He got weaker an' weaker. Finally he just died. I took Cherry to the funeral actin' like she was my girlfriend. But I think Sophie musta known sumpin' wit' the way that Cherry carried on. You know I don't think that there was a black woman ever lived would cry so hard for me as Cherry did for that fat old Jewish man."

Milton bit his lip and shook his head. He took the schnapps bottle out of his pocket but it was empty.

Socrates got down on the grass and stretched out. He put his hands behind his head and let his eyes wander with the big white clouds.

"They all gone," said the man who was named after a poet.

"Who?"

"Yo' friend. My friend. Cherry's alive but she ain't here no more. It's just all like a dream."

"What happened to Moses Junior?"

"I got him a job as a mail carrier. You know I tried to help Cherry out after Mo was gone. But I wasn't in on all that love."

Those were the last words Socrates heard for a while. He fell asleep with blades of grass waving in the breeze, tickling his bare arms.

An hour or so later he woke up. Milton was still sitting on the bench, watching the boats.

They rode home in amiable silence. When Milton let Socrates off at his alley door he said, "See you in a month, Mr. Fortlow?"

"I hope so," Socrates said.

◢ ◢ ◢ ◢

"Did you go to Mr. Burke's grave?" Darryl asked Socrates early the next morning at Bounty.

"Uh-huh." He was using the big floor buffer to strip the wax from aisle seven two hours before the doors to Bounty were due to open. Darryl had been given extra hours to help Socrates. He did that often so he could talk to the older man.

"Was you sad?"

"Sad?"

"Uh-huh."

Socrates lost himself for a few minutes in the pivot from right to left as he let the big, rotating, steel wool brush grind away the yellowing wax. Darryl followed with his squeegee pushing the extra water along behind the big chromium machine.

About half the way through Socrates stopped and pushed the red button between the handlebars. The motor died and the brush slowed, making the sound of a snake through the dead grasses of summer.

"No, I wasn't sad," Socrates said. "Uh-uh. I mean it was sad to see that nameplate on the ground. But you know Right made up his own mind. He took them pills."

They were the only people in the store. Both man and boy liked the solitude and freedom of their early morning jobs.

"I put your crystal down there. Luvia thought it was real nice'a you. But I wasn't sad," Socrates said again. "No, uh-uh. I went to the park with this man name'a Milton. We went to MacArthur Park downtown and he said about a man he knew that died. They was friends kinda like me an' Burke."

"Did you have some wine?" Darryl asked.

"He had somethin'," Socrates said. "But I didn't. You know you don't always have to be high to have a good time."

"Uh-huh, I know. I just asked is all."

"It was real pretty yesterday," Socrates said. "And it was strange too."

"What you mean?"

"You ever see one'a them big mural paintin's that they put up on the wall? The kinds about a whole big place with lots and lotsa people? The kind where nobody is special but they just doin' what they do? Sittin' on a park bench or throwin' a Frisbee."

"Yeah I seen 'em."

"And the pictures of the people ain't real good like no photograph. You know. Maybe somebody's head is just a circle or sumpin' but you know what it means, you know that it's a man or woman."

"Yeah."

"When I closed my eyes I could see all the people in the park just like in one'a them murals. I mean they were still in my mind. But it was like Right was there too and also this Jewish man that Milton was talkin' 'bout. There was some girl he mentioned too. You know what I mean?"

"Uh-uh," Darryl uttered, shaking his head to accent his confusion.

"It's like you take somebody with you even if they ain't there, even if they dead. It's like Martin Luther King. I can see him in my mind but I ain't never met him. Or like when I saw the boats they had on the pond there. I thought about you and how you'd like to get in one'a them and row around."

"So? That just mean you thinkin' 'bout somebody."

"Yeah. I was thinkin' an' I wasn't sad or mad. I was just thinkin' and everything was fine. Even though there was all this bad stuff and sad stuff in my mind everything was still fine. Yeah."

the mugger

"Hey you! Yeah you, mothahfuckah!" The man was young, not more than twenty, but built for power. He swaggered as he walked and his eyes had as much murder in them as Socrates had ever seen.

It was just sunset and Socrates had taken a shortcut down one alley that led to the alley that he lived on. He had just come from Tri-X Check Cashing on Central and had his full week's salary in an envelope in his pocket.

There was nobody else in sight. And even if there had been Socrates doubted if they would have interfered with the trouble about to come down.

"Stop right there, mothahfuckah!" the big man commanded.

But Socrates had already stopped. He spread his legs wide enough to give him both stability and power as the young giant approached. Close up he looked impossible with muscle and rage. Those murderous eyes were squashed down, murky things that searched out weak spots and gazed down long corridors of pain.

"Gimme the money an' you might get off with a ass-whippin'," the man said.

Socrates noted the smallness of the mugger's head in comparison to his hard, prison-built shoulders. He wasn't a man but a killing machine built on the body of a boy who had been sent off to jail and forgotten.

"Or you could try'n stop me." The young man reached for Socrates' neck. Socrates tried to block the hand but he was slapped down to the ground. Slapped down. The boy didn't even use a fist to knock Socrates to his knees.

The older ex-convict rose up delivering a powerful uppercut to the mugger's abdomen but he might as well have socked an oak tree or a granite rock. The mugger's next blow was a fist that sprawled Socrates out on the floor of the alley. Two kicks followed in quick succession. Then Socrates felt himself being lifted from the ground. He hadn't felt a sensation like that since he was a child. But this time it wasn't his mother taking him out from harm's way.

Even that powerhouse couldn't lift Socrates from his feet. There was more than two hundred and fifty pounds to the Indiana ex-con. He let his full weight hang dead and the mugger was forced to drop him.

"All right!" Socrates yelled from the ground. "You could have the money."

With that Socrates Fortlow, who had never lost a fight because in the world he came from there was no rematch, picked himself up and produced the drab green envelope that contained two hundred nineteen dollars and eighty-six cents.

The mugger took his prize.

"Turn out your pockets, old man."

"That's all I got," Socrates said.

"Empty out yo' pockets, niggah, else I'm'onna hafta hurt you." The mugger slapped Socrates across the face with the back of his right hand. It was too fast to block but Socrates didn't even try. The mugger was so smug that he didn't see the palm-sized stone that Socrates had picked up with his left hand. And once the slap was delivered the mugger had no limb with which to block the hard rock from crashing into the side of his head.

Socrates felt the bone crunching. He heard the high-pitched wheeze of the boy's last breath.

The killer child fell to his knees and then genuflected, pressing his meaty shoulder against Socrates' feet.

Socrates put the bloody stone in his pocket, reached down to retrieve his envelope, and walked the few back alley blocks to his home.

◤ ◤ ◤ ◤

He washed the stone and threw it away. He cut his pants into strips and flushed them down the toilet because of the blood in the pocket. Then he sat in a chair and waited for the police to come.

The police always came. They came when a grocery store was robbed or a child was mugged. They came for every dead body, with questions and insinuations. Sometimes they took him off to jail. They had searched his house and given him a ticket for not having a license for his two-legged dog. They dropped by on a whim at times just in case he had done something that even they couldn't suspect.

Because Socrates was guilty, guilty all the way around. He was big and he was black, he was an ex-convict and he was poor. He was unrepentant in the eyes of the law and you could see by looking at him that he wasn't afraid of any consequences no matter how harsh.

The police were coming so he sat in his chair waiting and wondering if there was some other man like that mugger waiting for him in jail. He wasn't afraid but it was a new thing in his life to be kicked around and beaten by a single man. When he was younger no one could have done that to him.

Socrates went through it over and over, the whole ninety seconds, in his mind. The slap that floored him. The humiliation and the threat. The fear he felt when he realized that he could not hurt the mugger. But when he remembered the stone in his hand and the crush of bone, that's when Socrates paused.

He could feel the police coming after him; could almost hear his name along with the word murder.

"Most people don't kill," he said to himself. "They don't have to go out and murder. But what else could I do?"

He wondered if there was a court somewhere

back in the old days of Africa where a man could lay out what had happened and decide, among his peers, if there had been a crime. If there was a world where a man had a say and was concerned about his own guilt. He didn't want to plead but to understand.

He thought about the boy hunched down over his knees paying final homage to the violence he lived by. In some ways there didn't seem to be anything wrong. It was all natural. The man made into a wild thing going against his ancestor who was now half tame.

It was after midnight when Socrates decided to go to bed. The police hadn't made it yet and he was tired, very tired and sore.

◪ ◪ ◪ ◪

They didn't show up at Bounty the next day either. Socrates was happy about that. He didn't want to embarrass his boss or to be humiliated in front of the people who saw him as a friend.

That evening he went to Iula's diner and ordered the fried chicken. It was the best-tasting meal he'd had in many years.

"This chicken's good, I," Socrates told her. "You doin' somethin' different?"

"It's just the same old chicken," Iula said. "An' it's just the same old me."

You look as good as it taste was what Socrates wanted to say but he didn't because he was a murderer again and a murderer had no right to flirt.

"What's wrong with you, Socrates?" Iula asked.

"How you'n Tony doin'?" Socrates asked back.

"He's okay I guess. He moved back out last Friday."

"Moved out? I thought you two was gonna get married again?"

Iula rubbed the back of her neck, raising her elbow as she did so. Socrates remembered that gesture when she was relaxed at his house late in the evening.

"I should'a known that he wasn't no different. Naggin' me about why I couldn't close the restaurant down and spend the day with him. You know a business cain't run itself." Iula looked directly into Socrates' eyes.

"I'm sorry about that, honey," Socrates said. "You need a good man. And you deserve the best."

"I don't know about all that," Iula said. "But I sure could use some company."

Socrates knew that in a few hours or a few days at most he was likely to lose his freedom, forever this time.

"Could I walk you home after?" he asked.

"If you want."

"I'll just wait for ya then."

"You will?"

"Yeah. Sumpin' wrong with that?"

"No. Nuthin' wrong but maybe just weird. I mean you don't come in on chicken night. An' you ain't been in at all in weeks. An' I thought you give up on walkin' me home, that you was with that Charlene Willert."

"An' I thought you chose Tony," Socrates replied.

Iula's nostrils flared. Socrates could see that she wanted to say more but didn't know how. She *had* decided on Tony. What Socrates did was none of her business.

"What night Topper come in?" Socrates asked hoping that he didn't sound desperate.

"Why?"

"Iula, can you get up off me an' be civil? I'm sorry if you mad. I thought you wanted to marry Tony. I stopped comin' 'cause I don't have no right to want you like I do if I cain't put up my nickel."

Iula's orangish skin brightened and her lips quivered with words that she held in.

"He be in in about a hour," she said finally.

When Socrates touched her arm she sighed.

"Hey, hey, Mr. Fortlow," Nelson Saint-Paul, more commonly known as Topper, said. "How you doin'?"

"Not so bad I guess." Socrates took a seat next to the pudgy undertaker who was named for the top hat he wore at services in his funeral home. "I mean I'm still breathin' and I'm still free."

"Would you like something to eat?" graciously asked the undertaker.

"Take some coffee if you offerin'."

"Done," Topper said. "Mrs. LaPort, please bring my friend some coffee and a slice of coffee cake."

Iula nodded but didn't move. There were a lot of customers in the diner that evening. Socrates didn't mind waiting. It was a little after eight o'clock and Iula wasn't off until eleven at the earliest.

He sat and discussed the day's events with Topper, who was one of the few men Socrates knew who read the newspapers each day. In prison there was a limited amount of news allowed to get out among the general population. Among a certain crowd talk about the news was like real cream in your coffee or a glimpse of the sea.

Sometimes Socrates sought Topper out to discuss the news but this day he had another purpose in mind.

After Topper and Socrates had dispatched with international and national events they discussed local comings and goings.

"I heard somebody got killed down near me," Socrates said almost incidentally.

"You mean that Logan child?" Topper asked.

Socrates shook his head. "Was that his name?"

"Ronald Logan. He was raised not five blocks from your house. Fell in with gangsters. Went to jail and came out wrong. It's amazing to me how they take these children and turn 'em into something that isn't even human any more. That boy was a terror on the street for

128

the whole time he was out of jail. Ten days. No. No I'm a liar. It was nine days. Nine days and then they found him dead in the alley right up the street here."

"Somebody shoot'im?"

"Crushed his skull. That's what his mother told me. And you know I believe that she was relieved. Relieved that the evil she released on this world was gone." Topper had a Bible group that met on Friday evenings at his funeral home, business permitting. He sounded like a minister but Socrates liked him anyway.

"You doin' the funeral?" Socrates asked as if just making conversation.

"When the coroner gets through with the body. When there's a murder the coroner has to take a look. He don't do much." Nelson Saint-Paul sneered in professional disdain. "Just take a look and then release the body. Only it usually take him a whole week to get to it because of the backlog they got. Backlog of death. You know that's a shame."

Socrates winced but remained quiet.

He was thinking about the bodies he had seen in his life. The dead men and women, almost all of them dead before they should have been. He considered Ronald Logan, who had just been a corpse until Nelson named him. Now he had a mother and a history.

"Socrates," Nelson was saying.

"Huh?"

"Where are you, man? Here I am offerin' you

129

employment and there you are examining your feet."

"Sorry."

"Well?"

"Well what?"

"You wanna try doin' a little work for me?"

"What you want? Some kinda janitor?"

"Naw. Janitor's easy to find. I need somebody to help with the embalming and the preparation for service. You know that's a real profession ain't gonna fall outta style."

Socrates put both of his hands on the table to keep his balance. He felt as if he might fall right out of his chair. Dumb luck, that's what they called it in stir. Dumb luck.

In prison, Cap Richmond used to say, *every day is April Fool's day. After 'while you begin to think that life is just one big gag.*

"Lemme see 'bout that," Socrates said. "You know I might have to go outta town a little while. But if I don't I'll be by."

◥ ◥ ◥ ◥

He stayed at Iula's house that night. They got there at about midnight. Four bright red numbers burned **03:39** when Iula finally said, "Baby, I cain't take no mo' right now. Not right now."

Socrates rolled back on his side and reached for her in the darkness. She took his hand in hers.

"I'm sore all over, honey," she said. "But that's not complainin'. I just ain't that young anymore." She chuckled for a moment and then added, "Maybe I wasn't ever that young. You

130

was goin' at it like you just got outta jail yesterday."

Socrates woke up at five. He sat around the big living room thumbing through old *Jet* magazines and waiting for the sun. Every now and then he'd wonder if the police had been to his house, if they issued a warrant once they found him missing.

"Mornin'," Iula said, breaking Socrates' trance.

"Hey, baby."

"What you thinkin' 'bout?"

"That it ain't true that a white man think we all look alike. That if there was a white man out there lookin' for me he'd know just who to look for."

"Why a white man be lookin' for you?" Iula's question was pointed but Socrates didn't care. Iula was a sharp woman.

"Any reason. I owe him money, kissed his daughter, forgot to take off my hat."

"Where you been wearin' that hat?"

"You ever?" Socrates said as the beginning of a question. But the question never came.

"I ever what?"

"You ever think that you the only one out here who cares? I mean that if the right thing gonna get done it's you got to do it 'cause nobody else even know?"

Iula frowned. She looked at the man who had worn her ragged with love. She shook her head

131

and then turned to leave the room. A while later Socrates smelled coffee brewing. When Iula returned with her tarnished, silver-plated tray she was still frowning.

Socrates raised his head as she handed him a white diner mug.

"You a good man, Socrates Fortlow," Iula declared. "Now drink your coffee and come on back down to earth."

◩ ◩ ◩ ◩

Killer was whimpering when Socrates got home. The ex-con thought his pet was hungry but the dog refused to eat and cried even louder.

That night Socrates let Killer's cries into his dreams. They were a perfect fit for his thoughts. Ronald Logan died over and over again against the screen of pain. And every time the boy fell Socrates sank lower. There were policemen eating ice cream cones, arresting old ladies and driving fast for fun. There were blind men walking past the murder scene ignorant of the criminal and the crime. Behind it all there was a trumpet playing. It was a jazz man playing but he was an angel too.

All angels ain't from heaven, his skinny aunt Bellandra whispered. *But you cain't choose your angels so you better not mind.*

In the morning Socrates realized that the police were not going to come, that he had gotten away with murder, that there was no price he had to pay.

He carried his freedom out the front door, past

the whimpering dog, and on the bus to work. His freedom wasn't light or happy or proud. People spoke to him but he didn't understand and had to ask them to repeat what they'd said. They'd oblige but still Socrates didn't get it. Finally he'd just nod his head as if he knew what they meant.

"Sumpin' wrong wit' you?" young Darryl asked him on their one forty-five lunch break.

"I don't know if it's me or everybody else, Darryl. Damn."

"What is it?"

Socrates looked at the boy. They were both killers. But Darryl still had a chance to be better.

"How you feelin', Darryl?" Socrates asked.

"Okay."

"How is it out there with Howard and Corina?"

"Okay I guess. I mean Howard always talkin' 'bout how good he is. 'Bout his job an' how him an' Corina wanna buy that house they rentin'. It's like he braggin' all the time but he okay."

"But you could talk to 'im, right?" Socrates wanted to know. "I mean if you got a problem you could talk to Howard."

"If I got a problem I could talk to you," Darryl said simply.

"But if you was home and you wasn't gonna come in to work," Socrates argued. "If you couldn't see me for a few days you could talk to Howard and Corina, right?"

"I guess," Darryl said, sounding no happier than Socrates felt.

It was sixteen miles from work to Socrates' home. He decided to walk part way, telling himself that it wasn't much longer than waiting for the bus to come.

On the way he had a talk with himself. A talk about what if.

"What if the cops drove up beside me right now?" he asked himself as he neared Robertson and Olympic. "What if they stopped me and said, 'Hey, niggah, what you doin' walkin' on the street up here? You live around here?'"

Socrates thought he might say, "I live in this city. I pay the tax pay your salary and fix these here streets. I guess I could walk if I want to." And then, in his daydream, he walked away from them.

But the cops followed him down the streets of his imagination. They stopped him on Fairfax and made him stand up against the wall. When they couldn't find anything in his pockets Socrates demanded their badge numbers because, he said, "Now you gone through my pockets and that's illegal 'less you got reason to 'spect me of a crime."

The scenario played itself out in a dozen different ways. In some he was shot and others the policemen were killed. In one long fantasy the people in the street rose up in a riot that lasted for fifteen days and leveled the streets of L.A. into the rubble of rage.

After more than two and half hours, almost

three, Socrates was tired but he hadn't been stopped by the police. He climbed into a bus and sat there exhausted. In the middle of a nap he decided to turn himself in.

It was well past dark when Socrates got home. He'd taken the shortcut past the place where Ronald Logan had died. He only remembered when he saw the spot where Logan had fallen. He stood there trying to feel something for the boy he had slaughtered but all he felt was wrong.

When he got home Killer was so sick that he couldn't even propel himself on his halter to greet his master. Socrates decided to put off turning himself in until the next day when he could make sure that his dog would survive.
He took the dog back to the veterinarian who saved his life when his legs were crushed. Dolly Straight told him that he would have to put the dog in a hospital where he'd have to undergo an operation if he were to survive. Socrates had never heard of an animal being operated on but he trusted the doctor and cared more about that dog than he cared for most people.
That night he considered Darryl and Killer, deciding that it would be wrong to leave either one by going to jail. Socrates wasn't afraid of prison; he wasn't afraid of anything. But he didn't need to prove that. What he needed was to make what amends he could and still meet his obligations.

"Okay now lift him," Nelson Saint-Paul said to his temporary helper Socrates Fortlow and to Stuart Lane, a regular worker in the funeral home. The two men were big but Ronald Logan was heavy with death. They had him all dressed up in a suit that was slit in the back so that it would fit. Nelson had slipped white silken socks on Ronald's feet but there were no shoes for the coffin.

Socrates had asked Topper if he could try out there for a while without pay. The first day he had helped to connect the tubes under Ronald's armpit to suck out the blood and replace it with the embalmer's fluid, the formaldehyde. He watched as Nelson put a placid visage on the boy's face and as he used makeup to replace a little of the life that Socrates had taken. He couldn't fully straighten out the dent in the boy's skull. The head was still a little lopsided.

The smell of the formaldehyde and the clammy touch of the boy's skin dismantled the hardened ex-con. The boy's deadweight did not leave his shoulders or strained heart even after laying the load down. And Ronald Logan's eyes were not fully shut. Socrates could see the dulled glimmer of his eyeballs through tiny slits. He was no longer human but neither was he gone. Socrates dreaded the three days he spent around that corpse. Every evening coming home from Bounty he clenched up anticipating the sneaky peeking of the boy he'd murdered.

Every evening he'd gone to the pay phone to tell Topper that he couldn't come in. But he never dropped the dime. He was like a dog, he knew, that needed his nose rubbed in his dirty business.

"Killin' ain't like a crap you could flush down the toilet," he said to Darryl one day before going down to Topper's. "The stink stays on you. Other people can smell it. I smell it in my sleep at night."

The boy didn't know why Socrates chose that moment to lecture him about guilt but he nodded, submitting the ex-con's words to memory.

On the first day, when he was alone with the naked corpse, Socrates stared at him; even in death the mugger looked menacing. A scar across his upper lip left him with the slightest sneer. The feet were pigeon-toed and the penis was small but hard. The hair was still growing, Topper told him that.

Socrates wanted to cry but could not. The feeling he was left with was worse than prison had been. Ronald Logan was a broken promise laid out on that table.

"You will never be forgotten," Socrates whispered. "Not as long as I live."

"Okay, now settle him in," Topper said. "You know how, Stuart. Make sure the fingers are in line, straighten out the suit. That's right. That's right."

137

"We see it all in here, Mr. Fortlow," Topper was saying. "They all come down to death. Even that princess over there in England. They had to bury her too just like anybody else."

Mrs. Yolanda Logan and her mother, Roxanne, came to view the body that Saturday morning at eight fifteen. Socrates stood toward the back of the little chapel and waited for some kind of sign from the grief-stricken mother. Yolanda was somewhere in her thirties but she looked as if she'd lived more years than her own mother. She was a heavy woman and her shoulders were sagging. Roxanne, a big woman too, stood near at hand in case her help was needed.

"Oh no there he is," Yolanda said. "There he is. It's him, Momma."

"He looks nice," said the boy's grandmother. "He looks peaceful. And his suit still fits him even after all that weight liftin' he did."

Yolanda put her hands up between her and the coffin trying to deny either the boy or his death. Topper, wearing his signature hat, came up with a stool. Roxanne guided her daughter toward the seat and then she took her turn visiting the coffin.

Roxanne's face was a study in cautious anger. She raised her head as far away as she could while still trying to see the boy. Her inspection was close and complete. When she turned away you knew that she'd have no nightmares about Ronald returning.

They stayed with the dead boy for half an hour or so.

When they started gathering themselves together, Socrates left. He went outside the chapel door and waited.

He had bought black rayon slacks and a button-up tan shirt for that day. He felt hemmed in and itchy, like a schoolboy in a new uniform.

"Mrs. Logan?" he said when the women came out.

"Yes?" Yolanda said.

"I wanted to say how sorry I am. About your son that is. About what happened."

The poor mother was beyond speech. She wore a dark brown dress and blue shawl with dark green and yellow flowers printed on it. She also wore white tennis shoes.

Yolanda took Socrates' hands in hers and stood there as if in prayer. The big man didn't pull away.

"What's your name?" Yolanda asked.

"Socrates Fortlow."

"He was a bad boy, Mr. Fortlow. I loved him but he was bad, crazy bad. It was just like havin' a wild animal right up there in the house wit' you. It was like when a old man forgets who his family is. Like when he don't remember his wife or daughter. When I looked at Ronnie I didn't even know him." Yolanda's hands were wet and so was her face. Socrates concentrated on keeping his grip from crushing her hands.

"That's enough now, Yoyo," Roxanne said.

She moved in to disengage the convict and his victim but they wouldn't let go.

"He loved you, Mrs. Logan. He prob'ly just forgot up in jail how to show it."

"Who are you?" Roxanne asked.

"I'm Socrates. I been in jail. I know how it hurts you and the ones you love too."

"Bless you," Yolanda said. "Did you know my son?"

"No, ma'am, I didn't. But you be strong now."

Roxanne pulled on her daughter's hands until finally she broke the bond. Socrates watched them climb into Topper's black Cadillac, which then drove off behind the hearse.

◪ ◪ ◪ ◪

A policeman was standing in front of Socrates' gate when he got home from work the next day. Albert Biggers had on a blue suit and buff shoes. Socrates thought that he looked ridiculous in those colors.

"Officer," Socrates hailed.

"Where you been, Socrates?"

"Nowhere. I ain't been nowhere. And I sure am tired so if you wanna arrest me please do it or let me pass."

"Why would I want to arrest you, Socrates? Have you done something wrong?"

That's when Socrates realized that some time in the last week the violence had drained out of his hands. He didn't want to hurt any-body. He didn't care that Biggers stood there in that silly suit trying to act like he was going to

140

trick Socrates into a confession. A confession to anything.

"Let me pass, man," was all Socrates had to say.

that smell

"A man cain't be a man if he don't make the money, honey," Leon Spellman said to Veronica Ashanti at the Saint-Paul Mortuary on a Wednesday night in June.

"An' here I thought you young men believed it was t'other way around." Veronica blew out a sweet smelling cloud of smoke from her short cigar.

"What you mean by that, Veronica?" Chip Lowe, the neighborhood watch captain, asked.

"I thought these male chirren believed that you cain't get no honey," Veronica paused for a beat between words, " 'less you let up on some money."

The older men, including Socrates, laughed at the joke. Leon glowered but even he smiled.

"All I'm sayin' is that a man has got to be responsible if he wants a woman to stand by'im," Leon said. "I mean a black man has got to be the bread winner. He's got to be a father and he's got to make a home where his wife an' family are safe. A black man has got to guide his people."

"And ain't that a man talkin'," Cynthia Lott chimed in. She was a tiny woman with a shrill voice that made Socrates' neck muscles tighten whenever he heard it.

"No need to attack the boy, Cindy," Nelson Saint-Paul said.

"You men always think I'm attackin' you," Cynthia said. "But I'm just sayin' what I hear. Leon wanna be the breadwinner, the father and the hunter all rolled up into one. What about the woman?"

"He didn't say that the woman couldn't help," Chip said.

"Help?" Cynthia cried opening her eyes as wide as possible. "Black women the ones *need* help. That's just the problem. You got this boy all of a sudden realizes he ain't been doin' right and now he just wanna walk in on a woman and say, 'Okay, baby, the boss is home now,' when what he should be doin' is askin', 'How can I help you, ma'am?' "

"An' does he have to get down on his knees too?" Chip asked angrily.

"Wouldn't hurt," said Cynthia. "Wouldn't hurt one bit. You know women been down on their knees cleanin' and beggin' while their men be drinkin' that wine and jokin' out here on Central and a hundred and third."

Socrates tried to hear past the piercing tones to get at Cynthia's words. He hadn't said much at Nelson's Wednesday meetings. Ever since he'd done a little apprentice work for Nelson, Socrates had an open invitation to the Saturday prayer meeting and the Wednesday night talk. Socrates usually spent his Saturday days with

Darryl and most weekend evenings, lately, with Iula.

But Socrates came to Nelson's on Wednesdays and listened to the men and women talk. There was no dress code but the men often wore sports coats and ties. Socrates wore a pair of tan slacks and a black dress shirt with a Salvation Army pullover sweater even on a hot day like that one.

"All us men don't do like that," Leon complained. "I'm here ain't I?"

"Here callin' me honey an' tellin' it like you was the boss." Cynthia's anger drove her voice higher.

"But men should be the boss," Leon argued. "Man was made to be the boss but somehow the black man lost his uh, his uh, authority."

"Oh please," Cynthia said with disdain.

"I agree with part'a what Cyn says," Veronica agreed. She was a pear-shaped woman with large hips and a small chest. Her face was luxurious and full featured, as dark and shiny as polished ebony. "I mean I don't need no man comin' in on me an' mine all of a sudden sayin' he the boss. But I don't want no man on his knees either." She paused, considering the imagined pose with her eyes. "Well, maybe sometimes."

The sly grin that the cigar-smoking woman revealed got everybody laughing again.

"But what I mean is," Veronica continued, "that I want a man to feel good about hisself. And men are different. They protect the home while the women raise chirren."

"Black men don't do shit," Cynthia said flatly.

"They come here," Nelson said. "I open my doors for you. Chip works on the neighborhood watch."

Socrates thought that Cynthia was biting her lip so as not to snap at Nelson. They all appreciated the Wednesday meeting because of the good conversation but also because of the chicken sandwiches and port wine that Topper served.

"Yeah," Leon barked. "You always wanna make all that's happenin' bad the black man's fault. It ain't all our fault. If you'd back us up more better maybe we'd get somewhere."

"You can't have it both ways Leon."

Everybody turned when they heard Socrates speak. Even Cynthia seemed interested in what the quiet man had to say.

"What you mean, Socrates?" Nelson asked.

"I mean if a boy wanna be a man he cain't be askin' for help. He just got to pick up and do what he have to do. Now Cynthia over here don't want him. Well, okay, don't ask her for nuthin'. There's some woman out here want your help."

"So you mean that it's on Leon not on black women?" Chip Lowe frowned. He was smaller than Socrates, but still large, with a gray mustache and black skin except for his hands and a big splotch on his face that had turned a milky white.

"It's on everybody, man." Socrates fought to keep the anger out of his voice. "Everybody think it's them or their people got it bad. We all got it bad, all of us."

"I don't know, Socrates," Nelson Saint-Paul said. "Some people have it better, easier, than some others. Some have homes, some are home-less."

"Yeah," Leon said bitterly. "Some is white, the rest sleep outside."

"You don't sleep outside, Leon," Cynthia said. "You live at home with your mother."

"All I'm sayin'," Socrates said. "Is that we all gonna walk out on Central Avenue when this talk is through. We all gonna be lookin' around in the shadows an' ain't nobody gonna feel friendly if you see a strange black face."

"So you think we're all in the same boat?" asked Veronica Ashanti. It was the first time she'd heard Socrates speak and she smiled at him approvingly through a haze of cigar smoke.

"And the boat is leakin' an' here we are arguin' 'bout which way is land." Socrates nodded with finality and everyone went quiet.

Even Cynthia was silent.

"Well," Nelson said. "On that note I guess we should call it a night. We all have something to think about until next time."

The watch captain Chip Lowe was the first one to stand up. Cynthia looked from side to side, scowling as if her final words were cut off.

"You wanna ride to your house, Ms. Lott?" young Leon asked.

"I guess so." She had to hop out of her chair because her feet didn't touch the floor.

"I'll take Veronica," Nelson offered.

They left through a door in the small back room that led to the chapel in the Saint-Paul Mortuary. At the front of the chapel stood a coffin faced by five neat rows of wood chairs. The ghostly audience seemed real to Socrates in the dim room. He wondered if there was a body up there waiting for the morning service.

Outside, Chip and Socrates saw the women and their escorts safely to their cars. Leon had a 1968 sky blue Pontiac. The prosperous under-taker drove a late model maroon BMW.

"You need a ride, Mr. Fortlow?" the watch captain asked.

"I could walk."

"I thought you said that we were all scared walking down Central?"

"We are. But there's a difference with me."

"What's that?"

"I ain't scared'a bein' scared," Socrates said with a grin. "If I was I couldn't even sleep at night. But I'll take a ride I guess. You know I'd rather be scared than have my feet hurtin' like they do sometimes."

◢ ◢ ◢ ◢

"I like what you had to say," Chip Lowe said to Socrates once they were on the way. He drove a 1959 pink and turquoise Chevy pickup. It looked as good as the day it was new.

The ex-con had no reply.

"I mean," the watch captain continued, "we got to settle this shit about men and women to get on with the problems we got down here. Don't you think so?"

"I don't know."

"But that's why we get together," Lowe said. This was the first time he'd been talkative with Socrates. Before that night he had been cold, even suspicious. "So we can talk all this stuff out. You know, everyday people talking. Not no Jesse Jackson or soul brother number one. Just folks. Right?"

Socrates looked over at Chip, who was looking back.

"I'ont know, man," Socrates said. "Talk is cheap." He was thinking about a man, J. T. Helms, who they said was having a conversation about the upcoming presidential election all the way to the electric chair. He talked until he died.

"But why would you wanna come to Nelson's if you don't think it matters?"

"I like chicken and wine," Socrates offered. "An' anyway, cheap is all a poor man can afford."

"But what you said back there to Leon came from your heart," Chip said with conviction.

"Maybe," Socrates admitted. "Maybe I felt it but feelin' don't make the difference. If all you leave wit' is a good feelin' you coulda stayed home."

Chip frowned and turned his eyes to traffic. Then he glanced at Socrates and looked away again. After he'd done this a few times Socrates realized that the man had something to say.

"You know there's been some talk about you,

148

brother," Chip Lowe said.

"Oh yeah?"

"Yeah. I mean I'm not the sort to get in a man's business but some people out here just ain't happy 'less they can run somebody else down."

Socrates' window was open. There was a scent in the breeze, the odor of human waste.

"I just wanted to tell you that people been talkin'," Chip said. Then he paused giving Socrates a chance to say something.

"Okay," the ex-con answered.

"Okay what?"

"Okay I hear ya. People been talkin'. I know, people talk."

The odor was picking up strength. Socrates tried to pierce the night darkness and see where the smell came from.

"It's just that I thought you should know about it," Chip said. "A man should know when he's bein' bad-mouthed."

"And now I know." When the odor began to lose strength Socrates gave up his surveillance.

"But you don't know what they said."

"I ain't askin' you about gossip, Chip Lowe. If you got somethin' t'say then just get on wit' it."

"It's the police," Chip said in a heavy tone.

"Yeah?"

"They said that they suspect you of killin' that girl, that Minnie Lee that they found four months ago near your place. They told the watch to be careful around you because you were in prison for murder and they think you still at it."

"How long ago they tell you this?" Socrates asked.

"I don't know."

"Yesterday?"

"No."

"Last week then?"

"Well . . ."

"How about last month? They tell you about me last month?"

"Maybe, maybe it was then." Chip looked up to see what cross street they were at.

"But you waited till now to tell me."

When Socrates rubbed his hand over his head Chip stiffened a little.

For the rest of the ride, only a few minutes, both men were silent. When Chip pulled up to the front gate in the back alley, Socrates waited before he opened the door.

"I don't hold it against you, Mr. Lowe. You got to wait before you can know if a man is trustworthy. But I cain't help ya either. I am who I am, you know what I mean?"

"Yeah. Yeah, I guess so."

With that Socrates climbed out of the truck and went in to pet and feed his dog.

◪ ◪ ◪ ◪

The next day he was at work again, bagging groceries and making deliveries around the Beverly Glen district. It was a hot day but overcast and gloomy. Socrates did his work without thinking much except every once in a while that odor came back to him. The smell of a man or

150

woman who had lost control and was sending out a scent that would bring predators and death.

"Socrates, can I talk to you?" Marty Gonzalez came upon him in the back room among the other older employees of the store.

Ben Rickman, Larry Cross, and Hal Crown all stood up to leave. They were white men, lifetime supermarket employees. Socrates was the only one of the group who hovered around minimum wage but he was accepted among them because of his age and maturity.

"What, Marty?" Socrates asked his boss.

"I can't hold that job open too much longer," the small bronze man said. There was no trace of a Spanish or Mexican accent in his words. "You know I've been without a produce man for six weeks now."

Socrates wanted to say that Marty should give that job to somebody else. He wanted to be left alone but somehow he couldn't get the words out. He thought about Leon and Nelson and especially about Cynthia and how she dismissed men. The smell from the street seemed to follow Marty's question.

"Well, Socco?" Marty asked. "What's it going to be?"

"Gimme one day, Marty. One day and I'll let you know for sure."

"Yeah I think you should do it," Darryl told his self-appointed guardian. "You could do that job

151

wit' no problem."

"I guess so," Socrates said. "And Marty's behind me, that's for sure."

They were having donuts and hot chocolate at the House of Donuts in a mini-mall eight blocks down from Bounty Supermarket. They watched five young white boys practicing on their skateboards in the parking lot of the mall.

"Then you gonna take it?"

"But what if in order to get this new job they got to look in my record again?" Socrates asked. He didn't expect an answer but Darryl had one anyway.

"They ain't checked yet. And so what if they do? You could get another job. But at least this way you got a chance t'get a better check."

"I don't know if it's worth all that bother."

"But if you get paid better," Darryl reasoned, "you could get a phone and maybe you could move."

"I don't need to move."

"But if you did I could come stay wit' you. If you lived in a place where nobody knew me, then I could stay at your house and you wouldn't have to think that the old gang might get me."

◪ ◪ ◪ ◪

Socrates got off the bus early on his way home, giving himself twelve blocks or so to walk and think. He meant to make a decision about Marty's offer to promote him to produce manager. It was a good job and he deserved it; at least he had done well at work.

But when he got off the bus Socrates caught a whiff of that same odor he smelled out the window of Chip Lowe's car. The smell of someone without a home or hope. The smell of someone dying.

For two blocks the scent gained potency. Socrates passed two liquor stores, a beauty shop, a travel agency and three times that in closed storefronts. He realized that the smell was coming from behind the block and so he went down a side street to an alley behind the stores.

Halfway down the alley he came upon a small wooden structure that was once meant to house trash cans for the weekly dump truck. The graying pine cube now contained the life of a man.

He wore white tennis shoes that had been blackened from the street. His jeans would have fit a child, and the pink shirt was unbuttoned, revealing parchment-like brown skin over brittle bones. The smell was heralded by flies that buzzed everywhere. Socrates recognized the trumpet player.

"Hoagland Mars," Socrates said loudly enough to rouse the man from his doze.

"I ain't," the small man whispered, "I ain't got it no mo'."

"Ain't got what?"

"I spent it on wine, man. Yo' money is gone, brother. Gone." Hoagland's eyes closed and then slowly opened again. "You still here?"

The odor intensified the longer Socrates stood

there. He already felt that he should go home and wash away the horn-player's stench.

"Get up," Socrates ordered. "Get up." He caught the soiled man by his shoulder, lifting him to his feet.

"Ow! Damn, man, what's wrong wit' you?" Hoagland was suddenly wide awake. He tried to pull away but Socrates held on to the boy-sized man. He held him at arm's length to keep from suffocating on the fumes released by lifting the wino.

"Lemme go, brother. I ain't got nuthin'. You cain't take nuthin'. Just lemme go or hit me an' leave." Hoagland was unsure on his feet but Socrates kept him upright, then he began to walk.

"Where you goin'?" the wino protested.

But Socrates didn't answer. He dragged Hoagland Mars to a phone booth on Ninety-second and made a call to a man named after a poet.

". . . and bring a tarp or sumpin' that we could put'im on, Milton," Socrates said into the mouthpiece, " 'cause he smell more'n a outhouse and he might vomit any minute."

The twenty-five-year-old gold Lincoln Continental pulled up twenty minutes later. Hoagland was sleeping on the sidewalk.

"Damn, man," Milton Langonier, semiretired gypsy cab driver, said. "That smell might get inta the seats."

"Just to Luvia's," Socrates said. "You can keep the windows open an' I'll pay ya ten bucks."

154

Socrates laid the unconscious jazz man on the painter's tarp that Milton used to cover his backseat. Milton drove with all the windows and vents open. He also turned on the air conditioner and waved one free hand under his nose.

◪ ◪ ◪ ◪

Socrates carried the man like a boy in his arms. He let the legs swing down and supported Hoagland with his right arm while he rapped on the door with his other hand.

He didn't know what to expect when Luvia saw the mess he'd brought to her doorstep. They had been at a partial truce ever since Socrates had started to pay for her monthly visits to Right Burke's grave. Socrates accompanied her, driven by Milton Langonier. He spoke very little and respected her few moments alone with the old man she'd taken care of and loved in silence.

Rail thin, and mean in a way that only some Christians seemed to master, Luvia opened the door and scowled at Socrates. She looked at Hoagland Mars dangling off the side of the ex-convict like a Siamese twin who had died and withered, leaving his brother the task of carrying him until the day that he too passed away.

Luvia didn't wrinkle up her nose or fan her face.

"This here is —" Socrates began.

"Bring him out back to the garage," Luvia interrupted. "I got a tub out there we could use. I usually use it for old clothes we get in but it'll do."

She turned and walked down the narrow hallway that went through the house and out a door into a small cement yard. Across the yard was a double door that led to a garage. Therein stood two washing machines, an industrial-sized sink, and a huge iron tub lined with cracked porcelain.

Luvia connected a small red rubber hose to the spigot and tested the water between hot and cold as if she were preparing to bathe an infant.

Socrates didn't need directions to undress Hoagland. It was impossible to tell if the man, who was semiconscious at best, had any objections. Socrates stood Hoagland up in the tub and then he took the hose from Luvia and formed a weak spray by applying pressure against the spout with his huge bone-breaking thumb.

Hoagland began to laugh. He giggled and assumed modest poses like a young girl walked in upon while dressing. He squealed and turned, using his hands to cover his genitals. Finally he sat down in the tub and allowed Luvia to scrub him with an oversized sponge.

Socrates gave her the hose. She just laid it down in the unplugged basin, using it to rinse off the places that needed it. Hoagland Mars lay back in a languorous euphoria allowing Luvia to wash him and move him with ease.

When it was all over the wino had fallen into a deep sleep. Socrates carried him to an attic room on the fourth floor of the house. He laid Hoagland out on a cot. Luvia covered the man and brushed his forehead with her hand. A smile came across the hard woman's face.

◢ ◢ ◢ ◢

"If you gimme a hunnert dollars a mont'," Luvia said in clipped words. "I could get that much again from the city an' then my church will come in with any extra if it's needed."

"That's what everybody stay wit' you has to pay?"

"Somebody got to pay it. I cain't make water into wine or pull bread out from a hat."

They were sitting in a small room on the bottom floor. Socrates sat on the sofa because no chair in the room looked like it would support him. Annie Rodgers, the feeble-minded woman whose mother had died when Annie was forty-two, stood in the hall watching Luvia.

"Who paid for Right?" Socrates asked.

"Right Burke was a guest in my house," Luvia said proudly.

She was still angry at Socrates. She would always blame him for Right's death. He accepted the burden. Guilt seemed to be the proper change for the kind of love he could give.

"My daddy was like that," Socrates said.

"Like what?"

"A drunk. Died on the street just like Mars was gonna do. They brought us to the hospital when they found him. He smelled just like that, just like Hoagland did."

"I don't have no sense'a smell," Luvia said as she batted the fingers of her left hand against her nose. "Smell don't bother me. I don't have to worry about it."

"You don't smell nuthin'?"

Luvia almost snarled as she shook her head.

"I'll come up with the money for at least three months," he said. "After that I'll put a clothespin on my own nose and mind my own business if he goes back on the street."

■ ■ ■ ■

"How much a produce manager get?" Socrates asked Marty Gonzalez the next morning at eight fifteen.

"It's a level twelve," the short man said.

"How's that in dollars?"

"Eleven forty-five an hour based on a forty-hour week," Marty replied. "But we expect a man in that position to work until he gets the job done. You only get paid for overtime if you have to come in special or stay overnight."

"That's near about five hundred a week." Socrates had always been good with numbers. He just thought about the equation and had a general notion of the result.

"Four fifty-eight," Marty said nodding. "A lot more than you get now."

"They might look at my record," Socrates said.

"Not if I don't check that box," Marty countered.

"I'll be sixty next year."

"Newman worked till he was sixty-nine down on Sepulveda. He only retired because his wife got sick. The way it works now is that a man's not old till he proves it. And you're stronger than any other man in the store right now."

Marty was smiling at the glower on his employee.

"You got three people workin' in produce right now," Socrates said. "What about what they say when you promote me over them?"

"Do you care what Kelly or Billings thinks?"

"Fuck no but you might."

"If I cared about a white man's opinion about me I'd be in a grave in East L.A. right this minute."

It was the first time that Marty had ever said anything about race or prejudice. Socrates had begun to think that Marty was one of those men who pretended to themselves that they were white. He wore a white shirt and tie, he spoke like a white man and married a white wife. But there it was — him and the white man, *them* and the white man.

Socrates liked Kelly and Billings. They were friendly and courteous. They asked after your health when you'd been sick and listened to what was going on with you. Marty didn't hate those men but he knew, Socrates did too, that colored men had suffered under white disapproval where when a brown man was angry it was spit in the wind.

"So what do I do?" Socrates asked.

"You take off that blue apron and put on a green one," Marty said. "I'll have the papers in my office tomorrow morning. Just practice your signature tonight and tomorrow make it plain."

◪ ◪ ◪ ◪

"It's a man's world," Leon Spellman said that Wednesday night at the Saint-Paul Mortuary. "From the president on down, from Martin Luther King on down, from Al Capone on down — it's a man sits on top and say what's what and who's who."

"And that's just why the world is in such a mess," Cynthia said with disgust. "We got a man in the driver's seat and he's drunk as a skunk."

"That's not fair, Cyn," Nelson the undertaker said. "The boy said Martin Luther King. You cain't call Martin Luther King no drunkard or fool."

"He was a good man but he was a man, Topper," Cynthia replied. "And a man wanna rattle his sword and shake his fist. A man wanna lead and the rest wanna follow. But when that man is cut down, we're lost. The head is gone, the man is gone and all the plans is gone too. A man, no matter how good he is, makes a mess."

"You know Cynthia's right there," Veronica agreed. "I don't want no man out there yellin' and fightin' when he could be home wit' me. It's the Bible tell me what's right. It's the Lord lead me. It breaks my heart when they kill our men like that, or when they kill each other. It breaks my heart."

"But what else can we do?" Socrates thought but he said it out loud too.

160

"Say what?" Chip Lowe asked.

"It's like nobody listens," Socrates said. "It's like you always alone. Most of the time it's like you got to yell or hit or somethin' 'cause nobody's listenin'. You got to do somethin'. You got to let somebody know. Other people don't have that problem. One of 'em look to the other one and they both nod and they know."

"What you talkin' 'bout, Socrates?" Nelson Saint-Paul asked.

"I don't know," Socrates said. "But it's somethin'. Cynthia's right. Other people don't have a leader you could point to and they seem okay. You got your Chinese in Chinatown and your Koreans with their language all over billboards and stores up on Olympic. And the Jews all over the country help each other without sayin' they need another Moses to set 'em free."

"What that supposed to mean?" Chip Lowe asked.

"It means that I'm tired, man. Tired," Socrates said. "We dyin' out here."

"I don't understand, Socrates," Veronica said as she lit her stogie. "What do you mean?"

"I don't know, baby. It's like there's somethin' missin'. Somethin' I ain't got in my head. I know what's wrong but I don't know what's right. You know what I mean?"

Veronica nodded slowly but the gesture seemed to say, *No, but I'd like to understand.*

Cynthia and Leon and Chip Lowe were all frowning.

"We all know what's right, Socrates," Nelson Saint-Paul said.

"All of us?" Socrates asked.

Nelson nodded while sticking out his pudgy lower lip with conviction.

"Then why do we have it so bad out here? Why don't we all get out in the street an' clean up what we got and then get together to take back what's been stolen?" Socrates' voice cracked and he blinked.

"It's complex," Nelson Saint-Paul answered. "Black people have been —"

"I know what it is stop me," Socrates said interrupting his host. "It's 'cause I'd be alone out there. I'd be crazy because I'm the only one and how can one man matter? It's like a butterfly in a hurricane."

For a few moments there was silence that befitted a mortuary. But soon there was talk again. Socrates listened. He heard what his friends had to say but he was thinking too.

He was thinking about the first time he heard Hoagland Mars play his coronet in the alley outside his door at three in the morning. The music was beautiful but it woke him up and gave him a scare. He was still scared and he was foolish. That combination of thoughts was enough to make Socrates smile.

◪ ◪ ◪ ◪

Six weeks later Socrates had a telephone installed in his home. He was produce manager at Bounty. He had a new pair of shoes and a

162

watch made from steel.

He walked to Marvane Street up to Luvia's front door. Even half a block away he could hear the jazz man playing out of the fourth floor window.

"He's upstairs," Luvia said, not frowning. "I'm sure you could hear it."

Hoagland put down his horn when Socrates walked into the room. He was wearing black jeans and a blue T-shirt, his feet were bare and his stiff hair was combed straight back.

"Yes?" Hoagland asked, not recognizing his patron.

"My name is Socrates."

"Oh yeah," Hoagland said. "You the one fount me and brought me over here."

Socrates nodded. Hoagland did too.

"You know," Hoagland said. "I have to thank you for bringin' me to Luvia. She just the kinda woman I need to keep my shit straight. I know she said that you thought I was dyin' out there, that I was hopeless and a drunk but you know it was just the intestinal flu."

"What?"

"I got put outta my place and then I come down with flu. That's what was goin' on. Just sick. But I thank you anyway. Even when I got better I prob'ly wouldn't'a found my way here."

"You need anything?" Socrates asked.

Hoagland shook his head to say no. "Luvia's church got a social club. They hired me to play 'em some jazz on Wednesdays. You could come on by and listen if you want. It only cost three dollars and you know I can blow."

"I'm busy on Wednesdays but good luck to you."

Hoagland Mars nodded and smirked. Socrates smiled to himself and said, "Well I better get goin'."

He turned and left the room without shaking hands.

walkin' the dog

On a clear day in August, when the hot air seemed to be boiling with flies, Socrates decided to take his dog for a walk. The ex-convict put on black sweatpants and a white T-shirt. He thought about putting a knife in his sock but, for a reason he couldn't explain, he went unarmed into the yard. There he found Killer capering expectantly with the help of the harness attached to his legless backside.

Socrates unhooked the short leader that connected Killer's halter to the suspension rope. He wrapped the bright yellow cord twice around his big fist and said, "Okay, boy. Let's go show 'em what you could do."

They walked a few blocks down the alley, Killer prancing proudly on his two powerful front legs. He was a heavy dog, seventy pounds easily. He had weighed more before the accident on the day Socrates saved him in the streets of West L.A.

Killer survived the amputations and, earlier on that summer, he made it through two operations. He was strong and brave too. Socrates would have said that he loved that dog if he ever said those two words about anyone or anything.

His right biceps bulged as the hot sun came down on his bald black head but Socrates didn't acknowledge the strain of his labors. Killer was the first pet that he'd ever owned. Other men in the penitentiary kept garden snakes, rats and pigeons for pets. Some of them swore that they had favorite cockroaches who returned each night for special crumbs they'd hoarded. But Socrates didn't love in prison. Love was weakness and Socrates' armor had nary a chink.

He never had a pet as a child. His father was a drunk and his mother worked too hard even to love Socrates most of the time. His aunt Bellandra loved him but she was crazy; she was too worried about her visions to have some furry creature mewling around begging for food.

"The white Christians call Him the Shepherd," Bellandra would tell Socrates, who was old enough to remember but not of an age to comprehend. "That makes them sheep. They made us pray like that, like we was sheep too. And you know what happens to sheep, don't ya? They cut off their woolly hair to humiliate 'em. They put the dogs on 'em. They slaughter 'em too. Now why would God want man to be lined up with sheep?"

Children were playing softball in the alley four blocks down. Socrates noticed that there were little Mexican children sprinkled in among the blacks. Too young to hate yet. Too young to separate and draw lines; to play a different game with guns and knives.

The children stopped and gawked at the big man and his deformed dog.

"Hey, mister," one black child shouted. "What happent to his legs?"

"Front part run so fast," Socrates responded, "that he left the back part behind."

"Huh?" the boy grunted, his friends mouthing the same wordless question.

But before they could say more Socrates was moving away, Killer barking joyously at the boys and their big white softball.

Socrates made a left on the next block. It was a street full of music and barbecue smoke, makeshift lawn chairs and people wandering back and forth. Down the middle of the street a gang of boys rode their bicycles in a swarm. Two or three old women sat on painted concrete porches fanning themselves and watching.

A few people motioned toward the dog, pointing out his deformity. If Socrates noticed them the gesture turned into a wave.

Killer tried hard to pull his master toward the smell of burnt flesh, but even if he had four legs he couldn't have budged the muscle built by so many years of prison life.

There wasn't a day that Socrates forgot the single cell, the smell of rust and sweat, the sounds of metal on stone that surrounded and imprisoned him. He was like a guerrilla soldier back then, secreted underground, waiting for the moment to rise and strike; waiting for freedom that he knew would probably come only in the form of a coffin.

But now, after twenty-seven years in storage and after nine years out, Socrates walked his crippled dog in the bright sun, unarmed and at an uneasy truce with his enemies.

The policeman, the salesman in the store, the newspaperman or TV anchor, Socrates didn't trust any one of them. He knew that their jobs were to hold him down and rob him, and then afterward to tell him lies about what had really gone down. It was a crazy thought, he told himself, but then he'd say, "But not as crazy as this world," and then he'd laugh.

He was laughing right then on the way to the park.

◪ ◪ ◪ ◪

From behind a sickly pine bush sprang a feathery red-haired dog. The animal, one-sixth the size of Killer, bared its sharp teeth and snarled. Killer saw no harm in the dog and danced on his front paws begging for a smell.

"Johnny, where are you?" a man called in a clear soprano. He appeared from behind the shedding, dying pine. He was tall and thin with a processed hairdo wrapped up in a nylon do-rag. He also wore a long-sleeved purple shirt, with fresh sweat stains in the armpits, and matching purple pants.

Even from a distance of a few feet Socrates

was assailed by the thick sweet scent of the man's cologne.

"Oh my," the younger man said. He held his hands in front of him in a cautious, almost feminine gesture.

"Yo' dog wanna fight and mine wanna make friends," Socrates said to help the purple man settle down.

"Johnny B. Goode, sit!" the younger man ordered.

The fluffy red dog obeyed instantly.

His master had a pencil-thin mustache and was older than Socrates had at first thought. Forty, maybe even forty-five. He had a slender scar down his left cheek and one eye was a light walnut, the other a deep mahogany brown.

"He like to growl but that's about all," the man said, still eyeing Socrates cautiously.

"Killer'd lick a razor blade if you'd let 'im. I don't think they taught survival in his brood."

"Yeah, I know what you mean. Sometimes Johnny be wagging his tail, snarlin', and takin' a piss all at the same time." The purple man smiled then he stuck out his hand and said, "Lavant Hall."

Socrates grabbed Lavant's right hand with his left because he was holding on to Killer's rope.

"Socrates Fortlow."

"What happened to your dog's legs?"

"Run over by a car," Socrates said, shrugging slightly.

"How come you call him Killer if he so

friendly?" Lavant Hall asked.

"I figger that if somebody hear me callin' him that they might stay offa my property on account'a the name."

Lavant Hall laughed and took a pack of no-name brand cigarettes from his oversized shirt pocket. He shook the pack at Socrates and a single tan filter appeared. Socrates took the cigarette. That was etiquette on the prison yard and a habit Socrates kept even though he rarely smoked after moving to L.A.

When Socrates leaned forward to take a light from the skinny man Killer got a chance to sniff the shiny red dog. Johnny B. Goode snarled but he didn't back away or snap. He was sniffing too.

"That's a fancy-assed dog," Socrates said with the familiarity of an old friend.

"Grand Long-Haired Red Terrier they call the breed," Lavant said. "It's a valuable dog but I ain't got the papers."

"How come you don't?"

" 'Cause I stole him off the street up in the Pacific Palisades."

Socrates took a deep drag on his cigarette and held the smoke for a few seconds before exhaling.

"Why you steal him?" Socrates asked. "You gonna sell him?"

"No."

"Hold him for ransom then?" Socrates was remembering Ahmed Jones, who used to say, on the recreation yard, that kidnapping favorite pets

170

of rich people was just as lucrative as kidnapping their children but that the law didn't get that crazy over a missing cat or a dog.

"I ride a bicycle," Lavant Hall said, smiling. "I ride it everywheres just so they don't think that they could keep me down here. I don't need to be white or rich or nuthin' to go up in the canyons or down to the beach. Not as long as I got my legs and my bike. . . ."

Johnny B. Goode jumped on Killer's head but the larger dog shrugged him off and barked. Somehow the motion started the two men walking on a zigzag path through Will Rogers Park.

". . . they cain't stop me from usin' the streets," Lavant continued. "Anyway I was up there at the Canyon Mall lookin' for a liquor store or some-place to get a soda pop 'cause it was hot an' I rode up all the way from down here. . . ."

There was a young couple lying near a bush in the lawn. They were kissing each other passionately, rubbing their hands all over each other's body. Socrates could see the big man's erection pressing urgently against his loose pants. The woman was holding on to it as if they were in a private room with the doors shut and locked.

"You see that," Lavant Hall said, nodding toward the lovers. "That's love right there on the ground. Ain't nuthin' t'be shamed about. An' if somebody don't like it then they don't have to look."

They passed the lovers and Socrates asked, "What about the dog?"

"Yeah," Lavant said. His smile flashed against a dark background of skin. "I saw this woman wearing a fur coat that was probably chinchilla. I say that 'cause the fur was like feathers, like Johnny look. That's not mink or nuthin'. Mink's heavy. But you know that white woman made me mad. There she had that cute dog and she was wearin' ten or twelve other animals on'er back that looked just like him, at least their hair did."

"So what you do?" Socrates asked. He was getting angry imagining the blood of some woman shed by a man who saw his own life in that of a dog.

"I followed her," Lavant said. "She went into a couple'a stores carryin' Johnny in her arms but then she come to this one place, this delicatessen. They wouldn't let no dogs in there. Even that bitch couldn't break that rule and so she tied his leash to a bike rack. That's all I needed."

The man in purple showed all of his teeth. "You know I pretended like I was lockin' up my bicycle but then that I changed my mind. I scooped up little Johnny and made a beeline back home. He's mine now. License, shots, everythang."

Lavant put up his hands feigning modesty at pulling off a great prank.

"Why?" Socrates asked.

"It's a war out here, brother," Lavant Hall said with conviction. "They wanna make us into slaves with the dollar. They wanna make us into slaves next to the TV. They even wanna make you a slave to taxes, my brother. You pay 'em yo' money an' they use it to buy your chains."

"Listen, man," Socrates said. "I done heard all that shit in the lockup. All day long you hear men talk about bein' political prisoners an' all that shit. What I wanna know is what's all that got to do with you stealin' that woman's dog?"

They had both stopped walking at the south end of the park. Socrates let Killer's backside down on the grass. But the dog didn't care because he was with his new best friend, barking and biting playfully.

"I didn't steal 'im I freed 'im," Lavant said with glee in his high voice. "I'm a freedom fighter. That's my job twenty-four hours a day, seven days a week. While you sleepin' I'm out fightin' for freedom. While you makin' chains I'm puttin' acid in the locks. While you countin' your pennies on a bare tabletop I'm partyin' with the people free from all the raggedy flags and law books of the Man."

"You do all that, huh?"

"Yep, I do," Lavant said.

"Then why ain't I heard about you, you so famous?"

"You done heard you just don't know. I'm all around you but I'm invisible like Ralph Ellison."

"I don't know him either. And I still don't see why you stole that dog. But I thank you for the cigarette." Socrates bent down to heft Killer's rope and said, "Come on, boy. Let's get you home before somebody wants to make you free."

"Hey, brother, hold up," Lavant Hall said. "What they have you in prison for?"

"I broke the law right on the jaw," Socrates said. "I fucked it up and they come down on me with a hundred tons of chain."

The man with the different-color eyes got serious.

"They can lock up your body," the purple man said. "But your mind is yours even if you don't want it."

Socrates stopped a moment to think over those words. He nodded and then nodded again. Then he gave a little half wave and turned away.

He walked back toward his own apartment. Before he reached his home he had forgotten about Lavant Hall; except for once in the middle of the night when he was awakened by a thickly sweet odor. He sniffed his left hand in the darkness and realized that it was the scent of Lavant Hall's cologne.

◤ ◤ ◤ ◤

September was hotter than August that year. One Saturday it was so bad that Socrates got a ride from the gypsy cabbie, Milton Langonier, out to Venice Beach where he and Darryl walked along the ocean with Killer at dusk.

Every hundred yards or so Killer would test the waves with his big red tongue, hoping to find fresh water somewhere in that vast ocean.

"How you like yo' new job?" Darryl asked. He was lanky and awkward but Socrates could see the beginning contours of a man's face coming out to replace the child's.

"They miss you down at the store, Darryl. Robyn and Sarah always askin' after you."

"Really?" the child said. "That Robyn's fine."

"They both cute." Socrates liked the black and white girlfriends even though they were wealthy and didn't know a thing.

"I miss 'em too but Howard won't let me work at Bounty no mo'."

"That ain't true an' you know it, boy. Me an' Howard an' Corina all talked to that vice principal. He said you got to buckle down if you wanna get good grades."

Darryl bent down quickly and picked up a fistful of sand, which he threw into the water. Killer barked and lurched against Socrates' grip, looking for the ball he used to chase when he had four legs.

"Come on, boy," Socrates said. "Let's go on up and get you a chili dog."

There was a big boarded-up building on the promenade. It was vacant but not abandoned. Men had been working on the inside changing it into some new business to sell trinkets or junk food at the beach. There was an unfinished pine plank blocking the main entrance. Socrates and Darryl sat on the step there eating their hot dogs and fries.

Pasted on the planking was a large yellow poster which was printed with bright red lettering.

It's War!

The racist and imperialist forces of Amerika are waging a war on you; a war in your schools, a war on your bodies and your minds. The poison in your food is chemical warfare. The lies in the schools are propaganda and nothing less.

Wake up! Wake up, Amerika! Don't let your children drown in the gutter. Don't let the so-called Democrats and their so-called free elections tell you what's on your mind. You got freedom on your mind. You got love on your mind. You got a good time with good neighbors on your mind.

They're using your money to kill in Rwanda, to kill in South Amerika, and right here in your own backyard. They put the blood in your hands but don't you drink it.

If there's a war you could win it. Just stand up and fight. Burn down the raggedy flags of the Man.

Rebel, Rebel

Socrates eyed the poster because of the bright red letters on the yellow paper. He looked closer

176

at the texture of the paper than at the words. It was rough fabric plastered with thick glue onto the wall. There had been attempts to tear it away but the poster had resisted. Looking closer Socrates realized that the words were handwritten, each letter painstakingly rendered between faint pencil lines. It was then that Socrates felt something familiar about the poster. Not the words but the poster itself.

"So you like it?" Darryl asked.

"Like what?"

"The produce job?"

"Yeah. Yeah, I like it fine," Socrates said. "Work hard though. Harder'n motherfucker when Marty gets a bug in his ass. But I make some money though. A poor man might think I was rich."

"You gonna move?" Darryl asked.

"I just barely got a phone, man. Gimme some time."

"It's just that they got some good apartments out around here. You could come live out here if you wanted." Darryl pulled his head back, indicating that it didn't matter one way or another if Socrates moved closer to him.

But Socrates knew better. He looked up at the poster again.

"Huh," the big man grunted.

"What?"

"I was just thinkin'," Socrates said. "You wanna come stay out at my house tonight?"

"Yeah," the boy said without hesitation.

The next morning they were both up early. Killer was ready for a walk. They went down to Iula's house where they made pancakes and pork links for her.

"We figure that you cook every day, I," Socrates told his weekend girlfriend. "At least one day a year somebody should make a meal for you."

Iula smiled and drank her coffee. She took only a bite of pancake, explaining that she never really ate until afternoon.

"But thank you for the meal, baby," she said to the boy while smiling for the man. "It's nice to be thought of any way you get it."

They ate in her small backyard under the thin branches of a pomegranate tree. Iula made the second batch of pancakes. Socrates helped by standing behind her with his hands on her hips.

"You ever meet a man name'a Lavant Hall?" he asked after kissing her ear twice.

"Mmmm," the diner owner crooned. "Smell like a whole bottle'a perfume done falled on his head. I always thought he was one'a them funny men. Why?"

"I don't know. I met'im 'bout a month ago. He had this fluffy red dog. He said somethin' that I didn't think about at the time but now I wanna talk to'im about it and I was wonderin' where he lives."

"He stay up in Theda Johnston's garage. He don't pay rent but I think he know somethin' about electricals and he rewired and did some other stuff for her."

Socrates and Darryl and Killer made it to Theda Johnston's house on Denker at two in the afternoon.

It was a big house for the block. Only one story but wide, with a front porch that almost ran the full length of the property. The porch was shaded by overhanging eaves. There was a sofa on either side of the front door and a huge dark evergreen tree in the front yard. Everything about the house looked cool and relaxing. Except for the loud African music coming from the backyard. The three Sunday strollers followed the music back to a garage that was newly painted yellow with crayon blue trim.

Johnny B. Goode leapt from some secret hiding place growling and barking and wagging his tail. Killer lunged forward to nuzzle his old friend.

"Dang," Darryl said, frightened by the sudden attack.

The music cut off.

"Who's out there?" someone shouted from behind the partially open yellow door.

"Socrates, Lavant. Me and a friend come by to see where you live at."

The door swung open and Lavant Hall came out holding a claw hammer in his left hand. He was wearing the same purple clothes with what looked like the same sweat stains. His eyes registered fear and distrust.

"You remember my dog don't you, Lavant?" Socrates found himself trying to put the man at ease again. "We met at the park last month. You remember."

"What you want?" the purple man asked.

"Just wanted to say hey, brother." Socrates hoped that his words didn't sound as unnatural as they felt in his mouth. "And to ask you somethin'."

"Ask me what?"

" 'Bout the raggedy flags of America, man. About them yellow posters you been puttin' up from here to the sea."

"Who told you that?"

"You did."

"Me?"

"I remembered you talkin' 'bout raggedy flags but even before that — I don't know, it was like that poster reminded me'a you. Neat but all handmade."

The wary look on Lavant Hall's face slowly turned into a smile. He lowered his hammer and called Johnny B. Goode. Then he threw the door to the garage open and waved an inviting hand at his uninvited guests.

◢ ◤ ◢ ◤

The garage had a high unfinished ceiling. The rafters were piled with junk, but it was neat. There was a platform loft halfway up the far end where Socrates spied a bed. The main room was dominated by a huge worktable supported by

180

boxes and sawhorses. On the table was a big rectangular tub full of a pasty yellow fluid. There were coffee cans that held artist's brushes. A yellow poster page was spread out in front of a high swivel chair that had been set up for Lavant to write out one of his political manifestos.

"This is it," he said proudly, holding up his skinny arms.

"Dog," Darryl said, looking around the darkly cavernous room. The only lights were one over-head lamp that shone down on the yellow sheet and another, smaller bulb that lighted the loft space above.

"It's sumpin'," Socrates agreed. "But what is it?"

"This is where the revolution's gonna come from," Lavant said. "Here and everywhere where people work for ideas instead'a for money."

"You mean these here papers you writin'?" Darryl asked.

"It's thinkin' that makes a man, son," Lavant lectured. "Ideas make us responsible for each other. Most people got money-colored glasses on. They think that they can put life in a wallet. They think they buy their souls when really all they do is sell 'em and then die and go to hell."

Darryl looked down to avoid the zealot's eyes. He nodded and mumbled something.

"I thought it was you," Socrates said. "I thought it was you and so I come by to see."

"That's what we need," Lavant said. "People who think about somethin' that ain't in your pocket, your stomach, or your crotch."

Darryl giggled at the last word and Socrates smiled.

"So you a revolutionary, huh," the ex-con said.

"Rebel," Lavant said in way of correction. "I don't have a revolutionary ideology. I fight anything that wants to keep a human being from being free."

"An' you think puttin' up these posters do all that?" Socrates' words were a challenge but Lavant could tell that his visitor wanted to believe.

"The truth *will* set you free, brother," the purple-clad fanatic replied. "Did you know that there were three black African popes that sat in the Vatican? Yeah. Saint Gelasius, Saint Miltades an' an' an' um, Saint Victor."

Socrates stalled for a moment, impressed by this impossible knowledge.

"You see?" Lavant said. "We could tear the walls down with that kinda truth."

Socrates wondered. He rarely spoke to anyone who told him anything new or hopeful. His Wednesday evening discussion group talked about all kinds of issues but Socrates hadn't learned much for all that talk.

"And that's not all I do," the younger man continued. "You know I help old folks fill out insurance and government forms and I taught two people how to read. I always bear witness when the cops make an arrest. And I preach to the young people in the streets."

"You crazy," Darryl said. "That's what crazy people do."

"Just remember what I say, boy," Lavant said with his eyes alight. "I might be crazy but you mark my words."

Lavant showed Socrates how he made the poster board from rags and permanent dyes. He read to them from past broadsides and showed them a wall map dotted with red pins that indicated where he'd placed his posters.

After that they drank Coca-Colas while Lavant questioned and corrected Darryl's history lessons from school. When the boy started fidgeting, Socrates stood up.

"Well." Socrates put a hand on Darryl's shoulder. "I got to see Darryl off to a bus so he can get home and get to bed in time to go to school tomorrow."

Outside the garage, under a strong-smelling bay laurel, Lavant asked Socrates, "You know where the Pink Lady is over on Jeff?"

"Yeah?"

"Two blocks south on the cross side'a the street is a boarded-up hardware store with a picture of a clown on the door." Lavant smiled. "Around the back, between the buildin's is a door. Come on round after ten and you see what a rebel can do when he's on the job."

Socrates put Darryl on a crosstown bus and went back to his place. On his butane camp stove he made scrambled eggs with chorizo sausage, garlic and onion. Alongside the eggs he had canned asparagus topped with lemon juice and mayonnaise. The smell of the sausages filled the house for hours. Socrates was reading about poisonous sea snakes in the South Seas in an old *National Geographic* he'd taken from the trash somewhere. He fell asleep reading and came awake a few hours later because of the smell. Not the sharp scent of spiced meat but a sweet odor.

It was Lavant Hill's cologne in the fabric of his clothes. Socrates smelled the hand that Lavant clasped while saying good-bye.

◢ ◢ ◢ ◢

There was a car service garage not far from Socrates' alley. Cigar-smoking Pete Roman ran the graveyard shift. Roman had Lamont Taylor drive Socrates to out near the Pink Lady for four thirty-five plus a one-dollar tip.

There was the sound of drums and strings coming out from the space between the condemned building, with the clown face on the door, and its neighbor. The passageway between the buildings was so narrow that Socrates had to hold his shoulders at an angle to make it down to the source of the music — a tin-plated door.

The man who answered Socrates' knock was six six at least. He wore black pants and a red vest with no shirt. His head was woolly and his hands were large. His arms were thin bands of steel.

"Who the hell you think you is?" the man demanded.

"Lavant invited me," Socrates said. He didn't want to hurt a man just because he didn't know how to talk.

"Lavant who?"

"Hall," Socrates said. "He said that he work here. He said I should come by."

"He went out," the man said searching Socrates face for signs. "But, uh, I guess you could come in if he invited ya. I mean, most of the people is regular but you don't look like no cop."

"Cop," Socrates sputtered and then he laughed.

The giant got the joke and backed away to let the new man in.

It was a big room filled with music and people. All kinds of people. Mexicans and blacks, whites and Asians. Men and women, young and old. There was a bar run out of a black trunk that stood on two tripods. There was also a white banner, with the bright red words **CLICK'S CLUB** printed across it, hanging down from the rafters.

The music was fiddle, clarinet, guitar and drums accompanied by three singers. It was rock and roll, kind of, and soul and blues for sure; improvisation from musicians who knew each other well.

It was truly a condemned building. Linoleum was ripped up to reveal the unfinished

185

wood of the floor. Walls were broken out so that there was just one big room between rotted timbers. It had been dusty but someone had gone through the place with a heavy-duty vacuum and a broom. In some places Socrates thought he could see where water had been sprayed to keep the dust down. There were jury-rigged overhead lamps like the one Lavant had used to illuminate the yellow broadside on his desk.

Many of the people were dancing wildly. Two women had taken off their blouses and were dancing, bare breasted, close to one another. There were lovers in the corners and lively conversations going on at makeshift tables and chairs.

"Drink?" asked a blond-haired black woman with three silver studs in her left nostril. She was standing next to the elevated trunk that was filled with bottles of liquor and wine.

"How much for a shot'a JD?" Socrates said, looking over the labels displayed.

The woman's wide face became a question. "You somebody's guest?"

"Lavant Hall invited me."

"Oh," she said, happy again. "This is Click's Club. All drinks one dollar. Everything else is free once you walk in the door."

The woman poured Socrates' drink in a paper cup and he handed her his dollar. She was young looking but in her forties, Socrates could tell by the lines near her eyes. She was heavy but shapely, responsible at her job but ready to laugh.

"How long you been here?" he asked the woman.

"My name is Venus," she replied.

"Socrates. How long this place been here, Venus?"

"Just tonight," she said.

"This your first night?"

"Naw, not like that. I mean it's our first night here. Saturday we be someplace else."

"You mean you move every night?"

"Every night that we convene. This place is click," Venus said snapping her fingers and tossing her hair. "We all put up the labor and then we party and congregate all over town."

"Hey, Venus," a woman said coming up to the bar.

"Hey, Shy. This is Socrates."

The woman named for bashfulness was wearing a see-through red wraparound with yellow lipstick. She had bleached white hair. She was a young woman and black too. Socrates had never seen anyone like her.

"Hi," Shy said with a friendly smile. "Venus, you got some rubbers?"

"How many you need?"

"Um," Shy mused, "three."

The bartender smiled knowingly and produced three square green packets from somewhere behind the trunk.

"You're the best," Shy said kissing the dark

woman with her bright yellow lips.

"A lotta that go on around here?" Socrates asked after Shy had gone.

"Everything go on when the Click flag flies," Venus said. "Everything but drugs and violence, but we don't put them down neither."

"Yeah, I could see that," Socrates said. He was looking at an elderly couple, even older than him, sitting next to each other on cinder blocks near the door.

"You do, huh?" Venus asked.

"Sure. People who wanna be free cain't have all that disruption. Fightin' an' drugs kill a good time faster'n the law."

Venus' laugh was friendly and inviting. She pressed her hand against Socrates' arm and smiled. "How do you know Lavant?" she asked.

"Our dogs are friends," Socrates replied.

"Oh," she said making eyes that spoke about something else altogether.

"Can we get some red wine, Veen," someone asked from behind. Socrates turned to see that it was a white man with a small Asian woman at his side.

Other men and women had come up to ask for drinks. Socrates allowed himself to be pushed away.

"Socrates," a high voice cried.

"Hey, Lavant. Where you been?"

The skinny man wore a purple dress jacket with camel-colored pants and white patent leather shoes. He was carrying two shopping bags.

"Out shoppin' for food at the twenty-four-hour Bounty over on Exposition. You know we ran outta cold cuts and dancin' makes you hungry."

Socrates took the two heavy bags and followed his host to a long table set up in what once was the storeroom of the hardware store. Helping hands were there to meet them taking bread and meat, catsup and mayonnaise from the bags and placing them around the table.

The music was playing loudly throughout the empty structure. Socrates looked around at the crowd.

"Somethin' else, huh," Lavant asked.

"You people ever get caught?"

"Sometimes. Especially when we hit some rich neighborhood. But all we do is walk away. Maybe a night in jail for one or two but you know this is two hundred people here. Nobody owns Click's." The tone of Lavant's voice changed and Socrates could tell that he was getting excited about his politics again. "The police can't stop a good time and they know it. Look at it, man. Every color and creed. One day all of America will get here."

"If nobody owns it how does it happen?" Socrates wanted to know. "I mean who sets up where you meet? Where does the money go?"

"There's a board like . . ." just then Lavant gestured at a skinny white woman who was kissing a heavyset man.

"Hey, Alice!" Lavant cried. "Save some'a that for me, baby." He laughed and turned back to Socrates. "We used t'be all political and had meetings about the world and how we was gonna change it. You know what it's like. Bunch'a men and women talkin' so hard that they sweat, thinkin' so hard that they get nosebleed."

Socrates felt the Jack Daniel's then. His smile turned into a chuckle and the music entered his bones.

"That's right," Lavant continued. "All we did was talk and grunt. One day we was all gonna live together an' have a dozen kids between us. The children would be an army that we'd lead into war. Next mont' we was all gonna go to Cuba and work for the revolution amongst the Afro-Cubanos down there."

Socrates had enough talk for right then. He wandered off for another whiskey and a few words with Venus. He didn't dance but stood near a mob of men and women shaking to the music.

Socrates nodded to people here and there but he didn't enter into any conversations. Lavant was talking to everybody and Venus was busy with her bottles and paper cups. So Socrates wandered the perimeter of the first floor, locating boarded-up windows and doors.

Once he ran into Shy, who was coming out of the shadows with a young white man. They were both smiling broadly.

"Hi, Socrates." The yellow lips wrapped themselves around his name.

"Tell me sumpin'," Socrates requested.

"What?"

"Do they like rent this place or what?"

Her smile was anything but shy.

"We know a lotta construction workers and supply people and just plain old folks in the neighborhoods. So when one'a them sees that a place is empty we check it out and make our plans. Sometimes we up in a nice area and somebody let us use their home."

"But this here is trespassin'?" Socrates asked.

"Only if we get caught." Shy puckered up her bright lips and kissed the air between her and Socrates.

For all his experience the ex-convict knew little about women. He had lived among men for most of his adult years. He nodded and backed away from her like a barefoot traveler who had come upon a snake.

"I'll prove it," someone said from behind a walled-off corner.

Socrates peered around the edge and saw a young black woman and a white man standing about three feet apart and staring hard into each other's eyes. She wore a black leather micromini with a tight-fitting elastic halter top. He held a large hunting knife in his left hand. Her eyes seemed to be pleading for this proof and so Socrates held back to see what would happen.

The white man, who was dark haired and half bald, raised his right hand and slashed the wrist. He dropped the knife holding the bleeding hand high. A look of deep satisfaction and grief worked its way into the young woman's features. She took a step forward and touched his bloody fingers. For long seconds she gazed into his unseen face.

Socrates was breathing hard. He'd never witnessed anything like this, not even in prison where suicide was commonplace.

The woman's mouth opened but no words came out. She pulled off the halter. If there wasn't so much blood being let Socrates might have been impressed by her nakedness. She used the halter as a bandage, wrapping it tightly around the wound. She gazed deeply into the white man's face with a need deeper than any love Socrates had known.

The blood was still dripping down between them but slower with the dressing. Socrates watched the lovers as long as they gazed at each other. But when they moved into an embrace he turned away.

A few minutes past three A.M., Socrates was talking to Lavant and the white woman, Alice, asking if there would be someone to give him a ride home, when someone yelled, "Police!"

"Com'on," Socrates ordered his friend. Then

he went toward the back of the building as the tin-plated entrance filled with cops in full riot gear.

Socrates made it to a window that had been blocked with thin plywood. Two well-placed kicks and Socrates, along with Venus, Alice and Lavant, was outside in a concrete yard.

With a nudge of Socrates' shoulder the pad-locked fence opened up. Then they were running down the alley, heavy footsteps not far behind.

Socrates allowed Lavant and the women to go before him while he caught a glance of the people behind. They were other refugees from the rave, stumbling along in their awkward party shoes.

From somewhere behind them came the command, "Halt! Police!"

"Keep on goin'!" Socrates told his friends. And then he ran hard with his head down. He knew that the cops would have their hands full with the other escapees. The only thing to worry about was a shot that might go wild.

But no shots were fired.

When the four reached the alley, Alice shouted, "My car's at the end of the block!"

It was a copper-toned Jaguar sedan. Socrates and Venus piled in the back. When Alice hit the gas, Socrates laid a heavy hand on her shoulder and said, "Slow it down to a walk, sugar, we ain't outta the bag yet."

He left his hand there for twenty blocks or

more, until Alice finally moaned, "You're hurting me."

Socrates sat back thinking about prison; about how they could have pulled him in for B and E. One small party and the rest of his life could have been spent in stir.

"Mothahfuckahs," he whispered.

Everyone else was silent.

The rage of the ex-con filled up the car but he was unaware of its effect. All he could think about was how small his cell had been. He couldn't even turn around comfortably. He couldn't play music or go through the bars for a bottle of wine. He couldn't even close his own door or open it for a visitor or friend.

It was cramped in Alice's car too. He thought about going home but his apartment was also small and cell-like. He was a prisoner-in-waiting on the streets as far as the cops were concerned.

Those thoughts played through his head again and again. Socrates paid no heed to the car's direction.

When Lavant sighed and said, "That was a close one," Socrates didn't hear him.

"You saved us," from Venus, could have been the passing blare of a horn.

The music from the party along with the scramble of feet on the gravel of the alley still filled Socrates' ears. He slipped into a daze that was closer to sleep than it was to consciousness. Sweat beaded up on his forehead and his blood ran cool.

Alice drove them up into Malibu hills, to her home.

The living room was sunken below the entrance hall. It was shallow and arching but over fifty feet wide. The walls were all glass. To the left you could see the million winking lights of Los Angeles and to the right there was darkness where Socrates knew the ocean lay.

"Nice, eh, Socco?" Lavant said at his shoulder.

"Yeah," Socrates said. "Yeah, this is more like it."

"If you like the view now," Alice said. "Wait until the sun comes up."

She wasn't yet forty, Socrates surmised, thin and plain, but the hunger in her eyes made up for a bad complexion. She wore a green, loose-knit sweater dress that came down to mid-thigh.

Lavant came up and put his arm around her.

"I can hardly wait," Socrates said. "To see the sun come up and not be in jail are the two best things there is."

Lavant and Alice went off to her bed. Venus touched Socrates' shoulder but he told her that he was going to stay up for a while.

Venus was well named but Socrates was too angry to be with a woman. He didn't feel safe in his own skin.

He opened the sliding glass door and sat out on the terrace that looked over Alice's rock garden, swimming pool and the sea. He couldn't make out the ocean but he could smell it and every once in a while there came the faint sound of breaking waves.

Two hours later the Pacific shifted into existence and morning gulls cried. Socrates sat completely still, afraid to move a finger lest the spell would break.

The smell of coffee came with daylight.

"Good morning, Mr. Fortlow," Alice said at the door. She came out with a cup of coffee in each hand.

"Mornin'," Socrates said. "Thank you."

His hostess wore a full-length white terry cloth robe. She sat down in the chair beside him.

"I love this view," she said. There were dark patches under her eyes and her hair was a mess.

"It's like we ran through hell and went right up to heaven," Socrates said. "Damn."

Venus and Lavant soon appeared and they went off saying that they would make breakfast. Alice joined them but Socrates stayed outside. He walked down through the rock garden, stuck his toes in the pool. He walked out to the edge of the property which looked down into a sheer gorge that led down to the sea.

"Where you wanna go, Socco?" Lavant called.

Socrates was standing near the pool.

Lavant and Alice and Venus came over to the edge when the big man didn't answer.

"Did you sleep at all last night?" Venus asked him.

"I don't think so," he replied.

"Why'ont you stay here and take a nap, brother," Lavant suggested. "Alice gonna take me down to Sam Flax in Westwood to get some razor blades and brushes. That's okay, right, baby?"

"Well," the homeowner stalled. "I . . ."

"He *did* save your butt last night, girl."

"Okay," she said after a long hesitation. "We're going for art supplies and maybe some lunch. We'll drop Venus off at work and Lavant promised to help me pick up a chair that I bought."

Socrates fell asleep on the sofa in the wide living room and dreamed of being in that house forever with the breeze from the ocean and the sweet sounds of the world.

He was walking on a large grassy field with Killer running around him on all four legs. There were sheep everywhere bleating and eating grass.

"Hey, Socco," someone called.

He turned and saw Right Burke approaching him wearing his sergeant's uniform from World War II. He was no longer crippled but he was still an old man.

"Hey, Burke, what's happenin'?" Socrates hailed.

"You think these sheep think they sheep?" Burke asked.

Killer howled in reply.

Socrates woke up half expecting Killer to be there. The house was still empty and he went right out the door. He wandered the narrow and steep pathways of the canyon, walking in the street mainly because there were few sidewalks up there. After some time he made it down to Sunset Boulevard. There he found a bus that got him to work by two fifteen.

Nobody complained about his absence. Socrates was a hard worker and respected among his peers.

When he got home that evening, Killer barked and stamped his forepaws to show how hungry he was.

"I learned a lot from that dog," he told Iula later that night as they lay together in each other's arms.

"What could you learn from a dog?" Iula asked playfully.

"That you can be hungry but you don't have to be mad." A wave of emotion choked off the end of his sentence. He stayed quiet for a few moments. "That bravery ain't no big thing. Bravery is just doin' what you do wit' what you got an' where you find yourself. But it's, but it's love that gives life. It's that that calls out for you."

"You don't need a dog to teach you about love. Everybody knows about love." Iula sounded angry.

"Not me," Socrates replied. "I never bled for nobody didn't bleed for me."

"What's blood got to do with it?"

"I wish I knew. I mean it seem like every time somethin' gets serious or important you got to put up blood and freedom just to stay in the game."

"What?" Iula said, exasperation filling her voice, "what are you talking about?"

"I'ont know what it means, honey. Just know that that's what I know."

mookie kid

The phone rang at 6:25 on Wednesday evening, just as Socrates got to the door. He took his time with the padlock and put the groceries down carefully before going to answer the phone. It was on the eleventh ring that Socrates picked up the receiver. Whoever it was had just lost heart and cut off the connection.

The big man put away his cans of tuna and bag of white rice. He had stripped down to his boxer shorts and was busy washing himself at the kitchen sink when the phone rang again. It only rang eight times before Socrates answered.

"Hello."

Nothing.

"Hello. Who is this?"

No response.

"Shit," Socrates said. Just as he took the phone from his ear he thought he heard something: a quick breath or hiss, maybe the beginning of a word, maybe the start of his name. But he was angry and slammed the phone down before he could be sure.

The ex-convict finished his toilet and then brought a saucepan half full of water to a boil on his butane stove. When the rice was cooked he added a can of tuna with onions, hot sauce, and soy sauce. He let that simmer for a while. He intended to blend in half a can of peas that had been keeping in his large Styrofoam cooler, but the ice had melted and the peas gone sour.

Lately he'd been thinking about getting another small refrigerator. The last one he had burned out because of a bad electrical connection. He could splice in another outlet off the 220 line and modify it for a 110 appliance. He'd learned how to do that from Michael Porter, an out-of-work electrician who liked to play dominoes in the park.

Socrates pulled away a section of wall shared with the vacant furniture store next door. With a flashlight he located the box he needed to use. There was one hot box left in the furniture store. Whether it was a mistake or not, Socrates had used the free electricity for nine years. His old landlord, Price Landers, said that the electricity came with the rent. But Landers had died years before and Michael Porter pointed out that the connection Socrates had was illegal.

Socrates was studying the fuse box, trying to remember what he had to do when the phone rang again. This time it rang over thirty times before the caller gave up.

Somewhere around midnight Socrates fell asleep speculating on how heavy the refrigerator would be. He also wondered if Stony Wile was still mad at him for going out with his woman-on-the-side, Charlene, for a couple of days.

Stony had a pickup truck.

That was the last thing on Socrates' mind, and then the phone was ringing again. He got up and pulled the plug from the wall. When the ringer cut off midtone Socrates relaxed.

◩ ◩ ◩ ◩

Bob's Used Appliances was on Grand Street in downtown L.A. The storefront led to a long and slender aisle piled high on each side with irons, radios, waffle presses, percolators, and just about every other electrical countertop appliance that existed.

Tony LaPort had told Socrates that Bob's was the best place to buy something used.

"Bob give ya a guarantee," Tony said. "One year and he'll fix anything go wrong."

Tony and Socrates were on friendly terms once more now that Tony had tried to live with Iula again but failed. Tony was happy in his bachelorhood.

"Five weeks with a woman was just about enough to last me the rest'a my life," Tony told Socrates.

Sitting immediately inside the door of Bob's Used Appliances was a surly-looking Mexican man. His gaze locked with Socrates' and there was a moment of recognition. The two men had never met but they had something in common: a toughness, a solitary self reliance. The nod they shared was the consolation of heroes home from a war that was lost.

Bob himself was a white man in his sixties but he still had a full head of dirty blond hair. He was seated behind a wood desk at the end of the narrow corridor.

"Tony sent ya, huh?" the white man said. "He got a good place down there."

Bob was missing one front tooth and the rest were worn down into nubs. For a moment Socrates imagined that the white man chewed on the metal utilities while fixing them.

"Refrigerator huh?" Bob said to himself. "Hey, Julio."

The man at the front of the store grunted something.

"I'm goin' out back with Mr. Fortlow here. You take over."

Julio raised his left hand in a halfhearted pledge and then let it drop.

"Come on," Bob said to Socrates. He pulled on a bookshelf to his left and it swung open like a door.

Bob led the way through a short hallway that was so cramped that Socrates' shoulders rubbed against the walls as he went. This hallway opened into an extremely large room full of appliances that would have never fit into the slender sales room. Washing machines, generators, TVs, there was even a giant strobe light in a far-off corner.

The room was organized according to appliance type. There was a whole row of full-sized refrigerators. Beyond that was a little cul-de-sac of small ones.

"Westinghouse is your best bet," Bob was saying. He patted the top of a two-foot-square drab green unit. "They built these suckers to last."

"How much?" Socrates asked. He felt oppressed in that dank atmosphere. The smell reminded him of his days in prison.

"Twenty bucks for this one," Bob said.

"That's all?"

"I took this one in for scrap and it worked. I opened her up but there wasn't anything wrong." Bob squatted down and rubbed his hand over the metal door. "You see they had these deep scratches in the paint. I figure that it was an eyesore and the owners just chucked it. That's America for ya. Nobody believes in utility. One day they'll start scrappin' kids for havin' crossed eyes or fat butts."

Bob looked up at Socrates and winked.

"Most the things I get in here still work," the fixer continued. "It's just that they went outta style in some way or they got marred."

Socrates looked around the vast workroom again. It reminded him more than ever of prison.

"How much it weigh?" Socrates asked.

"Twenty-five, thirty. Big fella like you could carry it easy. I got some rope over there. You could make a shoulder hoist and get it to your car."

Socrates nodded.

Bob helped him tie up the ugly green refrigerator. Socrates used the nylon rope to carry it over his right shoulder. It was a tight fit through the hallway to the front but Socrates made it. He paid his twenty dollars and then thought of a question.

"You got one'a them caller-ID gizmos?"

"Uhhhh, hm. Yeah I think I got one up on the shelf over there next to Julio." Bob was frowning. "Why?"

"You just connect it to your phone?"

"Naw," Bob said. "You gotta pay the phone company to let the information in. But there's a better way to do it."

"What's that?"

"Pick up the phone and ask who's there."

◤ ◤ ◤ ◤

Socrates spent his Saturday bringing in a double outlet for his refrigerator and caller-ID display. Michael Porter came over on Sunday to check the connections. Porter was a tan-skinned Negro who was small and round. His lips were thin and his nose was turned up like a bulldog's snout.

"She perfect, Socco," the little electrician said. "You don't need my help."

They played dominoes after that.

When Porter left it was after nine thirty. Socrates realized that the phone had not rung for three days.

That Monday he called the phone company and had his caller-ID turned on. When the phone rang that night the name Howard Shakur shimmered in green across the small screen.

"Darryl?" Socrates said. "Where you been, boy?"

"How you know it was me?" the startled boy asked.

"Who else gonna be callin' me this time'a night?" The glee of a secret was in Socrates' tone.

"I don't know," the boy answered uncertainly. "But anyway Howard and Corina and them havin' a picnic next weekend and they wanna know if you comin'."

"What day?"

"Uh, hold on." Darryl put his hand over the receiver and shouted something then he said, "On Sunday afternoon."

"I'll be there," Socrates said. "How you doin', boy?"

"I got a A on my math test."

"You did?"

"Uh-huh. I like to divide an' stuff."

"I always knew you were smart, Darryl."

"So how did you know it was me on the phone?"

"But you not that smart."

At about eleven P.M. the small glass screen shimmered, then the phone rang and the name Moorland Kinear appeared with a number beside it. Socrates had a pencil and a pad of paper ready to jot down the information. In case

206

of a blackout he didn't want to lose the memory in his first computer device.

He didn't answer the phone. Instead he studied the name for clues to the caller's purpose.

It might have been a white man's name except that Socrates felt something familiar when he mouthed it. And there weren't that many white men who knew his name, not to mention his number. In his nine years in L.A., from Dumpster-diving for cans and bottles to working at Bounty Supermarket, he couldn't think of anyone named Moorland.

Thinking back over twenty-seven years in an Indiana prison didn't reveal the name either. But it was there.

A man in prison wouldn't have used a name like that. *Moorland* would get some of the uneducated cons, and guards, upset. They'd think that just having a name like that would be putting on airs. He'd have to have a nickname, a handle. But that could be anything. It could be his size or color or the shape of his ears. A nickname could be based on the kind of crimes you committed or the thing you were the most proud of in the outside world. Loverboy, Big Daddy, Longarm and Loose Lips were all handles that might have hidden a name like Poindexter, Archibald or Moorland.

If he's just a salesman, Socrates thought. *Then why didn't he say something when I answered the line last week?*

But maybe this was the first time that Moorland Kinear ever called. Maybe the call last week was somebody else.

But why is that name so familiar?

Because they callin' you, fool. It's somebody who knows you and wants to talk.

If Socrates had had that conversation with another man it might have come to blows. In turns he decided to answer when the phone rang again, to tear the phone out of the wall and discontinue the service, and to get an answering machine and never respond to a call unless the caller stated his business clearly.

He wished he'd never gotten that phone in the first place. He never had a phone as a child or as a convict. It was just another way that people could reach at you, could cause you trouble.

The best kind of life to live was with no contacts and no way for people to find you, Socrates believed. At least that's what part of him believed. But ever since he'd met that boy, that Darryl, he'd been pulled out of his shell. Trying to help Darryl out of trouble, he'd got himself all tangled up with people and confused. He'd gotten the phone so that Darryl could call if he had to.

Socrates lay in his bed thinking that he should disappear, that he should take the money he had buried in a jar in the yard, and leave L.A. He could go to Oakland and start over.

He went to sleep in turmoil, twisting and grunting to the rhythm of his dreams. He saw himself in prison fights and in the *dungeon,* the place where they sent you if you had discipline problems. He remembered wardens and assistant wardens, head guards and new recruits. And then suddenly, in the middle of all that dreaming and worry, Socrates woke up and spoke. "Mookie. It's Mookie Kid the first-floor man."

Mookie, sometimes known as Mookie Kid and sometimes as the first-floor man, that was Moorland Kinear. He bunked down the row from Socrates for five years. Mookie was a burly man, not very strong but imposing. He liked to find businesses that kept their money and valuables in locked rooms instead of a safe.

"You could always cut through the flo' on a locked room," Mookie would say. He was christened the first-floor man because, unlike the cat burglar, the second-story man, Mookie usually cut a hole up from the cellar to the first floor.

Mookie was a career criminal. He had never held a job that didn't lead to a crime. Most of his life had been spent eating off tin plates at long tables alongside of rough men.

Socrates issued a harsh syllable that stood for a laugh and then went back to sleep.

It was a sound sleep. No rolling around or dreams that had words or faces or names.

He went to work the next day without fear of being seen or sought out. He got a citrus delivery from Florida Inc. and a shipment of berries from the Central California Farmer's Union.

Socrates handled much of the purchasing for his store even though the purchasing office for Bounty would have been glad to handle it for him. Socrates liked his job.

It wasn't until that afternoon that Mookie Kid came back into his thoughts.

Should he call Mookie and see what the ex-con wanted? He already knew what Mookie was up to. Why ask? It was some grocery store or five-and-dime that kept their receipts in a storage room over a poorly guarded basement. Maybe it was some upscale place that wasn't used to criminals with pickaxes and sledgehammers.

Whatever it was Mookie was up to, it had to do with getting caught. Mookie's lifetime of prison food attested to that. Socrates decided not to call. He wouldn't answer any calls from Mookie either.

But why should he hide from Mookie Kid, Moorland Kinear? He wasn't afraid. Nobody could tell him what to say or who to talk to. He could talk to Mookie on the phone if he wanted to. His parole had been up for four years. No one could tell him what to do.

Socrates decided that when he got home he'd call Mookie and say hey. But then, on the bus, on the way home he reconsidered. Why did Mookie Kid want to call him anyway? How did he even get his number? How did he know that Socrates was in L.A? The more he thought about it the more suspicious he became. Better to stay away from someone who was so sneaky as to come up on somebody when he wasn't expecting it. And why didn't he say anything when Socrates answered the phone the first time?

◢ ◢ ◢ ◢

The phone was ringing when Socrates got to his door. He took his time again but the phone kept ringing. The green screen again read MOORLAND KINEAR. Socrates' heart was thumping, even his fingers were sweating. Here he was a man who could face death feeling little more than surprise, even at this late age, and a ringing phone terrorized his soul.

Fury replaced fear and Socrates grabbed the phone. He intended to throw it but then there it was in his hand. A tiny voice said, "Hello?"

Socrates put the phone to his ear.

"Hello?" the voice asked again.

"Mookie, is that you?"

"You remember my voice after all these years?" the first-floor man asked. "And over the phone too?"

"Man, why you callin' me? Where'd you get my number?"

"I looked it up in the phone book," the voice said. "Really, I called information an' they give it to me. Lionel Heath said that he saw you somewheres down Watts a few years ago . . ."

"Lionel?" Socrates said. He remembered seeing a man, an old man, who reminded him of someone. The man said something but Socrates was collecting bottles back then and had few words for anyone. It could have been Lionel

Heath, or maybe his father.

"Yeah. You know that drug life caught up with him somethin' bad. He said you didn't even recognize him."

"I'idn't ask the phone company to list my name," Socrates said.

"They do it automatic," Mookie said. "You got to pay to be unlisted."

"Shit."

The expletive led into a span of silence. Socrates for his part was trying to deal with all the new information he had just received. Lionel Heath's reconnaissance, the phone company's deceit.

"When did you talk to Lionel?" Socrates wanted to know.

"I don't remember, man. He been dead three years. I didn't see him for a while before that. You know they had me in jail up north for eighteen months."

"He died?" Socrates felt a momentary sense of loss. Lionel Heath knew how to tell a joke. He would have been a comedian if it wasn't for heroin.

"Yeah," Mookie said. "It was Slim, you know, AIDS. He took it in with the drug an' it ate him alive."

Socrates pulled up a chair and sat down heavily.

"Damn," Socrates said. "So what you want, Mookie?"

"I don't want nuthin', Socco. I remembered

the other day that Lionel seen you an' I thought I might try you on the phone. So I did. You know. You was straight up in the joint, man. I thought maybe we could grab a drink or sumpin'. You know."

"I'm pretty busy," Socrates said. "I been workin'."

"Where you work at?"

"Post office."

"Mail carrier?"

"Naw. I'm a sorter. Work all kinda hours."

"That pay good?"

"Good enough."

"How they hire you with a record like you got?"

"I cain't let up on all my secrets now, Mookie."

"So," Mookie Kid the first-floor man hesitated, "you wanna get together?"

"Lemme call ya back later this week," Socrates offered. "I got a tight schedule but I'll see."

"You want my number?"

"Yeah. Shoot."

Moorland recited his number and Socrates repeated it pretending he was writing it down.

"I'll call the end'a this week, Mookie. You take care."

After that Socrates put Mookie Kid out of his mind. He worked the rest of the week managing the produce section at Bounty. The purchasing office sent him two double orders of highly perishable fruits and greens. The head dispatcher was a man named Wexler who would never admit to having made a mistake and so Socrates had to find three other stores that would be willing to share the order. That took most of his week.

On Saturday he painted the walls of his sleeping room white. It took the whole day and he was light-headed at the end because there was no cross ventilation in his house and the fumes were powerful.

He was still light-headed when he walked Iula home at midnight. While they were making love he passed out.

As with many of his dreams Socrates found himself in prison. This time his cell was a cave. He had a cellmate but the man died somehow and the guards had not yet removed the body. The corpse had been covered with a blanket but it was rotting and the odor was almost unbearable.

Socrates went to the bars at the entrance of his cell and looked out into a long dark tunnel that was lit by weak blue electric bulbs. There were no other cells that he could see and no one coming.

A fly buzzed in past his ear and Socrates knew that soon the corpse would be alive with maggots. No sooner had this thought entered his mind than a loud buzzing started behind him. Socrates turned and saw waves of small flies rise out of the blanket. It was like the mist in the

214

morning rising off the pond near his aunt Bellandra's home.

"He's free," escaped Socrates' lips in Iula's high feather bed.

"What, baby?" she asked.

"Free," Socrates repeated and then, unaware, he turned away from his girlfriend to burrow deeper into the cell of his imagination.

The haze of flies washed over Socrates on their way toward freedom. He felt them as a cool breeze in early autum. He closed his eyes and there was a surge in his chest. The flies were gone when he opened his eyes again.

"A million eyes came forth," a voice in the dream said. "And now he's free to see every-where."

Socrates did not remember the dream in the morning. He was still dizzy from the paint fumes and the failure of his passion.

"You okay?" Iula asked. She was already dressed and ready to leave for her diner.

"What time is it?" Socrates asked.

"It's eight fifteen. I wanna get in early 'cause I'ma make a pork roast for the special this afternoon. But you sleep, baby. Come on down later if you want somethin' t'eat." Iula kissed Socrates on his forehead and patted his hand.

"Sorry 'bout last night," the big man said.

"You ain't got a thing to be sorry for, Socrates Fortlow." Iula looked hard at him. He could see small knots of imperfection in the whites of her eyes; scars that made her all the stronger.

When she was gone Socrates pulled himself up and got dressed. He was still dizzy but there was the Shakurs' picnic that he had to go to. And there was something else, a dream that he couldn't remember. He didn't want to remember it but still it was on his mind.

◪ ◪ ◪ ◪

"Hi, Mr. Fortlow." Corina Shakur came up to him near the fence at the front of their small yard. Howard, Corina's fat husband, was still cooking ribs on the barbecue grill. Loud R&B music issued from the boom box near to his feet.

"Hey, Corina," Socrates said. "You got some nice friends."

Eight or nine guests had come for the Sunday afternoon picnic in the Shakurs' front yard. It was just a patch of grass that stood a foot or so above the sidewalk. The ocean was just a block and a half down the street.

"Howard got some nice friends down from work," Corina said, leveling her gaze at the ex-convict's chest. "Wayne's funny."

Wayne Yashimura was the shift supervisor from Silicon Solution's computer operations center. He was tall and handsome, with funny jokes and a pocket full of joints that he shared with Corina's girlfriends up from Watts. They had smoked the drug in the backyard, over the canal, while Socrates talked to Darryl out front.

Now everyone was together in the front yard

216

laughing and drinking beers.

"How you doin', Corina?" Socrates asked the young woman that he coveted on dark lonely nights.

"Fine," she said. "I mean Howard's doin' good. He make good money now and I ain't got to worry."

"You happy?"

"I'ont know," the young woman answered. "White lady across the street got kids too. We get together sometimes, you know? An' it's nice but you know we never laugh real hard like I do with my friends." Corina gestured with her head toward the young black women who mingled with the men around the barbecue grill.

"A real friend is somebody know your heart," Socrates said and instantly he was sorry. He didn't want to let his feelings out about Corina. She was Howard's wife. She stood in for being a mother to Darryl.

"Yeah," Corina said. "It's like you an' Darryl."

"What you mean?"

"Howard try an' be like a father around Darryl. He tell him what to do and how to make it in the world. And Darryl listen, but not like when you talk." Corina took a deep breath and seemed to swell with pride. "When you talk, Darryl's eyes light up an' he's open like. That's how I feel around DeeDee. She just makes me happy. I guess I miss her. You know everybody always sayin' that they wanna good job so that they can move away from South Central, but I miss it. I miss my people, you know?"

On the bus back home Socrates thought of Corina and what she'd said about Darryl. He allowed himself a rare sigh of pleasure.

"That was nice, huh?" Monica Nealy, one of Corina's friends, asked. Socrates had agreed to ride with her, to see her home. The rest of the young women had gone to hear music on the beach with Howard's friends.

"Yeah," Socrates replied. "Howard can burn some meat."

The young woman turned away to look out at the dark street. She was big boned and husky but not overweight. And she had hungry eyes. The kind of eyes that drove young men wild with the promise of her kisses.

"Mr. Fortlow?"

"Yeah, Monica?"

"Nuthin'."

Socrates didn't mind her sudden indecision. By then he was deep in the memory of the dream about a dead man's soul becoming a haze of flies that could go where the man could not.

"Mr. Fortlow?"

"Uh-huh?"

"Did you talk to Wayne?"

"Li'l bit," Socrates said. "He's a nice guy."

"It's funny how Howard got friends who's white an' Mexican an' Japanese."

It was true. Howard had only one Negro friend from work. All of Corina's friends were black women.

"Yeah," Socrates said. "When you start workin' serious, you get to know all kinds."

"You think that's okay?" Monica asked, but there was another question that lay behind.

"They was nice. I don't care what color you are if you treat me okay."

"Uh-huh," Monica agreed. She lowered her head and stuck out her lips. Even though she was in no way pretty, Monica, Socrates realized, was close to beautiful.

"What's wrong, girl?" Socrates asked. "Why you poutin'?"

"I ain't poutin'. I'm thinkin'."

"Thinkin' about what?"

"Wayne said he goes to Las Vegas almost once a mont'," Monica said. She looked over her shoulder to make sure that there was no one listening from behind.

"Uh-huh," Socrates grunted to prompt the reluctant woman.

"An' when he said that, I said that I heard it was nice but that I ain't never been. And he said that he was gonna go soon and if I give him my number he'd tell me when, and if I could go he'd drive us out there in his Trans Am." The words came out clearly and quickly as if she'd been going over them again and again.

"Uh-huh," Socrates said again.

"What you mean uh-huh?"

"Well, it ain't a surprise that a young man wanna drive you somewhere. Men musta been askin' you t'get in their cars since you was a child."

The look on Monica's face was an acknowledgment of the truth.

"So," Socrates continued, "why you surprised that this Wayne wanna take you away?"

"He Japanese." Monica said the words as if she was explaining to an inexperienced driver that he needed gasoline to run his car.

"Monica, look," Socrates said. "You like that boy?"

"He nice."

"You like how he looks, the kinda car he drive. He got a job. And he think you cute enough to see again." Socrates itemized these facts on four muscular fingers.

"Yeah but —" Monica began.

"Monica." Socrates held his hands up for her silence. "You spend eight hours a day sleepin', two hours in the bathroom, and at least a hour and a half at the table eatin'. You spend fifty hours every week gettin' to work, comin' home or workin'. Either that or you got kids and that's every hour of every day. You got to wash dishes, get dressed, get mad, go to the store, go to school, go to the doctor. An' every day you on your feet walkin', walkin', walkin'. Except sometimes you're sick an' then you cain't even get up."

"Word." Monica smiled and then grinned. She

put up a hand to testify to the truth of Socrates' claims.

"Now how many minutes do you think a man spends givin' you what you want? A lotta men spend a whole lotta time tryin' to get what they want from you. But how many'a them gonna get off the dime and do for you?" Socrates found himself reaching out to hold Monica by her elbow. "If that man got yellah skin it don't seem so bad, not if you like that skin. And if he work hard to buy a nice car and then he wanna drive you somewhere, well then maybe you should tell 'im you wanna go some place close by first — just to see if he's nice."

Monica ducked her head and smiled. She also leaned into Socrates' hand.

"But suppose somebody see?" she asked.

"Ain't nobody gonna care, honey. And if they do it's only 'cause they jealous or stupid."

Monica frowned and reared back like a wary kitten.

Socrates imagined her sensual lips kissing the handsome Asian's face.

◪ ◪ ◪ ◪

"Hello," a woman's voice said.

"Can I speak to Mookie?"

"I think you must have the wrong number," she replied.

"Hold on," Socrates said quickly to stop her from hanging up. "Mookie is my nickname for Moorland Kinear."

There was silence from the other end of the

221

phone. For a moment Socrates wondered if the woman had hung up, leaving the phone line caught in a few seconds of silence before the harsh buzz.

"Who is this?" Her voice had turned cold.

"Tell 'im it's Socrates."

"I'll go see if he can come to the phone right now."

There came a hard knock of the phone being put down and then loud voices speaking unintelligible words. One voice, a man's, became louder and louder until Socrates could make out, ". . . he's just a friend, Delice. Aw come on, honey, don't be like that . . ."

"Socco," was the next word that the man's voice said, this time into the receiver, "is that you?"

"Hey, Mookie. Sorry if it's a bad time."

It was seven fifteen on the Tuesday after Howard and Corina's barbecue. After talking to Monica Socrates decided that he didn't have to be afraid of talking to Mookie. He could make his own decisions and nobody could talk him into going bad. But still he hesitated until Tuesday evening.

"Naw, man. I ain't busy. Delice just get like that sometime. How you doin'? You know I didn't think you was gonna call me. I thought that you had broke it off with the life. You married?"

"Uh-uh."

"But you gotta good job," Mookie said. "Good

job and your own phone. Hey, who woulda believed it back in the day?"

"Half of 'em still there," Socrates said.

"Yeah." Mookie's tone turned somber. "I heard that Joe Benz passed two years ago. He was still locked down. You know it's a shame."

Socrates felt something snap then. It was in his mind but he felt just the same as when the assistant warden, Blake Riordan, broke his nose while three guards held him down. The break itself was just a snick in his sinuses — the pain came later. And when it came it spread over his whole head.

"He was sixty-seven," Mookie continued. "And he'd been up there forty-eight years."

Socrates took a deep breath and closed his eyes.

"George Wiles got cancer and they let him go home to die," Moorland said. "I guess you could call him lucky. He called my brother to get my number out here."

"How long you been in L.A., Mookie?" Socrates asked to make him talk about something else.

"Seven years," Mookie replied. "At first I was still up to breakin' in. But after that eighteen months in Folsom I cleaned up. Broke my back, you know. Cain't walk."

"Broke your back?"

"Had a disagreement and it got outta hand. That's why they let me out. You know, it was too expensive to take care'a me and I cain't ply my trade in no wheelchair anyway."

"I'm sorry to hear about that, Kid. Shit. A wheelchair."

"I'm the lucky one, man," Mookie said. "You know George Greenfield got AIDS like Lionel. Hurly got in a argument broke his head. At least I still know my own name. And my daughter, Delice, come out to live wit' me and see that I eat."

"She do all that for you?" Socrates was looking for anything good to hang on to.

"Yeah. Her husband went up for larceny. He was beatin' her pretty bad up until he was arrested. Now she here with me and you know I got a gun. If he come out after her I'll pay my debt killin' him for her. You know ain't nobody scared'a no niggah in a wheelchair."

"I gotta go, Mook," Socrates said.

"Why? You just called."

"I'll talk to you later, man." Socrates hung up the phone and pushed it away. He unplugged it from the wall and set it in a drawer next to the sink. Then he went to the door to check that the latch was secure and the bolt was thrown.

The next day he would call the phone company to change his number for a new, unlisted one. He thought about moving again, about changing his name.

His hands were shaking.

"Twenty-seven years in the Indiana prison and I wasn't never as scared as I was after talkin' to that Mookie," Socrates told Darryl a few weeks later.

"You scared that he was gonna try an' get you in trouble so you'd have to go back to jail?" Darryl asked.

"No, boy," the big ex-con said. "I'm scared'a livin' in my own skin, I'm scared of all the evil and sad I know."

"What you mean?"

"Mookie don't know shit," Socrates explained. "If a man put a gun to his own head an' pull the trigger Mookie'd a tell ya that the man just died. That's all. He don't see what's happenin'. That's what scares me."

"How come?" Darryl asked. "It ain't you. If you know then that's all that matters."

"Yeah. But suppose I don't know? Suppose I'm just as blind and stupid as Mookie Kid? Maybe if I'd just stop and look and listen I'd see that what I'm doin' is fulla shit. That's what scares me. Just like when I didn't know that the phone company list your name if you don't tell 'em not to. Just like when I woke up after killin' my friends and I didn't even know. I mean just 'cause they let you outta prison that don't mean you're free. And if you in jail that don't mean you're guilty or bad."

Socrates did know that the frown furrowed in the skinny boy's face reflected his own.

"It's okay, Darryl."

"It is?"

"Yeah. I think so. You see, since then I realized that it's okay to be scared and unsure. Scared teach you sumpin'. Uh-huh. Yeah.

225

Scared make you ask the question. Sometimes it's only a scared man can do what's right."

Darryl nodded, not quite so sure that he understood what Socrates was saying.

Socrates laughed because he wasn't too sure himself.

moving on

As Socrates came home from work that afternoon he was almost completely satisfied with life. He had a good job and friends who he could talk to when he was lonely and a door that he could unlock any time he wanted. He had a girlfriend and a telephone and new shoes that didn't hurt his feet. He was a free man, just as long as the police didn't know about his hidden handgun and no one found out about a fight or two he had had in the streets. There was a young boy who looked up to him and even though they lived under different roofs everyone who knew them thought of Socrates and Darryl as father and son.

But on the way home from the bus stop a dark cloud passed over Socrates' heart. He remembered the deepest lesson a convict ever learns: you never trusted in your own good fortune.

"Anything good they could always take away from you," old man Cap Richmond used to say in the Indiana slam. "And what's already bad they could always make worse."

Even at the corner of the alley he knew something was wrong. Killer, his two-legged dog, was barking wildly from the small garden plot in front of Socrates' door. When he got to the gate he found that the padlock had been cut and half of his belongings were strewn in the yard. Two large men were carrying his sofa bed into the alley. They dropped it like it was some kind of garbage and not a man furniture at all. He saw his old radio crushed on the ground next to the sofa.

"Hold up!" Socrates cried running toward the men. "What the fuck you think you doin' here?"

The men were large and black. They had done hard labor for their entire lives but they weren't old like Socrates. Neither one of them had seen his thirtieth birthday.

"What the fuck you think, old man?" one destroyer said. He had close-cropped hair and wore overalls with no shirt underneath. The sweat on his dark brown skin made him glisten with the promise of violence.

His friend wore no shirt at all and had long dreadlocks cascading down on his corded shoulders. The men stood together against the foul-mouthed intruder, as if daring him to speak again.

"I think," Socrates said slowly. "That you lookin' to be two dead men."

In his younger days Socrates would have already crushed these men. They might have already been dead, but Socrates was a changed man. He gave his enemies a warning, a five-second window in which to drop what they were doing and run. The man in the overalls had enough sense to put up a protective arm before

Socrates hit him. The arm padded the blow enough to save him from a broken jaw or a trip to the morgue. His friend tried to do what was right. He threw some kind of karate chop at Socrates' head. He even connected while grunting loudly to increase the force of his blow. Socrates grabbed the man by his long hair and sent him sliding across the dirt and broken glass of the asphalt alley.

Then Socrates picked up one of the steel pipes that he always left lying around his yard in case he needed a weapon quickly in the middle of the night. The man in the overalls was semiconscious but his friend was aware and on his feet.

"You get the fuck away from here, man," Socrates warned. "Or the next time I touch you will be last thing you ever feel."

Dreadlocks knew what Socrates said was true. He wouldn't even cross the alley to help his downed companion.

"It's you in trouble, man," he yelled at Socrates. "That ain't your place. You in there illegal and they hired us to move your stuff. The cops gonna come after this. The law gonna come down on you now."

The man in the overalls was trying to rise. Socrates pulled him up by his straps and pushed him toward his friend. Together the house wreckers stumbled away from Socrates' home, down the alley to report their failure. Socrates watched them, willing himself to stay where he was and not go after his hidden handgun.

229

"You showed 'em, Mr. Fortlow," Irene Melendez shouted from her own backyard across the alley. "I told 'em they didn't want to mess with the master of that house but they didn't listen. They didn't listen and now they got to go to the clinic an' get all sewed up."

The small Louisianan woman was so happy that Socrates smiled again.

"Where they say they was from?" he asked his neighbor of nine years.

"First they told me it wasn't none of my business. Told me to go back in my house and shut up. But when I said I was callin' the cops they said it was Mr. Lomax from Cherry Hill Developers. They said that Mr. Lomax owns these here stores and that he wanna sell 'em so you had to go."

Socrates nodded and gave her an evil grin. "We'll see about all that," he said.

◪ ◪ ◪ ◪

The police showed up within two hours of the fight but Brenda Marsh had already made it to Socrates' back alley home. The slender, mocha-colored woman had hair that she'd dyed blond and wore a rose-colored two-piece suit with a bright yellow blouse underneath. She had represented Socrates once before when he had been arrested for assault. And even though he didn't like her hairstyle or way of talking Socrates kept her number because a poor man didn't necessarily have to like his friends.

She met the three officers at the door.

"My client is not here at the moment, officers," the young lawyer said. "He had to go out but I am aware of the events that took place this afternoon."

"Leon Burris and Almond Trapps have sworn out a complaint against Mr. Fortlow," Officer Wayne Leontine said. "Where is he?"

"Mr. Fortlow was protecting his property from those men, Officer Leontine. They broke into his home unlawfully and threw his property into the street."

"That's not for me to judge, Ms. Marsh," Officer Leontine said. He had come with two other uniforms. Socrates watched them from Mrs. Melendez's house across the alley. He smiled when he saw three cops.

They always send three, he thought to himself. *That's 'cause they scared'a what they might get.*

"I have a witness," Brenda Marsh was saying, "who can tell you that these men broke into Mr. Fortlow's domicile."

"They were working for the owner, Ms. Marsh," Leontine said impatiently. "Your Mr. Fortlow was trespassing."

A brilliant smile came across the lawyer's face. It was fierce and triumphant. "That's not true. Mr. Fortlow is the rightful tenant of Price Landers, the original owner of this property. I have the rent agreement and the receipt for the first and last months rent that Mr. Fortlow paid over nine years ago. I also have the canceled stubs of twelve money orders that Mr. Fortlow

231

sent to Mr. Landers in 1990. These money orders were returned with no forwarding address being given. The stubs show that Mr. Fortlow intended to pay his rent but could not locate the landlord."

Leontine stumbled then.

"I don't know anything about that —"

"No, officer," Brenda Marsh interrupted. "And neither do you know that my client's actions were unprovoked. I have proof that this apartment is my client's legal domicile. I also have a witness saying that she saw your Mr. Burris and Mr. Trapps illegally break into Mr. Fortlow's home. I am willing to make an appointment with your desk sergeant for Mr. Fortlow to come in and face his accusers but first I have to get an injunction against the men who sent Burris and Trapps to vandalize my client's home."

"Do you know where Mr. Fortlow is?" Leontine asked in a last-ditch attempt to take control.

"Not at this time. But we have an appointment to speak by phone tomorrow morning at ten o'clock. I will contact your desk sergeant after that. But first I am telling you that this property is legally in the possession of my client at this moment in time and that if it is in any way molested by Trapps, Burris or some other agent of their employer it will be a crime. And because you have been informed of this situation and because you have spoken to the vandals and they have admitted their illegal activity, although presenting it as their legal right, I hold you responsible for the protection of Mr. Fortlow's property."

"I'm just trying to uphold the law, lady," Officer Leontine said.

"The law," she replied, "works for the poor man as well as the rich."

"I didn't say it didn't," Leontine answered. After that he left with his friends.

At seven that evening four men arrived at the gate of Socrates' apartment. The man in the overalls, Leon Burris, was armed with a baseball bat. Killer was the first to see them but soon Stony Wile, Howard Shakur, and Chip Lowe with four members of his neighborhood watch appeared out of Socrates' home.

"What you want here?" Howard said boldly to the intruders.

"What business it to you, Negro?" Burris growled.

"I could see by that swolled-up jaw that you done got yo' ass whipped once already," Howard said. "This time we might just have to break it up permanent."

Socrates watched the demolition thugs back off and retreat. A feeling of power thrummed in his heart. He felt like a Cadillac cruising on a full tank of gas.

The next morning Socrates Fortlow and his

lawyer, Brenda Marsh, stood before desk sergeant Tremont LaMett. Sergeant LaMett had to decide whether or not to allow Officer Leontine to execute a warrant issued for the arrest of Socrates.

"Did you hit him?" LaMett asked the burly ex-con.

"My client was protecting his property," Ms. Marsh responded. She and Socrates had agreed that he would stay silent during the interview with the police.

"Silent is my best thing," he had told his blond Negro lawyer.

"I was asking him," LaMett said to Ms. Marsh.

"I am representing Mr. Fortlow, sergeant. I have here an affidavit from Mrs. Irene Melendez who says that she had warned the accusers that they were trespassing and that when Mr. Fortlow confronted them that they approached him in a threatening manner. I also have photocopies of Mr. Fortlow's lease with Price Landers and his canceled money order stubs. I have been granted an injunction against the Cherry Hill Development Company and Mr. Ira Lomax preventing them from taking any further action against Mr. Fortlow or his property until this matter can be settled in front of a judge."

Socrates knew that all Brenda Marsh was going to do was get him arrested. He knew how to talk to the cops better than she did. She *knew* the law but LaMett and Leontine *were* the law. Their blood and bones and fists were the letter

234

and the last word.

"Did your client strike Mr. Burris?" LaMett asked patiently.

"In defense of his property."

"Then I'm going to put him in a cell."

"You can't do that," Brenda Marsh said registering deep shock.

"You know what to do, Wayne," LaMett said to Leontine.

Socrates laughed again. This time it wasn't the good life that made him smile but the presence of an old enemy; somebody he had fought against for so long that he was almost like a friend.

He didn't fight against the handcuffs. And he wasn't angry at Brenda Marsh. She'd tried.

They took him to a room behind the sergeant's desk and chained him to a long line of other prisoners. All of them black or brown. All young too. The chain of men were led from the back door of the police station to a waiting drab green bus. The men were taken to their seats and their chains were threaded through steel eyes in the floor. The windows were laced with metal grating and the way to the exit was obstructed by a door of metal bars.

Two guards and a driver took their posts up front and the bus drove off. The boys and young men began talking in the back. It was the beginning of the pecking order. Socrates had taken that ride before.

"Hey, old man, what they got you for? Stealin' wine?" It was a young Mexican kid. He wore a sleeveless shirt that revealed green and red tattoos from his wrists to his shoulders. The designs spoke of love, gang affiliations, his mother, his nation and a few aesthetics about death and pride.

"Youngsters tried to empty out my house," Socrates said. "But I guess I was a little too rough. Little bit."

"Hey, pops can hit," another young man said. "You mean the cops had to pull you off 'em?"

"They was workin' boys," Socrates said in a remote tone. "They went to the cops and then the cops come to me."

"Man that's some chickenshit," a tubby boy said. He was a Negro with scared green eyes. "You know they shouldn'ta called cop."

"Shut up, faggot," a well-built young man said. Socrates sized him up as the would-be leader. "Nobody wanna hear from your fat ass."

The tubby boy shook, trying to hide his fear.

The well-built young man was seated two rows in front of Socrates. He had hair only on the top of his head. The rest had disappeared in a severe fade. The name Lex was tattooed on the right side of his head. Socrates couldn't see the other side.

"What you lookin' at, mothahfuckah?" Lex dared Socrates.

"When we stop, dog," Socrates said. "When we stop and you come a little closer I will show

236

you a lesson that your daddy forgot to tell ya. I'ma show you how to roll over an' beg."

Lex didn't say anything to that. The rest of the prisoners stayed quiet for a second too. The fat boy studied the situation with desperate green eyes.

The bus drove for over two hours to a detention facility in the foothills. It looked like an old abandoned school. A dozen or so reinforced salmon bungalows with bars in the windows and a razor wire fence over eighteen feet high around the perimeter.

The men and boys were hustled into a large room with long tables and made to sit for lunch while still in their manacles.

Lex started giving the fat boy, James, a hard time but he stopped when Socrates said, "Eat your slop and shut up."

Lex was the oldest of the bunch, except for Socrates. He was maybe twenty-seven and dull eyed. He was big and strong. That counted for something in the street but you needed more than bulk against the desperation of incarceration. In the lockup you needed courage and concentration, you needed friendship and you could never back down even when going ahead meant for sure that you were dead.

Before Socrates finished his meal he palmed a small glass saltshaker.

"What you in for, James?" Socrates asked the scared fat boy. In two days James had been beaten up twice. The other young men sensed his weakness and ganged up on him. Lex left him alone, however, because Socrates made it clear that he didn't want Lex to mess around.

"Stealin'," James said. "I broke into a Stop n' Save market but they caught me."

"You don't look like you been starvin', man. Why you stealin'?"

"I'ont know. I wanted some money."

"What kinda money you gonna get outta some little store?" Socrates asked. "If you get a hundred dollars that would be a lot."

James pouted and looked away. He tried to hang around Socrates because the other young men left him alone under the older man's gaze.

"You been busted before?"

"Once."

"Stealin'?"

"Uh-huh."

"How old are you?"

"Seventeen. I look younger but I'm seventeen."

Socrates watched the baby-faced green-eyed boy.

"You got to learn how to fight if they put you in jail, James," he said finally. " 'Cause they gonna tear you down in here. Tear you up."

"I know."

"Uh-uh, boy. You don't know. I know. I been there and there ain't no nothin' like it that you could think of. This here is just a lark compared to what you got in store."

For two days Socrates and his chain mates had been quartered in a barracks. They had a small recreation yard that was blocked off from other similar barracks and yards. Each compound contained about eighteen prisoners that were being held for trial or something else. Some of the barracks held very tough men who made kissing noises through the razor wire at the young men who were held with Socrates.

"If you was in one'a them other cages, James, they would eat you up."

James' fearful eyes flashed for a moment and then he clamped down his jaw to crush the fear.

"Get you somethin' sharp, James," Socrates said. "Some kinda knife or edge. And you stand up. You fight, son. 'Cause you already here an' ain't nobody gonna help you when I'm gone."

Two hours later Socrates was transferred out of the Trancas detention facility. As a good-bye present he gave James the jagged bottom of the broken saltshaker.

◢ ◤ ◢ ◤

They met in the judge's chambers. It wasn't a trial, just an inquiry, that was what Judge Radell said. He was an older white man with white hair and blue veins at his temples. There was a hint of blue in his washed-out eyes and an air of certainty about him that made Socrates nervous.

"Now is this a property disagreement or a question of assault?" Judge Radell asked.

"A little of both, Your Honor," Kenneth Brantley, the Cherry Hill Development Com-

239

pany lawyer, said. He was there with Burris and Trapps. The two men were dressed neatly in suits. Burris's jaw was still swollen and there were cuts across Trapps's face from his spill in the alley. "Mr. Fortlow was illegally occupying our property and he assaulted Mr. Trapps and Burris when they were merely executing their job."

"That's not true, Your Honor," an unusually subdued Brenda Marsh said.

"What isn't, Brenda?" the judge asked.

"None of it. I've presented Mr. Fortlow's documents. These men were destroying his home and property. My client is gainfully employed and he has tried to pay his rent."

The judge lifted the cover of a manila folder on his desk. He didn't read much.

"He sent a few money orders nine years ago and that makes him the legal occupant? Sounds rather slim, counselor."

"He paid first and last month's rent, Your Honor. No one ever tried to evict." All of her brash tone was gone. Socrates thought that maybe Brenda Marsh had learned something even if James had not.

"Okay." Judge Radell smiled and put up his hands. "Why no eviction procedure, Mr. Brantley?"

"We have no legal relationship with Mr. Fortlow. I don't know whether that document is real or not but Price Landers died almost ten years ago. He owed back taxes and Cherry Hill bought the estate. The fact that the property went through government hands absolves us from any responsibility."

"Absolution?" The judge's eyebrows rose and the question seemed more like an accusation. "You throw a man's bed into the street and call that absolution?"

"It was our property, Your Honor. Mr. Fortlow had to know —"

"Where was he going to sleep that night?" the judge asked. And before Brantley could reply, "Why couldn't you just knock on the door and say that he needed to move? Was your company going to lose money? Were you planning to build something next week?"

"There is no law compelling us to take such an action." Brantley, Socrates could see, was used to better treatment by the law. "Mr. Fortlow was trespassing."

"Oh. Huh," Judge Radell said. "And here I thought it was the court's job to make those kinds of decisions."

Kenneth Brantley's left eye closed of its own accord. There was no apology or courtroom wisdom there.

"And this court says that Mr. Fortlow is the rightful tenant of the property in question, that he will be exonerated from paying the past rent because it is an unreasonable expectation for the current landlords to expect remuneration. And I further stipulate that no development can be made upon any section of that property until Mr.

241

Fortlow has vacated his residence. As far as assault charges are concerned I am willing to hear Mr. Fortlow's charges against Burris, Trapps, Lomax, and Cherry Hill. That will be all."

The last four words silenced Brantley.

Socrates remembered to keep his smile to himself.

"Thank you, Ms. Marsh," Socrates said to his lawyer outside of the downtown courthouse.

"You shouldn't thank me, Mr. Fortlow. If it wasn't for me you wouldn't have spent forty-eight hours in jail."

"Don't you worry about that," Socrates said with real warmth. "I seen a lotta jail in my life. Two more days ain't nuthin'."

"What do you want to do now?" Brenda asked.

"What is it you wanna do?"

"Cherry Hill isn't going to let this drop. Radell put a hold on a multimillion project. They aren't going to let that alone for long."

"Yeah, I know."

"We can take Cherry Hill back to court and seek a settlement," the young lawyer said. "I think that they'd be happy to see you in court. That way they'd have an opportunity to settle, to pay you."

"To pay me off, you mean."

"Yes."

To anyone looking, Socrates might have been staring off into space. But really he was appreciating the swell of Ms. Marsh's buttocks and breasts. They seemed to him in perfect balance.

242

Not large but firm.

"Mr. Fortlow?" Brenda Marsh said. "What do you want to do?"

"I think I'ma go see Iula down at her diner and have a home-cooked meal," he replied. "Yeah. Some home cookin'."

"But what about Cherry Hill."

"I'll call ya on Friday, Ms. Marsh." Socrates touched her forearm with two big fingers and inhaled deeply the scent of her perfume.

◪ ◪ ◪ ◪

"Four hundred and twenty-five dollars a month, Mr. Fortlow," King Malone said in a rumbling bass voice. "That includes utilities."

It was a small garden house in the middle of a green lawn. Killer hopped up and down on his forepaws. Socrates held up the dog's legless hindquarters with a harness attached to a bright yellow nylon rope.

"The dog likes it," Socrates said. "What you think, boy?"

"Cool," Darryl crooned. "It's bad."

There was a large lemon bush in the center of the lawn. Five feet high and wider still. Golden bees buzzed around the tiny white flowers. A snow white cat flitted in among the leaves of the roses that lined the high redwood fence circling the yard. The sun was hot on Socrates' bald head. He did his best to suppress a grin.

"All I ask is that you keep the lawn mowed and that you rake up after your dog," King said.

The air was sweet with lemon blossoms. Socrates feared that the image in his eyes would somehow disappear if he blinked or sneezed.

"Topper says that you'd be a good tenant. He said I wouldn't have to worry 'bout you messin' up or havin' them wild parties," King said.

"Don't party. No," Socrates said. "And I put all my trash in a big plastic bag."

"They pick up on Tuesday afternoons," King said.

"Say what?"

"The trash. They come pick it up in front of the house at about four but you'd do best to have it out there by noon. I got the new rubber cans that the dogs can't knock over."

Socrates stared at the small crippled man before him. He was trying to decipher the words he just heard. He remembered the smell of the trash fires when he was a boy living outside Indianapolis. He remembered the brown paper bags they gave him for trash in his prison cell. It would take two months to fill that bag.

Inside, the house had real oak floors made from wide planks of cured and stained wood. The walls were painted white with a deep green trim and the windowpanes were so old that they presented a mild distortion of the outside yard. There was a kitchen with a gas stove and a built-in sink. The bedroom was large and surrounded by windows. And the living room was big enough to contain three single cells.

"Whyn't you take it?" Darryl asked later that day when they returned to Socrates' home.

"I'm thinkin' 'bout it, Darryl. You know four hundred and twenty-five dollars is a whole lotta money for a man ain't paid a dime in nine years."

"You get paid. They pay you at Bounty."

Socrates loved Darryl and he trusted the boy above anyone else. But he didn't know how to express the fear he had of moving on to some place as beautiful as King Malone's garden home. He'd never lived anywhere that he couldn't leave without a backward look. "Home is where I hang my hat," he used to say.

". . . or where they hang your neck," Joe Benz, a fellow inmate, would always add.

"Lemme think about it a couple'a days."

"But s'pose Mr. Malone rent it before you make up your mind?"

"Then I guess I just have to stay here."

"But I thought you said that Ms. Marsh said that they gonna kick you out?"

"Yeah." Socrates had no desire to stifle his grin. "Yeah, I'd like to see 'em try."

◪ ◪ ◪ ◪

The Cherry Hill Development Company was on the twelfth floor of the Astor building on Crenshaw. It had glass doors and a beautiful black receptionist who wore African cloths cut in a western style. When she looked up at Socrates to ask his business, his heart skipped once and he forgot everything that he had come there to say.

"Yes?" the child asked.

"Has anybody told you how beautiful you are yet today, uh, Malva?" Socrates asked looking at the nameplate on her desk.

Her smile was a gift that only a man who'd spent half of his life in prison could appreciate.

"Not yet," she said. "Who are you?"

"Socrates Fortlow."

The frown that came across Malva's face brought back the business at hand.

"Oh," Malva said. "Please sit down. I'll call Mr. Lomax."

"Come in, Fortlow," Ira Lomax said. His office had a glass wall that looked out over the Hollywood Hills. His desk, which was shaped like the body of a guitar, was made from white ash.

Lomax was tall and well dressed, black and a little greasy. He stood taller than Socrates but lacked the bulk to reinforce his height.

"Sit down, why don't you?"

Socrates took a seat. Lomax remained standing.

"I'm surprised to see you, Fortlow. But I'm glad that you're here. Maybe we can get a few problems ironed out without any more diffi-culty." Lomax was a crook. Socrates knew that from the moment he walked into the room. A man who was too smart to rob a Stop n' Save but too stupid to fly right.

"You see," Lomax said when Socrates stayed quiet, "you're costing this company money. You attacked my employees. And just because some foolish judge doesn't know the law that doesn't mean you can hold us up."

The silence that followed Lomax's declaration didn't bother Socrates. He looked the sleek land developer up and down and sucked on a tooth.

"Heavy fists won't stand up to my kind of power, Fortlow. All I have to do is make a quick phone call and your apartment will disappear. If I stay on the line a minute more you could be gone too."

When James came into his mind Socrates knew that he was experiencing fear. James, he thought, was afraid of getting beaten or raped or killed. Socrates wondered if the boy had used his saltshaker on Lex.

With that thought Socrates stood straight up from his chair. Ira Lomax stumbled backward and took in a gasp of air.

"Listen to me, Ira," Socrates said. "I know that you know people. I probably even know some'a the people you do. I been to Blackbird's bar an' I'm sure you have too. But I'm not like they are. I don't do it for money, brother. I ain't a thief or a leg-breaker, I ain't a robber or con man. I'm a killer plain and simple. A killer."

Socrates paused to allow his words to have their meaning then he continued, "I lived in that place for nine years. If you added up the money I owed it's probably ten, twelve thousand dollars. So if I turn that around then it would be you owe me instead'a I owe you. I'm sure your banker bosses would think that was a good price."

"I ain't payin' you shit, niggah." Lomax's voice

was harsh but his eyes were like James's.

"Then you better not miss," Socrates said before he turned and walked out of the door.

For a week or so there was talk about Lomax around the hood. Iula heard a few things in the diner and Chip Lowe got the word through members of the watch. There were men willing to inflict pain for money but Socrates was nowhere to be found. He rarely showed up at his alley home. Killer moved across the street to stay with Mrs. Melendez for a while.

One evening Socrates showed up at Blackbird's bar. He took the new owner, Craig Hatter, to the side for a powwow.

Late the next morning Socrates showed up at Lomax's big home in View Park. He wasn't admitted by the housekeeper and so he merely left the expensive box of chocolates he brought as a gift. The box was big, red and velvet, in the form of a Valentine's heart.

In the next week Socrates spoke to Brenda Marsh three times. Lomax had called her, the police did too. The cops wanted to know if her client had delivered a box of chocolates to Lomax's address. Brenda asked them if delivering chocolates was a crime.

Craig Hatter met with Socrates at Bebe's bar and said, "Lomax is a pussy, man. He asked me who I could get to kick your ass."

"What you tell'im?" Socrates asked.

"Last I heard Mike Tyson was in jail."

The money exchanged hands in Brenda Marsh's office on Pico and Rimpau at the end of that week. Lomax looked scared and tired. He handed over the cash and Socrates signed the letter Brenda had drafted that said he no longer contested the apartment between the furniture store walls.

◪ ◪ ◪ ◪

The only things Socrates took from his home of nine years were a suitcase full of clothes, a few cooking utensils and the photograph of a painting of a disapproving woman dressed in red.

He bought a king-sized bed, and twelve folding chairs that he put in his closet with a fancy folding table. He also bought a folding cot that he kept in a corner for when Darryl stayed with him. He had a phone installed. Other than that his house was bare and pristine.

He walked around the rooms smiling. He had a home that he loved but still he could disappear leaving nothing behind.

rascals in the cane

"What I wanna know is if you think that black people have a right to be mad at white folks or are we all just fulla shit an' don't have no excuse for the misery down here an' everywhere else?" The speaker, Socrates Fortlow, sat back in his folding chair. It creaked loudly under his brawny weight.

Nelson Saint-Paul, the undertaker known as Topper, cleared his throat and looked to his right. There sat the skinny and bespectacled Leon Spellman. The youth was taking off his glasses to wipe his irritated eyes. The irritation came from Veronica Ashanti's sweet-smelling cigar.

"Is that why you had us come to your new house this week?" Veronica asked.

"It sure is a pretty house, Mr. Fortlow," Cynthia Lott cried in shrill tones.

Chip Lowe sat back in his chair glowering, his light gray mustache glowing like a nightlight against the ebony skin of his upper lip. His hands were clasped before him. They had turned almost completely white with the creeping vitiligo skin disease that was slowly turning the skin of his hands and the right side of his face to white.

"How long you been here?" Leon asked.

" 'Bout two months." Socrates took a deep breath to keep down the nervous passion that had built up before he asked his question.

"You need somebody to help you pick out some more furniture," Veronica Ashanti said. Her eyelids lowered and her hand moved to cover her small bosom. Almost everything Veronica said seemed to contain a romantic suggestion.

But she was right. Socrates' living room was empty except for six folding chairs and a folding table, all of which had been stored in a closet before the Wednesday night discussion group had arrived.

"I like it spare, Ronnie," Socrates said. "I like it clean."

"But you need some kinda sofa," Cynthia Lott screeched, her stubby legs dangling from the sharp-angled wooden chair. "Some place soft for a woman to sit comfortably."

"I use these same kind of chairs at the funeral home," Nelson Saint-Paul said. "We meet there all the time and you never complained."

"But that's not a house, Topper," Veronica explained. "You expect more comfort in a house. Here Mr. Fortlow got this nice new place and a yard with flowers and fruit. He should have a nice big sofa and a chair and maybe some kinda rug. That's what you expect to see in a house."

"I like the yard, man," Leon said. "It's fat."

"And if you had some lawn chairs . . . ," Veronica began to say.

"What kinda shit you mean by that, man?" Chip Lowe, head of the local neighborhood watch, blurted out.

"Excuse me?" Veronica did not like the interruption.

"I said what the hell does he mean by that question? Do black people have the right? Do I have the right? Who is he to question me?" The anger rolling off Lowe's voice was like a gentle breeze across Socrates' face.

"I was talking about lawn furniture," Veronica said icily.

"I don't care 'bout no damn furniture," Chip said. "What I wanna know is what he mean questioning me?"

"He didn't say nobody in particular, Mr. Lowe," Leon quailed. "He just said black people."

"And what the hell you think I am?" Lowe said.

"That's why I asked you, brother," Socrates said. "I asked you 'cause you the one know. If you don't know then who does? I mean you read the paper an' you got white people writin' about it. You got white people on the TV talkin', on the radio, they vote on it too. You got white people askin' black people but then they wanna argue wit' what those black people say. Everybody act like what we feel got to go to a white vote or TV or newspaper. I say fuck that. Fuck it. All that matters is what you'n me think. That's all. I don't care what Mr. Newscaster wanna report. All I wanna know is what we think right here in this room. Right here. Us. Just talkin'. It ain't goin' on the midnight report or the early edition or no shit like that."

Silence followed Socrates' declaration. A police helicopter passed overhead but it could not have suspected the conversation unfolding below. And even if the policemen knew what was about to be said they wouldn't have wondered or worried about mere words.

"Wh-wh-what do you mean, Mr. Fortlow?" Nelson asked after the loud rush of the helicopter passed on. "I mean we all know what's been done to us that's wrong. We all know what we got to do to make our lives better."

"We do?" Socrates stared hard at the middle-class mortician. "We don't all look the same. We don't all talk alike. We ain't related. The only things we got in common is what's on the TV an' in the papers. And ain't nuthin' like that made from black hands or minds."

"But we know," young Mr. Spellman said.

"What is it you know?" Cynthia Lott asked the boy.

"I know I'm a black man in a white world that had me as a slave; that keeps me from my history and my birthright." Leon spoke proudly and loud.

Tiny Cynthia waggled her dangling feet angrily. "First off you ain't a man you're a boy. You wasn't never a slave. And as far as any birthright you live wit' your momma and play at like you tryin' to go to school. As far as I see it you ain't got nuthin' to complain about at all. I mean if you cain't make somethin' outta yourself with all that you got then all they could blame is you."

Cynthia sucked a tooth and looked away from the young man.

Leon was trying to think of something to say but he was trembling, too furious to put words together.

"But I didn't ask if he could blame somebody, Cyn," Socrates said. "I asked if we got the right to be mad. All of us is mad. Almost every black man, woman or child you meet is mad. Damn mad. Every day we talk about what some white man did or what some black man actin' like a white man did. Even if you blame Leon for his problems you still sayin' that there's somethin' wrong. Ain't you?"

"Only thing wrong is that these here men you got today ain't worth shit." Cynthia curled her lip, revealing a sharp white tooth. "Black men puffin' up an' blamin' anybody they can. He say, 'I cain't get a job 'cause'a the white man,' or 'I cain't stay home 'cause Mr. Charlie on my butt.' But the woman is home. The woman got a job and a child and a pain in her heart that don't ever stop. I don't know why I wanna be mad at no white man when I got a black man willin' to burn me down to the ground and then stomp on my ashes."

Cynthia's high-pitched voice always made

Socrates wince. He swallowed once and then prepared to speak.

But before he could start Leon opened up again. "I don't know why you wanna be like that, Miss Lott. Some man musta hurt you. But I'm doin' what I can. I am. I got a job. . . ."

"What kinda job you got?" Cynthia demanded.

"I work at the drugstore on Kinkaid on the weekends."

"That's a child's job," the tiny woman shrilled. "Come talk to me when you doin' man's work."

"Come on now, Cyn," Veronica Ashanti chided. "You know Leon's a good boy and he tryin'. And you know ain't no man start out perfect. No woman neither. I know a lotta black women out here mess up just as quick as a man. Quicker sometimes."

"Yeah," Chip Lowe said. "Leave Leon alone. I got a job and a family. I live at home with my wife and my daughters. I work hard. Harder'n any white man do the same job. That's why I got the right to be mad. I come in early an' leave late and they still pass me over for some lazy motherfucker don't know how to tie his shoelaces."

"No need to curse, Chip," Topper said. "But you are right. We all have difficulties that are incurred by our skins. We all know that we have to work harder and longer hours to be recognized. We have to be extra careful and honest not to be fired or even arrested. And if one black man commits a crime then we are all seen as crimi- nals. All of us share that legacy."

"But do you have the right to be mad?" Cynthia Lott asked. It was rare that Cynthia would dare to question Topper and she seemed to take pleasure in the grilling.

"Certainly," Saint-Paul said. "We are held back not because of worth but because of preju- dice and racism. That is reason enough."

Socrates looked at his friends with harsh satis- faction. He had been thinking about the ques- tion for months. It had been on his mind for years. Every time he saw a white man he'd get mad. Sometimes he had to leave the room so as not to yell or even attack some man who was just standing there. His ire was as natural as the sun- rise. It was more like an instinct than like the higher faculty of reason that supposedly sepa- rates people from other creatures.

Socrates had long wanted to ask the question but he couldn't get out the words in the Saint- Paul Mortuary. He was afraid of the big room and the many doors all around. Somebody might be listening; he knew that it wasn't true and even if it was that it didn't matter. But Socrates' throat was clamped shut. So he had decided to invite the group to his new home in King Malone's backyard, next to the sweet-smelling lemon bush. If anyone came around, the two-legged dog Killer would bark.

In the nearly empty rooms of Socrates' home he felt his heart beating and the air coming into his lungs. There he could believe that he was the master.

He had made lemonade and ham sandwiches, bought two fifths of Barbancourt Haitian rum. He had put the small bounty on his folding table and set up chairs for his friends as they arrived at the door. But even with all of that he could barely get the words out. When he started to put his question into words his face had flushed with fever and the room seemed to shake.

"But I know what you mean, Miss Lott," Leon said in a voice that was devoid of feeling. " 'cause when it come to tearin' down a black man it's a black woman the first one on line. Like when I come here to talk. You always be ridin' me even though I ain't never done nuthin' to you. Even though I give you a ride home every week an' you never say thank you or offer me somethin' like a drink of water or maybe a dollar for all that gas. There's a white woman work at the pharmacy speaks nice to me every day. She treat me better than half the black women I ever meet."

"Well if you so hurt then why you come here?" Cynthia Lott said. Her voice was less angry than it was strained. "Why you give me a ride? I don't ever ask you. I don't ever ask you for nuthin'. I don't ever ask no man for nuthin'."

There were tears in Leon's eyes but he didn't seem to notice. The muscle and bone at the hinges of his jaw bulged out. "I come here 'cause I wanna be around black people who talk about stuff other than just complainin' or lyin'. I want to be somebody other just some nigger or gangbanger."

Cynthia almost said something but then she held back. Socrates thought that this silence was an answer to the boy's hurt feelings but that he would never know it.

"My aunt Bellandra," Socrates began, "used to tell me a story."

Everybody in the room seemed to understand immediately that this was the real beginning of the Wednesday night talk, that everything up until then was just like an introduction.

"It was a story," Socrates continued, "about slaves that were set free by a freak storm down on a Louisiana sugar plantation a long time before the Civil War. She said that it was a big wind . . ."

". . . *that blew out of the Gulf of Mexico.*" Bellandra's words came back to him. He was a scrawny child again rapt in the frightening tales of his severe auntie. "And it tore down the ramshackle slave quarters and tore out the timbers that their chains was bound to. Many of the slaves died from the crash but some of them lived. They cut away the corpses from the long chain that bound them all together and then moved like a serpent toward the overseer's hut.

"This overseer was a man named Drummond and he was evil down to the bone. He heard the slave quarters crash but he didn't do nuthin' to help because the wind scared him and so he stayed in his hut. He didn't know that the chain gang was movin' toward him. He just laid up with Rose, a slave girl that he took to his bed sometimes. Outside the wind was howlin' and the trees were scratchin' at his roof. It was like hell outside his do' an' he wasn't goin' nowhere." Bellandra, Socrates remembered, paused then and glared down at the boy. He felt as if he had done something wrong but didn't know what it was.

"An' then the knockin' started on his do'. It was a loud thump and then the drag of chain and then another loud thump. Rose called out in fear and her master cringed. But the knocking got louder and the chain sounded everywhere all around the house. Then there was the angry cry of men. If it wasn't for the storm that cry would have reached the plantation owner's ears. He would have called out his men and his dogs but the wind ate up the slaves' voices. Only Drummond could hear them men and he wasn't even sure that it was men. He was afraid that ghosts from some shipwreck had blown in on the winds of that storm. He was tryin' to remember a prayer to send them ghosts away when the do' shattered and so did the shutters on his windows. And then four men came into his shack one after another, manacled hand and foot and chained in a line. There were two empty shackles that were bloody from where the dead men had been cut away.

" 'Carden, is that you?' the overseer cried. ' 'Cause if it is, you had better get ret ta die. Ain't no slave gonna come in on me in my home!' The overseer stood up to thrash Carden the slave but another slave, Alfred, raised his chain and laid the overseer low. Drummond lay on the ground bleedin' while Rose cried from his bed. 'Give us the keys, man,' Alfred said. He held the chain above the overseer's head and that broke him down. He took the key to the fetters from a string on his neck. And when he freed them they set on him with the loose chains and while they beat him, do you know what he said?"

"Uh-uh," little boy Socrates said to his auntie.

"He said, 'Why you killin' me? I freed your bonds.' But the slave Alfred said, 'You just dead, white man.' And he was dead even before he could hear those last words.

"And they took Rose and freed whatever slaves there was left alive in the wreck. And then they set fire to the master's home and ran out into the sugarcane fields and hid. There was twenty-two escaped slaves. Man, woman, and child. They went up into the swamplands and laid low. And after a day or two they got strong on fish and birds they slew. Small groups of white men came looking for the escaped slaves but they died and their weapons went into the hands of Alfred Africa, the leader of the runaways.

"Everywhere in the parish white folks was scared of them slaves. Bounties was put on their heads, but after the first search parties disappeared most folks were too scared to go after Alfred and his gang. But the runaways was scared too. Scared that if they ever left the swamplands and the cane they would be hunted down and killed for their sins. Because they knew that killin' was wrong. They knew that they had murdered old Drummond and Langley Whitehall, the plantation owner, and his family and men. So they stayed in the wild and went kinda crazy. They attacked white people that traveled alone and burnt down houses and fields of cane. Nobody was safe and they started to call Alfred and his gang the rascals in the cane. And it wasn't only white people that was scared. Because if Alfred's crew came up on a slave and he was too scared to go with'em then they would say that that slave was their enemy and they would kill him too.

"They called the state militia finally but they never found Alfred's crew. After a while that whole section of farmlands was abandoned because nobody felt safe. Nobody would brave the rascals in that cane. Every once in a while one of 'em would get caught though. If one of 'em got tired of the mosquitoes and gators and he wanted to leave. And if one of Alfred Africa's men was caught they'd torture him for days to find the secret of where the runaways hid. But they never found out. After a long time the attacks stopped and the plantation owners came back. But they still went with armed guards. And they set out sentries at night who had to stay at their posts even in the worst storms. Because everybody said that the soul of Alfred Africa lived in the eye of the storm and that one day he would return and burn down all the plantations everywhere in the south."

Socrates looked up and saw the faces of Cynthia, Veronica and Chip Lowe. He was surprised because he half hoped to see his long-dead auntie Bellandra. He wondered if he had really told the story that he'd only just remembered after more than fifty years.

"It sounds like a true story, Mr. Fortlow," Nelson Saint-Paul said.

"Yeah," Socrates said, still partly in the trance of his memory. "Rose, the woman that the overseer raped, was my aunt's great-grandmother. She was the only one of the escaped slaves to survive. She caught a fever and wandered away. Indians took her in and she wound up in Texas. She had a child and became an Indian but the army massacred the tribe she traveled with and she and her baby were sold as slaves. After the war she came to Indiana with her son. That's where my family is from."

"So what you tryin' to say, Socrates?" Chip Lowe asked. "What's that story supposed to mean?"

"Depends on what part you're talking about," Veronica Ashanti said on a cloud of blue smoke.

"What you mean by that, Ronnie?" Chip asked.

"Could be the storm or the killin', could be that they thought the killin' was sin even though they killed a sinner." Veronica counted out each point on a different finger.

"Yeah," Leon added. "Or maybe that they stayed around and fought against the people who persecuted them."

"They should'a run," Cynthia said. "But no doubt that Alfred Africa wanted to fight instead'a doin' somethin' right."

"Maybe they couldn't help it," Leon argued. "Maybe it was like Mr. Fortlow's aunt said and they couldn't escape. That's like us. We cain't escape. We here in this land where they took our ancestors. How could you run from that?"

"I don't know," Veronica said sadly. "But maybe Miss Lott is right when she says about men always wantin' to fight. Our men always on the edge of some kind'a war. All proud'a their muscles. I mean I like me a strong man but what good is he if he's all bleedin' an' dead."

"Sometimes it's better to fight," Chip Lowe put in. "That's why we got the neighborhood watch. Sometimes you got to stand up."

"But not like no fool," Cynthia said. "Not like them, uh, what you called 'em, Mr. Fortlow?"

"Rascals in the cane. That's what they were called." Socrates was happy to hear his question discussed. He didn't need to say much because everybody else was alive with words.

"Yeah," Cynthia said. "Rascals. That's just like a man. So busy fightin' that he gets killed and his woman and child go back into slavery."

"But what is the storm?" Topper asked Socrates. "What does it mean?"

"Why's it got to mean anything?" Cynthia

263

screeched. "It's just what happened."

"No," Topper disagreed. "No. Every story, everything that happens has a meaning. A purpose. That's why Mr. Fortlow asked that question and then told his auntie's story. The story is the answer. The answer to his question."

"Is that right?" Veronica asked. "Is what Topper say true?"

Socrates looked at the beautiful, black, pear-shaped woman. It was the first time he ever heard her ask something without the twist of sex in her tone.

"I'm not sure," Socrates said. "I mean I been thinkin' about bein' mad at white folks lately. I mean I'm always mad. But bein' mad don't help. Even if I say somethin' or get in a fight, I'm still mad when it's all over. One day I realized that I couldn't stop bein' mad. Bein' mad was like havin' a extra finger. I don't like it, everybody always make fun of it but I cain't get rid of it. It's mine just like my blood.

"But I didn't remember Bellandra's story until we were already talkin'. It just came to me and I said it. And now that Topper says that the answer is in the story I think he might be right. Maybe not the whole answer but there's somethin' there. Somethin'."

"But why you wanna ask the question?" Chip Lowe asked.

"Because I'm tired'a bein' mad, man. Tired. I see all these white people walkin' 'round and I'm pissed off just that they're there. And they don't care. They ain't worried. They thinkin' 'bout what they saw on TV last night. They thinkin' about some joke they heard. An' here I am 'bout to bust a gut."

"Maybe they should have left the cane fields," Leon said. "Maybe they should have forgotten all about all that fear and guilt."

"Yeah," Cynthia added in an almost sweet voice. "And they sure shouldn't'a killed those black folks that was too scared to run with 'em. Sure shouldn't."

"Uh-huh," Veronica agreed. "And Alfred should have taken Rose and gone north or south or west. If he ain't had a home to go back to he should have made a new home rather than stayed in the cane fields with them mosquitoes and alligators."

"Maybe that's what Mr. Fortlow's aunt was saying," Nelson Saint-Paul said. "Maybe they couldn't leave the plantation. Maybe they were stuck with those white folks that put'em in chains and the blacks who stayed slaves."

"This sure is some good rum, Socrates," Cynthia Lott exclaimed. She had taken a small paper cup and filled it. "That's just about the best liquor I ever tasted."

"Made from sugarcane by black hands in the Caribbean sun," Socrates said.

Everyone had a drink and then they all had another.

Socrates felt secure in his secluded home with his black friends and smooth liquor. They ate the ham sandwiches and talked about white people and how they felt about them.

"But do we have the right?" Socrates asked Nelson Saint-Paul.

"We got reasons," Nelson answered. "We got reasons. But reasons and rights ain't the same thing."

"I don't know what it means really," Cynthia Lott crooned, her voice calmed by smooth rum. "I mean so what if you don't have the right? You still gonna be mad."

Socrates smiled and rested his big hands on his knees. He stood up saying, "Well we can't figure all that out in one night anyway. It was just a question been on my mind."

"Oh my it's midnight," Veronica said. "I better be gettin'."

"Damn," Chip Lowe said. "We usually out by ten. That rum loosen up the tongue."

The Wednesday night group gathered themselves up quickly and left Socrates' home. He wondered if Leon drove Cynthia and what it might feel like to kiss Veronica's big lips.

"Bye," he said at the front door.

He noticed a light on in the front house. Maybe tomorrow Mr. Malone would complain about his little party.

After everyone left Socrates went to fold his collapsible chairs but then he stopped and stood there in his living room. He looked at the chairs, imagining that they still held his guests. Snobby

Topper, angry Cynthia Lott, and all the rest. He thought about being angry himself. Somewhere in the night he realized that it wasn't just white people that made him mad. He would be upset even if there weren't any white people.

"How come they didn't go down in Mexico?" little Socrates might have asked his stern auntie.

"Because the road wasn't paved," she would have answered.

Socrates laughed to himself and poured one last shot of rum. He left the chairs out for the night because they felt friendly.

rogue

He stood in an alley across the street from Denther's Bar and Grill on Normandie. It was drizzling slightly but Socrates wore a canvas hat and a water-repellent army surplus fatigue jacket. His hands were in his pockets, each of them holding a pistol.

There were two small wood framed windows in the wall of the old stucco building. In one the word *Café* shone in neon blue. In the other **Open** burned red. Beyond the lights Socrates could see men and women laughing and talking and touching. The sight of all that happiness and warmth sent angry tremors through Socrates' big hands. He had to release the guns for fear of shooting himself in the legs.

There was one white woman that he could see at the lower corner of the right window, near the bottom of the *n*. She had hair that was golden and lips drawn red. She was smiling and moving her head to music that Socrates could not hear. The man she was with was a policeman, Socrates knew that. All the men who went to Denther's were cops. It was, Socrates thought, a world of cops. Your good men, your fools — your killers too.

The ex-con took a deep breath to keep his nerves down. In each of the fourteen pockets of his jacket there was a clip full of bullets. He was ready to fight through to the end but he would stop shooting when the target he came for was dead. He didn't want to kill any innocent cops that he didn't have to. Only the name Matthew G. Cardwell Jr. was on the hit list in his mind.

Thin and too tall for his hands or features, Cardwell was a black-haired killer.

"You see what he done to my boy?" Stony Wile had asked three months earlier. They had just broken a long silence over a woman when Socrates stopped by Stony's house to bring his family a crate of week-old peaches from Bounty.

Reggie was laid up in a bed, his features swollen and bloody. He was out of his mind with pain and concussion. The emergency room doctors said that he needed a week of observation in a hospital bed but the nurse on the admitting desk didn't see how Stony's insurance could pay for that. They brought Reggie home where at least somebody could pray.

"They didn't arrest him," Stony wailed. "If he did some kinda crime bad enough to near kill'im for, then how come they didn't take him to jail?"

Socrates didn't have an answer for his friend. Tildy, Stony's wife, wilted over the bed, crying.

"He was out with his friends," Stony was saying. "He was raisin' some hell an' bein' wild. But he didn't have no gun or no knife. He didn't hurt nobody. Maybe he did somethin' but how

269

can that excuse the law actin' like the lawless? Who can I go to about this?"

"Nobody," Socrates said to himself. He repeated the word standing there in the shadows of the alley across the street from Denther's Bar and Grill.

Reggie mended quickly. He was out of bed in a week. And the day he got up he enrolled in Los Angeles City College. Maybe, Socrates thought at the time, the beating was just what young Mr. Wile needed to set him straight. After all, Socrates had taken, and given, some horrendous beatings in his life.

But then there was Inger Lowe, whose features favored the best sides of her black mother and her Swedish father. Inger was raped, that's what Iula said she said. Raped and sodomized by Matthew G. Cardwell Jr. She was stopped on Morrisy, that's what she said.

Inger didn't tell many people about it. She was too afraid that it would get back to the police. Cardwell had told her what could happen if she complained.

He'd told her that he'd come visit some time soon at any rate. Inger moved up to Oakland to live with her brother.

"She left all her furniture and belongings. Hardly even packed a suitcase." That's what Iula, who gave Inger airfare, had said.

Socrates was mad even then. But one woman raped and a boy being beaten wasn't much in the eyes of a man who had done worse in his own life.

Socrates began to hear other tales about the rogue cop. Beatings, molestations, and humiliations. Even the pimps started talking about how their jewelry always disappeared after a bust. And if anybody complained they received a visit, if not from Cardwell then from one of his friends.

Socrates had heard the stories but they didn't stick. He'd learned to live next to suffering in prison. He awoke in his cell many nights to the sound of some young man being raped for the first time. Once he saw a man hit so hard by a guard that his eye came out of his head. With that kind of pain in his mind there was little that some cop could do to displace it.

But then Cardwell killed Torrence Johnson. It was in the *L.A. Times*, on page three. A three-quarters profile of a smiling young boy with the words *tragedy* and *death* in the headline. He was only fourteen, just two years older than Darryl. Shot down running from the police, from Matthew G. Cardwell Jr. Socrates read the news report. It was intimated that Johnson was involved with gang activity. There was a turf war or something like that. Torrence was involved. He ran.

From that point on it was a straight line for Socrates. He went to the Johnson home even though he didn't know them. He brought white flowers that he took from the Saint-Paul Mortuary. He stayed on the front porch to give his

271

condolences but even from there things didn't seem like what the police had said.

Mr. Johnson was a short man and broad. He didn't like the idea of Socrates at his door.

"Did you know Torrie?" Mr. Johnson asked.

"No sir," Socrates said. "I just read about him. I just read it and wanted to come and say I was sorry."

"Sorry about what? Were you there?" There was a hysterical note in the fat man's voice.

"No sir. I just felt for you and I wanted to say that a lotta people feel it's wrong to have happen what happened to your son."

The Johnsons lived in what some people called *the jungle,* below View Park and above Crenshaw. Socrates found a mother and a father and a well-kept house. The other children weren't gang members. Socrates took the bus home wondering why the article got him so upset.

The boy was fleeing, the article had said. *Fleeing.* He was involved in gang activity. *Gang activity,* Socrates thought to himself, *what's that?*

He didn't sleep that night and the next day he called in sick to work. He was sick too. The words fleeing and gang activity wore on his nerves like some kind of virus that eats away the senses.

His lips were numb. Colors hurt his eyes.

Fleeing. Gang activity. Shot down. Tragedy.

All the suffering he'd witnessed in prison came back and added itself to Torrence Johnson's father's pain. Socrates thought about Inger fleeing to Oakland, about Reggie scared into school.

"That ain't why people s'posed to do things," Socrates said to Stony at Stony's house one day.

The bronze-skinned welder lit a cigarette and nodded.

When Socrates put his glass down it broke on the red Formica.

That was the first night he stalked Denther's. He saw Cardwell leaving to go home at one A.M. The rat-faced beanpole wasn't even being charged. The police investigation proved that Torrence wasn't armed but another boy, Aldo Reams, was. They discovered the gun in young Mr. Reams's pocket after Torrence was already dead. There was no evidence. No tattoos or gang colors. Somebody broke a window and the boys made some kind of hand signs. The cops came. The boys ran. Cardwell shot but he wasn't answering fire. The unfired and unseen gun was taken from a scared Aldo Reams, who fell to the ground with his hands outstretched when Torrence was hit. The puzzle pieces did not fit the story. Socrates saw that a boy was slaughtered over a broken window and the finger. All he did was run.

Socrates was drawn to Denther's every night for two weeks. He learned Cardwell's pattern with no intention except to nurse a feeling of hatred that was so familiar he sometimes wondered if the hate was older than him.

For hours every night in cold wet weather he stood at absolute attention. He didn't go through the problems at work in his mind. He didn't think about Darryl or Iula. All that existed was Cardwell and his movements. Socrates had become a predator, a hunter. He was a wild thing with a too fast heart.

"The chains on a black man," his old aunt Bellandra had said, "go down through the centuries. They once made us slaves to the plantation but now they make us slaves to the slaves we was."

"Huh?" the small boy Socrates asked.

"A good word and a gentle touch is like a cloud that passes on a nice day, Socrates," she replied. "But pain, real pain last forever. It hurt your son and his son and his. The slave is still cryin' even though his chains ain't nuthin' but rust, even though he's long gone and forgotten."

There had been guards who he thought about every day and every night for months, even years. Their names were still in his mind even though sometimes he couldn't remember his mother's face. Craig Kimball was one. Warden Joseph Simon was another one. They were just as much murderers as Socrates. They tortured and broke simple men for no reason. Socrates was sure that he'd hunt both of them down if he ever had the chance. But he never did. Kimball had beaten three men to death in their cells. Simon ordered sick men into the dungeon when any fool could have seen it would kill them.

But Socrates didn't try to find Simon or Kimball after his release. Now the hatred welled up again. Socrates was still in prison. Cardwell was the new evil screw assigned to his block. Bellandra's words came back to him again. *Everything fades except for pain.*

An angry old woman, long dead and forgotten by everyone except one frightened nephew, pronounced Cardwell's death sentence.

Socrates bought guns and ammunition at Blackbird's bar. You could get anything at Blackbird's if you were brave enough to go there. Fourteen clips of 9mm shells was like an extra-generous baker's dozen from a friendly grocer.

Cardwell came out of Denther's. If Socrates had looked at his watch he would have known that it was two fifteen. But the wristwatch was in his pocket with the hand on the gun. The murder in the air came in through his lungs and from there to his blood. Socrates, who knew that he had been prepared for centuries, was finally ready to answer a destiny older than the oldest man in the world.

Cardwell obliged and walked toward the dark alley. He was smoking a cigarette, moving at an unhurried pace. He was thinking about something. Socrates breathed deeply and tasted the air. It filled him with a sweetness of anticipation that he had not felt since the first time a woman, Netalie Brian, had helped him find his manhood.

"It was the air, no, no, no, the breath of air," Socrates told Darryl the next morning on the phone. "It was so good. I mean good, man. You know I almost called out loud. I saw Cardwell walkin' my way an' my hands was tight on them guns. You know he was a dead man an' didn't know it. I pulled them pistols outta my pockets. I was thinking about him dyin' but at the same time I was wonderin' what was goin' on in my mind. You know what I mean, Darryl? How you could think about somethin' an' still be thinkin' 'bout somethin' else?"

"Uh-huh," Darryl grunted. Socrates hadn't slept that night. He'd called the Shakurs' house at seven A.M. and gotten Corina to get Darryl out of bed. Darryl was the only human being that Socrates trusted completely. "You mean like when it's almost three but the teacher talkin' 'bout the Civil War but you thinkin' 'bout basketball?"

"Yeah like that, like that. But I was gonna murder that man. I was gonna kill him. But I was thinkin' that I had never felt nuthin' like that deep breath I just took. An' even though I was gettin' ready to kill I had to take just one second to think about how I felt. You know?"

"I guess I do," Darryl said. "But how did you feel?"

"I felt free," Socrates said in a soft voice. "All my life I ain't never felt like that. I was ready to die along with that man. My life for his — you cain't get more free than that."

"Did you kill him?" Darryl whispered the question so that Howard and Corina wouldn't

276

hear if they were close at hand.

"I meant to. The guns was out and he passed not three feet from me. But I just stood there — smiling, thinkin' 'bout how good it felt to be in my own skin."

▰ ▰ ▰ ▰

Socrates took his newfound freedom to work that day. He smiled at people and asked after their health. He told gentle jokes and paid more attention to the details of the produce department than he ever had before. He was tired from two weeks with little sleep and suffered from a slight cold from all those nights spent in the alley. He detected a whiff of staleness about his person like the smell of old clothes taken out of the bottom drawer after many years.

It was the finest day of Socrates Fortlow's life. Death held no dominion that day. And if his aunt Bellandra's blue god was in his heaven Socrates had no quarrel with his remoteness.

The elation lasted deep into the night. Socrates turned off all the lights in his small garden home and walked around in bare feet touching the wood and metal and glass of his house with wonder and joy. He lay down on the new sofa in the living room unaware that he would fall asleep. He just sat down for a moment and then stretched out with a silly glee. Sleep came upon him like a highwayman who had been lying in wait.

The dream was a variation on an old theme. A small room with a single cot on which the ex-convict slept. The pounding on the door that roused him was like artillery fire in a war film.

Socrates simply opened the door for the ebony giant who was stripped to the waist and powerful in a way that only wildness can breed. The big man towered over Socrates but there was no more fear in the bald ex-con. Their gazes met and somewhere Socrates knew that he was dreaming. He also knew that he had to go along until the end.

"What you want from me?" Socrates asked.

"I only wanna know what you gonna do now. You done the first job. You done dug up all the dead an' set 'em free. Now what you gonna do with all that power?"

Freedom was old hat in twenty-four hours.

"You know I couldn't believe it, Darryl," he told the son of his heart that weekend. "Here I been lookin' to be free for my whole life. Whole life. An' when I get it it's just like a pocket fulla change somebody done give to me 'cause I looked wretched an' poor. Now that change is just jinglin' in my pockets but there ain't nuthin' I got to buy. Uh-uh. I could just pass it on to somebody else now. Yeah, pass it on to somebody like you."

Darryl looked a little stunned into his friend's eyes, his skinny boy's body moving with the rhythm of his breath.

◪ ◪ ◪ ◪

"I need a favor, Lavant," Socrates told the self-styled anarchist. They were sitting in the garage where Lavant slept and created the bright yellow broadsides that he hoped would be the clarion call to revolution for the working men and women of L.A.

"What's that, Socco?" the black zealot asked.

"I need to know everything I can about somebody and then I need your printin' skills."

Two weeks later Socrates took the first paid vacation of his life. He gave short notice and Marty Gonzalez was hard pressed to explain to the main office that it was worth it to give their new produce manager a week off after only six months on a job that had benefits.

"You know they don't like it, Socco," his boss said.

"I don't like it either, Marty. But you know I got to take the time, got to."

Saturday he spent with Iula. He went to work with her early in the morning and helped her get ready for the day. He managed the big pots and did some of the little jobs that she never got around to. When he wasn't working he sat at the counter drinking tea with lemon, something he'd always pined for in prison but never drank once he was on the outside.

That night they made love, speaking hardly at all. Iula could tell that there was something wrong but she kept silent.

Sunday he went down to Venice Beach to see Darryl with Corina and Howard Shakur. They all went down the beach with the children, Winnie and little Howard.

"That's a good job you got down at Bounty now." Howard's statement seemed to contain a question.

"I guess." Socrates was distracted by the sound of the waves and the wind. The ocean's power always made his heart race.

"How you think I'd do in a grocery store?" Howard asked.

"Better'n me that's for sure."

"Why you say that?"

"You young, Howard. Strong too. Bounty got stores all over the West Coast. You could work all the way up the top ranks if you tried. Add that to the computers you know and you could make it big."

"You think so?" Howard puffed up with pride.

Socrates looked at Howard. He really couldn't call the man his friend. All Howard did was brag and gloat over others who had less than him. He was jealous of his own children where Corina's affections were concerned. But Socrates felt generous that day on the beach.

"Yeah, Howard. But you got to remember, man."

"Remember what?"

"All that money don't mean a thing if you want to see your momma smile but your momma's dead."

Howard frowned and almost said something but instead he raised his bulk out of the aluminum strap chair and walked over to his wife.

Socrates set his alarm for five A.M. but he didn't get out of bed until seven fifteen. He made tea with lemon and had wheat toast with eggs. He ate standing at the kitchen sink, looking out of his window at his landlord's backyard. Fuzzy bees hovered around the lemon bush, eyed by the white cat that sometimes came from next door. The ear of the teacup was too small for Socrates' finger to fit through. He pinched the small handle though and that worked all right.

He hadn't yet bought a radio or television. Now he thought that he never would. He liked the idea of a radio, voices that he could spy on and then turn off when he got bored or annoyed. But that morning all he had was sunlight and that lemon bush, bees and a white cat.

Against the front door lay two stiff yellow boards connected by purple straps spaced for a head to fit between them. Each board was filled with red lettering and illustrated by laminated photographs.

But Socrates wasn't looking at the board right then. He was savoring his hot tea and breathing the still air and silence.

At ten thirty he showed up across the street from the rogue cop's police precinct. He stood there in his camouflage army surplus coveralls wearing the sandwich board that detailed the crimes of Matthew G. Cardwell Jr., *POLICE*

OFFICER and KILLER, the homemade poster board read.

A five-by-seven photograph of Cardwell, seen laughing and smoking a cigarette, was at the center of each board. Below that was a copy of the list of allegations of police brutality brought against the cop. This list was an enlarged photocopy of the public record. Above his photo and to each side were the names and photographs of his victims. Reggie Wile was there, his face battered and swollen. A picture of Inger Lowe was accompanied by the question *Where is she now?* The photograph of Torrence Johnson was from the newspaper. Its caption read simply, *Killed by Officer Cardwell.*

Socrates stood for a while facing the station. Policemen came in and out without paying him any heed. Now and then a car would slow down but the words on the sign were too small and no one stopped to get out of their cars. A few rare walkers stopped and read the words, avoiding the sandwich man's eyes. But they needn't have worried, Socrates wasn't there to talk.

There was a Pick-an'-Save drugstore on the corner of the block and Brother Joe's Coffee n' Cake across the street from the station. Both of these stores were patronized by black and brown people who did stop to look for a moment before getting on with their day.

Socrates began to pace the block across the street from the station after an hour or so. He walked solemnly and slow as if to the beat of a single military drum. As the day went on, more and more people came to read his sandwich board. Children ran after him laughing, then fleeing gleefully when he turned to walk in their direction. Men passed by seemingly oblivious but reading every word with sideways glances.

By noon the police had noticed him too. Most of the cops went to a small diner next door to the station but one or two black officers got their coffee from Brother Joe. They stopped to read Socrates' sign and then went away to work.

Finally, at a little after twelve, two uniformed cops approached him.

"All right now," a burly white sergeant said. "You had your fun, now move along."

Socrates kept walking.

The second officer, who was also white and large, stood in front of Socrates pressing the five fingertips of his left hand against the hard sign. "It's time for you to leave."

Socrates showed no concern. He took two steps backward and turned to walk in the opposite direction.

"Halt!"

Socrates stopped. He didn't turn around though.

The policemen flanked him.

"It's time for you to leave," the sergeant said again. He had a small purple scar underneath his right eye. Socrates tried to pick out some recognizable shape in the mark but there was none.

"If you don't go," the other cop said, "you're going to spend some special time with us across the street."

Socrates began walking again. He'd taken two steps when the sergeant's hand tried to close around his right biceps. There weren't many human hands that could encompass Socrates' muscle.

"Show me some ID," the policeman said.

It was a direct order. Socrates didn't want to talk to the cops. All he wanted was to stand there in silent testimony to the crimes of the man named Cardwell.

When he reached into his back pocket the officers came out with their guns.

"Stop what you're doing," the sergeant commanded.

"But you asked for my ID," Socrates said.

"Put your hands where I can see them."

Socrates put out his arms like a Christian accepting the cross. There were policemen coming out from the station from across the street. The other cop grabbed Socrates by the wrist. He had a pair of handcuffs in his other hand but he couldn't figure out how to put the big man's wrists together.

"Hey, what you doin'?" a man complained. It was one of the men who had read Socrates' sign. "This is a free country ain't it? A man could tell the truth if he want to."

"This isn't any of your business," the police sergeant said. "Clear out."

"I'ma stay right here!" the man yelled. "I ain't leavin' my brother for no pig to shit on."

The second policeman, not the sergeant, released Socrates and approached the new man threateningly.

"You better get the fuck outta here if you know what's good for you."

But by then men and women had begun to come out of the diner and from out of the Pick-an'-Save down the street. One car full of young men blasting loud music parked at the curb and the men piled out of the black Buick.

"What's goin' on?" people were asking.

"They tryin' to arrest a man just 'cause he wanna protest."

"I know that Matthew Cardwell."

"He the one murdered that boy."

The police from across the street advanced. They pulled truncheons and canisters of Mace from their belts.

"Why you wanna arrest this man?" a woman demanded. "It's that cop oughtta be arrested. It's him did all them things the sign says."

Socrates felt the handcuff clamp down around his left wrist. Before the policeman could grab the other wrist a man in a lime green shirt and dark green pants ran up from the crowd and pushed the policeman hard in the chest. The cop fell down at his sergeant's feet. The sergeant helped his partner up and they both started moving back toward the precinct.

There were twenty or so black men and

women surrounding Socrates and yelling at the cops. There were just as many policemen, most of them white, but there were Mexicans and black men in uniform too.

"He just carryin' a sign!" yelled the small man who first came to Socrates' aid. "Cain't we even say what we thinkin'? Is that what the police supposed to do? Keep a man from speakin' his mind?"

The policemen had gathered into a group that stood there in the middle of the street. Their numbers grew only slightly where Socrates' protectors seem to appear from nowhere. Men and women and boys and girls came out of buildings and from around corners as if they had just been waiting for this moment.

It had taken no more than ten minutes. Before that Socrates was alone. Now he was on the front line of a battle.

The policemen moved back toward their headquarters. They were pushed and yelled at and reviled.

Socrates watched them, the chain dangling from his left wrist. All around him men and women were shouting and waving their fists. A glass broke somewhere.

More missiles were hurled and the doors to the station closed. The picture window of the Pick-an'-Save shattered. Three car alarms went off. One of them was a magnified voice that kept repeating "Stand away from the vehicle!" in a threatening tone.

The street was blocked off with angry women and men. Traffic stopped at the intersections and more and more people came. Socrates was at their center but he didn't wave his fists or shout. He didn't do anything but watch and maybe wonder a little at all those people so ready to break out in violence.

A police car was turned over. A trash can was set on fire at the precinct building's front door. Socrates, who had left home that day ready for death, worried for the first time that he might not die alone.

The police doors flew open after a few minutes of the fire. Cops in plastic-visored helmets and see-through shields came pouring out of those double doors. Three trails of smoke came out over the advancing army's head and the familiar burn of tear gas raked against Socrates' eyes and gouged into his nose and lungs.

Forty-seven policemen plowed into the crowd of hundreds, firing rubber bullets and hurling canisters of gas. They sent nine people to the hospital and arrested twenty-seven more. One policeman had a broken jaw. No one died. The worst injury was Lou Henry, the proprietor of the Pick-an'-Save, who had a heart attack trying to drive a handful of looters from his store.

Socrates saw very little of what happened after that first whiff of gas. He fell back from the fumes and the advancing army of lawmen. Whatever else he saw was on the faces of black people and brown folks who were too angry and tired to be scared.

Socrates called Iula at her diner from his backyard home. He asked her for a metal saw and a
transistor radio. She brought them both, tempo-
rarily closing down her restaurant for the first
time in over fourteen years of business. She told
Socrates that she'd stay with him but he told her
to go.

"I just need to think," he explained.

It took four hours to hack through the metal
cuff. While he worked at it the scratch radio re-
ported on the violence.

The miniriot flared up sporadically through
the day. There was a curfew set anywhere within
eight blocks of the police station. There were
four cops assigned to a cruiser, each one armed
with a shotgun. They looked like space invaders,
one eyewitness claimed, because of their helmets
and heavy gloves.

By the time morning had come there was a
sense of fear spread over Los Angeles. The
schools were closed and store owners from
all over town had taken up posts at the doors
of their establishments, fearing looters but
not, it seemed, death. News vans representing
every TV station, and many radio stations,
were parked on the street in front of the precinct headquarters where the violence had
flared.

Late that night Iula brought him a baked

chicken dinner with beer and half a blueberry pie.

"You want me to stay with you?" she asked while he picked at the meal.

"Yeah."

She held him through the night, but in the morning he pulled away. He donned his overalls and his sandwich board.

"I'm afraid they might kill you, baby," Iula said as he went out the door.

"I hope not," he replied. "But if somethin' does happen will you tell Darryl to look after my dog?"

Men and women in heavy makeup stood before video cameras talking about the debacle. It was six o'clock but the morning traffic was lighter than usual. It was a holiday of violence which most people stayed home to observe.

Everything from a certain point of view seemed ordinary, almost orchestrated. The policemen in their fancy war dress, the anchors and their cameramen, a day to stay home from school.

But then Socrates Fortlow, in his sandwich board, came through an alley into the street across from the police and their chroniclers. He planted his feet defiantly and stood with his message still intact. The bloodred letters seeming prophetic now; the questions and accusations a bit more serious.

Katy Moran of *The Pulse*, a TV news program that Socrates had never seen or even heard of, was the first to notice him and register his potential to her career.

"Excuse me, sir," she asked. She had run up to him followed by a cameraman and someone else who held a microphone on a pole. "Were you here yesterday morning when the violence began?"

She was a beautiful white woman dressed in a tan two-piece suit. Her lips were a deep peach hue. Her blouse was brown silk and there was a green jeweled pin on the lapel that folded over her heart. Socrates wondered about the pin while other news broadcasters came his way. He wondered if she had decided to wear that pin because somebody would see it on TV and like it. He wondered who that somebody was.

The microphone was hovering over his head.

"Were you the one who was here yesterday?" Katy Moran asked.

"It's right here on my sandwich board," Socrates said.

"What does it say?" Katy Moran asked. Five microphones were jammed in front of his face.

"All you got to do is read it," Socrates said.

The newscasters and reporters stood back to allow their cameras to record the document. Then the police broke through. They pushed the reporters aside and grabbed Socrates, throwing him to the ground. They ripped the sandwich boards from him and put on a new pair of handcuffs and dragged him toward the station.

"Are you arresting him for starting the riot?" Katy Moran's voice asked.

"Does this man have rights?" a man's voice shouted. Socrates thought it was the voice of a black man but he wasn't quite sure.

He was dragged into the station and thrown into a room. He was surrounded by at least a dozen angry cops. All of them pushing and swearing.

For a moment Socrates thought that he was going to die. He could tell when there was murder in the air.

"All right, back off!" a plainclothes black police officer shouted.

The white sergeant from the day before pressed his chest up against the detective. "Who the hell are you?"

"Sergeant Biggers. They called me from Watts because I know this man."

"This nigger's mine," the burly sergeant replied.

Instead of answering, Biggers slammed a beefy fist against the sergeant's jaw. The man went down and out.

Socrates had never been so surprised in his adult life. The men yelling, blood coming from the mouth of the downed sergeant. Biggers shouting, "Back off!"

Another man entered the room then. His uniform was that of some high rank. Maybe a commander, Socrates thought. This man didn't say anything, but his presence brought silence to the angry men in the room.

"Biggers," the commander said. "Bring him down the hall, to alpha room."

"He hit Sergeant Taylor," a uniform complained to his commander.

"Somebody had to one day," the commander replied.

Socrates' hands were freed and he was sitting in a fancy wooden chair. Detectives Biggers and Beryl stood around him while the captain sat behind a simple table before a window that looked out on a brick wall.

"What are we going to do now, Fortlow?" the commander asked.

Socrates, who felt like he was dreaming, said nothing.

"Answer the man," Inspector Beryl, another old aquaintance, demanded.

"Where's my sign?" Socrates asked.

"It was destroyed during recovery," Beryl said. "Now answer the commander."

"Commander," Socrates repeated the word.

"You in some serious shit, Fortlow," Biggers said. "You better fly right."

"What you want?" Socrates was looking directly into the black policeman's eyes.

"Have you ever been arrested by Officer Cardwell?" the commander asked.

"What's your name?" Socrates asked the man in charge.

"DeWitt," the man said after a moment's silence. "Commander DeWitt."

"Your officer Cardwell killed a boy. He done raped, beat, stole from an' threatened black men and women all over your precinct. I ain't never had nuthin' to do with him, though I considered killin' 'im at one time."

Beryl asked, "But you didn't know him?" The short but well-built white man had his thumbs in his belt loops, which held back his jacket and revealed his shoulder holster and gun.

Socrates did not reply.

DeWitt stared at Socrates while Beryl and Biggers stared at him. Socrates wondered what they were doing when DeWitt said, "Book him on inciting to riot. Tell Mackie to put him in the special vault on three."

Socrates stayed in a cell called the vault on the third floor of the police station for three days without seeing anyone. He had a commode and a sink. There was a cot to sleep on and pizza three times a day.

He didn't mind. He'd known from the day he was let out of prison that he'd be back in a lockup somewhere. It was nice to be alone without responsibility or noise. It was a real vacation, just like he told Marty he'd take.

For the first time in his life Socrates had leisure time. There was light and food and there were no guards or fellow prisoners to negotiate. There was no job to go to, no cans to collect. There was no booze to get him hungover. And if there were screams in the night, they were too far away for him to hear them.

He didn't eat the pizza.

All he did was sit and think about what had happened.

"All them men and women, white and black, police and civilian ready to go to war," he said to Darryl a few weeks later. "It was so much power, like fire out of nowhere. There was somethin' to that. Somethin' I always knew was there but I never really thought about it."

But he had three days to think and remember. Three days to reflect on the fire he'd sparked. Socrates never expected anything to change. All he thought was that he had to stand up without killing. Because killing, even killing someone like Cardwell, was a mark on your soul. And not only on you but on all the black men and women who were alive, and those who were to come after, and those who were to come after that too.

But there was power in his standing up. Power in words and pictures just like the crazy self-centered Lavant Hall had said. And he had swung that power like a baseball bat.

At night Socrates attended his dreams almost as if he were awake and watching a movie screen. He saw the images of his mind and questioned them or laughed at them. He never lost the strand of his investigations during the whole three days he was the guest of John Law.

And then the police came to the room and took him to another room where he found Marty

Gonzalez's cousin, the lawyer Ernesto Chavez.

"Mr. Fortlow," the well-dressed lawyer said. His smile was perfect and his mustache was a razor's edge. "Looks like you're in the fire again."

"I still cain't pay you, man," Socrates said. He had to sit down because he was weak after walking down the stairs.

"You okay, bro?" the lawyer asked.

"Food ain't too good here," Socrates said. "I want some'a Iula's corn bread. Yeah, that's what I need."

"Well we'll see what we can do about that," Ernesto said with an irrepressible smile. "And as far as money, I should be paying you for a chance like this."

"Huh?"

"You're famous all over the world, Mr. Fortlow. China, France, everywhere. They got your picture holding up that sign on *Time* magazine and in the *New York Times*. Cardwell's history. And it was you wrote the book. You don't really need a lawyer. It's them who need the lawyers, man. You got them on the run."

The video cameras that captured the image of the testimony against Cardwell had played on every TV station though they must have known it would cause violent tension in the black community. There had been demonstrations at the police station. Sporadic violence had broken out over the three days. The mayor himself had called Ernesto because he was the only lawyer on record to have represented Socrates in L.A.

"They shit on your rights and that Cardwell is a bad dude. Even the Republicans like you, man. You could run for office after some shit like that." Ernesto smiled at his client, checked over his shoulder and then winked. "But I say you should go for the money, Mr. Fortlow. You could clean up after a mess like they made."

"Can I get outta here?"

Ernesto snapped his fingers and cocked his head to indicate that it was already done.

◢ ◢ ◢ ◢

Commander DeWitt apologized to Socrates on behalf of the police chief and the mayor.

"They have suspended Officer Cardwell," he informed his recent prisoner. "I guess we never put together all of the information like you did on that sandwich board."

If Socrates were to go by the tone of the commander's voice, instead of his words, he would have been looking for a fist rather than the handshake offered.

They removed Socrates by a side entrance and took him to the Saint-Paul Mortuary where his friend Topper had offered a place to stay.

"Reporters been callin'," the mortician said to his friend. "What are you going to tell them?"

"I ain't got nuthin' to tell the papers, man," Socrates replied. "They can make up their own lies without me helpin'."

"But, Mr. Fortlow. You got power now. You got the ear of the press. You could make a difference out here."

"I know what you sayin', Nelson," Socrates told his prosperous black friend. "But it ain't nuthin' I could say that they don't already know. Them reporters know all about Cardwell an' cops like him. They know all about men who been in prison. They already know. It's us who don't know."

"Us?" Nelson Saint-Paul said. "Every black man, woman and child knows what it's like to be poor and mistreated and held back. Even me. You know they didn't wanna know about me at the funeral directors' society. I had to make all kindsa stink just to belong."

Socrates looked at his small friend and shook his head. It wasn't a conscious move and he was sorry when he saw the pain in Saint-Paul's eyes.

"What do you mean that we're the ones who don't know?" Nelson asked again.

"We had the whole city scared, Nelson. But nuthin' changed. No one said, 'Hey, lets get together an' vote or strike or just get together and say somethin' true.' Me complainin' to some newspaper is like me tellin' the warden that I don't like his jail."

"But this is different . . ." Nelson Saint-Paul began.

"Ain't nuthin' different. Just look out here in the street. No, Nelson. Me talkin' to the newspaper or the TV is just like if they made me into a cartoon. A goddamned cartoon."

"They fired you," Marty Gonzalez said on the

297

phone. Socrates had called to see if there was any fallout from his being in the papers. "Mr. Ricci himself read the article that said you were a murderer and a produce manager in his store. Shit. I almost lost my own job. I'm sorry, Socco."

"You don't have to be sorry, Marty," Socrates consoled. "I knew it couldn't last. You know some men just born to be fools. And they signt me up when I was only a child."

Socrates moved in with Luvia Prine for a while after his incarceration. She shooed away reporters and served his meals at eight, one, and six thirty. He didn't ask her for the respite. She called Howard Shakur and told him to pass the offer on.

Their relationship was cold because Luvia would never approve of a man like him.

"But you did what you could and they treatin' you hard," she told him on the first day he moved in. "And Right would'a asked me to shelter you I know. And even if he's dead I will still respect his wishes in my home."

Socrates was looking out of his window on Marvane Street while Hoagland Mars played his trumpet across the hall. The music was so loud that Socrates barely heard the weak knock at his door.

"Yeah?"

"It's me. Darryl."

"Come on in."

He was an inch taller than the last time Socrates had seen him. His chest was wider too.

"Hey," the boy said.

Socrates nodded.

"What you lookin' at?"

"Just outside," the ex-convict said.

"I went over your house to feed Killer and Mr. Malone said that you went here."

"Yeah." Socrates nodded again.

"Mr. Malone said that you could come back though. He said that you'n him could work sumpin' out on the rent if you ain't got a job."

"He said that?"

"Uh-huh."

"Damn."

"What you gonna do now?" Darryl asked. Socrates could see that he was worried.

"I lost my job."

"I know. You gonna try'n work someplace else?"

"Got to eat," Socrates said. "An' if you wanna eat then you got to work."

"How you gonna get a job?"

"Sit down, boy. Sit in that chair."

Darryl obeyed and Socrates sat on the sill of the open window.

"I got some money put away. I got enough for a year or so if I don't eat too many steaks. You know, it was the money they give me for movin'."

"Uh-huh."

"Maybe I'll go back home, back to King Malone's place. Maybe if I take enough time I can figure out a business or sumpin'."

"Like what?"

"I'ont know. But not where I'm workin' for somebody who if they find out who I am they gonna let me go. 'Cause you know there ain't nuthin' wrong with me."

"But you ain't gonna leave?" Darryl asked nervously.

"Leave where?"

"Howard said that the best thing for you to do is to get out of California. He said that they know who you are now and once they know that about a black man he got to go."

"A smart man maybe," Socrates agreed. "But I ain't all that smart."

"You smart. You the smartest man I know," Darryl said. "Not like in a book maybe but books cain't make you smart anyways."

"I'm not leavin', Darryl. I'ma stay right here or maybe down at King Malone's. Some place. And I'm gonna do sumpin' too."

"What?"

"Ever since I saw all those people jump up to save me from the cops I knew that there was sumpin' goin' on. Not like Lavant says. Not like Nelson Saint-Paul says neither. Poster board don't get it. Goin' on TV with white people don't get it neither. You cain't see it or show it, not yet."

"Then what if you cain't say it or see it?"

"You got to dream it. You got to make it up. And when you get it right then it'll be there."

Luvia brought up lemonade and ginger snaps for the man and boy. After a little coaxing Darryl started to talk about his grades and his new girl-friend. Socrates listened happily.

After the boy had gone Socrates laid back on the bed and listened to Hoagland Mars practicing across the hall. It was a sweet sound from a sour man but it was better than any radio.

"It's just that one sweet note," his aunt Bellandra said in his dreams. "Just that one sweet note and everything is sometimes turnt around."

The employees of G.K. Hall hope you have enjoyed this Large Print book. All our Large Print titles are designed for easy reading, and all our books are made to last. Other G.K. Hall books are available at your library, through selected bookstores, or directly from us.

For information about titles, please call:

(800) 223-2336

To share your comments, please write:

Publisher
G.K. Hall & Co.
P.O. Box 159
Thorndike, ME 04986